My**Diet**Starts**Tomorrow**

A NOVEL

My**Diet**Starts**Tomorrow**

A NOVEL

LAUREL HANDFIELD

A STREBOR BOOKS INTERNATIONAL LLC PUBLICATION

DISTRIBUTED BY SIMON & SCHUSTER, INC.

Published by

Strebor Books International LLC
P.O. Box 1370
Bowie, MD 20718
http://www.streborbooks.com

My Diet Starts Tomorrow © 2003 by Laurel Handfield

ISBN 1-59309-005-6
LCCN 2003109344

Distributed by Simon & Schuster, Inc.
1230 Avenue of the Americas
New York, NY 10020
1-800-223-2336

Cover art: André Harris

First Printing August 2003
Manufactured and Printed in the United States

10   9   8   7   6   5   4   3   2   1

ACKNOWLEDGMENTS

I would first and foremost like to thank God for allowing me to find a gift that I am able to share with others and believe me, I've searched and searched. He gave me strength when I needed it the most and guided me to where I am today.

Thank you to my lovely husband. I know I got on your nerves making you proof my books but you did a great job and I love you for it. Thank you to sweet Savannah. You are the person who has given me the most motivation to be the best person I can possibly be. I love you sweetie.

I would like to thank my parents. Without them, I wouldn't be. They have been nothing but great to me and I thank you for the wonderful childhood that you have bestowed upon me. You have always supported me even if you didn't agree with me. Thank you to my sisters, Dawn and Sharon for their never-ending support inside and outside of the literary world and for sending information to my publisher when I was unable to do so due to time constraints.

To my brother Steve who is just cool to the fifth power. You're too dang big to tease now.

To my new family, Jeanie, Remus, Yvonne and Chris. Since day one you have been there for us. Without your help, I probably wouldn't be here today. I love you guys.

Thanks to my best friend Alicia. We have been through some crazy things together. I appreciate and value our friendship, and always will. Thanks to Tara G. and Lynn who have been with me throughout the years and provided great companionship when I most needed it.

Thank you to Sydney, my cat. You have been through the best and the worst with me. Let's hope the rest is smooth sailing.

To those people who have inadvertently shaped the person you see before you today. I thank you. I wouldn't have changed a thing, good or bad.

To all fellow writers at Strebor Books. I have genuinely appreciated the advice you all have given me. As a new author, I have truly needed it. To those hard working people at Strebor, even though I have yet to actually meet you, I thank you for putting the finished product together and making it look good.

I would like to thank the wonderful author Zane for even giving me this opportunity to express myself. I may not have told you yet, but you are an incredible person for allowing new authors to go for theirs. I really do appreciate it and hope we are able to work together for a long time to come.

Lastly, I would like to thank those readers who have enjoyed my book and those future readers who will enjoy my book. This was made for you.

Never cease the struggle for personal success. I haven't and never will.

Laurel Handfield

To MY WONDERFUL HUSBAND AND MY BEAUTIFUL DAUGHTER.
Without you guys I wouldn't have been able to make it.
I truly mean that.
I love you!

Chapter 1

M y eyes opened up around seven in the morning. As I stared at the ceiling, I lay there thinking what the hell just happened last night? My head was pounding from the night before and lying there, it all started coming back to me slowly but surely.

That damn date. That's what it was. The first date in three months, and I couldn't believe that I actually went, but Charlize, my best and closest friend had insisted. After all, she was the one who set it up.

"Stop being such a fuddy-duddy," she had said to me.

Fuddy-duddy? I started to laugh out loud as I thought about it. When was the last time I heard that term?

My best friend could be a little—let's just say—weird at times. To me, Charlize and I were extreme opposites. Where she had short hair (when not wearing one of her many weaves), my hair was longer. She was short and I'm tall. In my personal opinion, she was a bitch whereas I am... I guess in that respect we were *slightly* similar.

At least I admitted it.

I got out of the bed and stretched my five-foot-ten-inch frame. I forgot to tie my shoulder-length hair up last night when I came home, so I knew I was in for a real treat when I went to wash my face and look into the mirror.

I put my slippers on, headed for the bathroom and tripped over my dang cat.

"Good morning, Sydney."

"Meow," was her reply, and that was only because she was hungry.

If cats were bitches, then mine would be the queen.

I got to the bathroom mirror and almost laughed my head off. There I was in all my glory or should I say gory? Not only was my hair every which way, but also my makeup was still on my face in smears from the night before.

I bet Mark would've loved seeing me like this last night.

Mark was the guy I went on a blind date with, and let me tell you it wasn't pretty. Charlize had insisted that he was the best thing since Billy Dee Williams. Well, Billy Dee Williams back in the day. I guess now it would be D'Angelo or whoever was the latest guy to compare other guys to in that superficial way.

He was tall and a consultant and the best thing since sliced bread, according to Charlize. I'm not sure what he consulted, but you have to really watch out for some of those job titles out there. I found out that mechanical engineer could also mean janitor.

He was from the Bethesda, Maryland area, so it was not far from me. Even after our date last night, that was pretty much the only thing I knew about him.

We'd agreed to meet at Fu Shi, which was one of those chi-chi Chinese restaurants. I wasn't really big on Chinese food, but as long as he was paying, I was going. (I know; trife but a sista was hungry.)

I'd decided to wear my sleeveless floral print dress. It showed off my curves, and it was perfect for a beautiful July summer night, so that's what I wore. I had my hair out straight and chose dainty earrings with a matching choker. I believed simple was better.

That was me and Mark's first difference.

When I met him outside the restaurant, I immediately knew it was him from our phone conversations. He had always talked business in at least half of our conversations, and when I saw a man in a dark blue flawless suit on his cell phone outside the restaurant, I knew that had to be him. I had to admit he looked good. He had these incredible broad shoulders that looked, well, broad in that flawless suit.

I noticed that when he was talking on the phone, he repeatedly used his free hand to make a point to the person on the other end—business call no doubt.

I got out of my Mustang (cool points for the Mustang) and casually walked up to him, but when I went to introduce myself, I got the finger. You know; the I-am-not-ready-to speak-to-you-just-yet-so-please-hold-on-for-one-moment finger.

So I stood there and stood there and stood there until *he* was ready. Thank goodness I had decided to have that vodka martini at home before meeting him, because if I didn't, I might have actually felt a bit embarrassed just standing there looking like an idiot.

So there I still stood contemplating whether or not to just go ahead home and call it a night, but just as I turned to leave, I heard him say something to the phone indicating the conversation was concluding.

"I'm sorry," he said, giving me a wink and a smile. "I had to take care of this. You know how it is."

He did have a nice smile with all those pearly white teeth. (How much you wanna bet they aren't natural?)

"Actually, I don't. I'm in between jobs right now, but yeah, I remember those days," I stated.

You think I would've just passed gas or something because just then his face dropped to the ground. Maybe I shouldn't have divulged that bit of information at this point.

"Oh, I thought Charlize said that you were in sales and marketing?"

"I am, or rather I was. I quit about a month ago and moved out here."

There was that face again.

"Why would anyone in their right mind do something like that?"

Now he was insinuating that I was crazy. How nice.

Did you ever get the feeling that something was doomed from the beginning? Well, I had that feeling. It kind of felt like gas that was pent up right in the pit of your stomach ready to explode at any sudden movement.

To make a long story short, we ended up having a quick dinner, and then, for some strange reason, the food seemed to not agree with me all of a sudden, and I really had to go home to rest from this humongous headache, stomachache, whatever, take your pick. Go figure.

As I got into my car, I ended up calling Charlize, and we met at Quimby's on the waterfront and had two chocolate martinis—or three or four—I couldn't remember. I do remember that we joked all night about the so-called date I had earlier.

Even though she set it up, I could never have been mad at her. I knew she had the best intentions, but sometimes I just wanted to take her intentions and shove them right up her...

"Are you mad at me?" Charlize asked with a grin on her face.

I could tell she really was concerned if I was mad at her or not, especially with her grinning in my face like that.

"No, I'm not mad, but let me ask you something I should've asked you before 'the date,'" I said, doing the finger thing to indicate a quote. (I don't know why I do that; I hate that, too!)

"You're just as single as I am, so why didn't *you* go out with him?"

She began to giggle a bit, and then she began to laugh and then burst out uncontrollably.

"Monica, when I met him I knew he was the type of guy that was—shall we say—a little pretentious? You had always stated that you wanted a man who had a good head on his shoulders, was business-minded and to sum it up, 'had it goin' on.' So that's what I found. He fit all those descriptions. Ever hear of the term be careful what you wish for?"

She started laughing again but this time I joined her.

"In all honesty," she began between gasps of air, "I actually thought you two just might hit it off, but I guess now all I can say is oops."

"In that case," I stated still laughing. "Let's toast to oops."

As we lifted our glasses, that began our first monthly Martini Night.

And that, my friends, was the wonderful blind date I had last night.

How could I have had any reservations?

~❤~

I pinned my hair up and stepped into the shower that was spitting out cold water. I reached through the streaming water and turned the far left knob all the way to the right, turning on more hot water and then jumped in. It was as if I were washing away the night before along with the smeared eye makeup. I noticed that my sit-ups were working. Next month would either make or break me. I would either keep up the crunches or I would go back to my chicken fingers and fries, which where my favorite, especially with extra honey-mustard sauce. We'd see.

Just as I turned off the water, I heard my phone ring. I grabbed a towel and ran to pick it up. It had to be nobody but Charlize this dang early in the morning.

"Hello?" I answered quickly without looking at my caller ID.

"Good morning," a baritone voice said. "And how are you this morning?" *Who the heck was this?*

"I wasn't sure if I should call this early, but since you got sick, I thought I might give you a ring to make sure things were okay," the voice said.

Well, that did it. It had to be no one but Mark from "the date" last night. I looked at my caller ID and, sure enough, it was.

Wait, I thought we were both on the same date last night, but maybe I was wrong. Maybe it was a dream or rather a nightmare. I never expected to hear from him again. Actually *hoped* was more the word. I mean sure, after standing around waiting for him to finish his phone call on his cell and being called a dummy, we did have an okay time at dinner, but nothing to write home about.

"Uh, yeah, I actually feel okay now. I do have a slight headache though," I stated telling the truth.

"Yeah," he said laughing. "All those martinis you had will do that to you." *Busted!!!!* But I thought I'd try to play it off anyway.

"What?" I said as I walked to my living room to look for Sydney. "Martinis, what are you talking about?"

Damn, that sounded phony as all hell. (Did you ever get caught in a lie, and you know you're caught in a lie but you insist on playing it out anyway? I think there's an actual word for that in the dictionary.)

"After our date last night, I happened to pass by Quimby's, and I saw you and Charlize at the bar."

Now I'm thinking, do I go the route of making up an excuse like as-soon-as-I-left-your-tired-ass-I-felt-better-and-decided-to-call-my-friend-to-get-a-real-party-on?

Nah, caught was caught and what did I care anyway? He didn't know me like that.

"I was actually just trying to let *you* off the hook. I got the impression you weren't having the best time," I said trying to save face. (Okay, semi-lie).

"You're absolutely right...we didn't have a good time because I was rude. I can get that way at times, but it wasn't intentional. I just happened to have had a bad day, and I carried it out on our date. I don't blame you for wanting to leave and I do want to apologize."

This was nice of him and I was impressed. It didn't make me like him any more, but this was actually refreshing.

"No problem, I've been there done that," I said, realizing how stupid that sounded.

Just then, Sydney jumped up on my lap and made herself comfortable.

"I apologize myself for lying, but I figured I was doing both of us a favor," I said, laughing.

He laughed at that, too.

Looked like everything was copasetic.

Beep.

"Can you hold on?" I asked, brushing Sydney off my lap and walking back into my bedroom.

"Sure."

I checked my caller ID and clicked over. It was my girl.

"Hey, Char, guess who I'm talking to?"

"Uh, lemme guess. I'll say Mark," she said.

"How did you know?"

I went into the kitchen and poured myself a glass of ice-cold orange juice.

"I'm psychic. Just kidding. He called here this morning and told me some shit about last night. Are you sure you two went on the same date because he couldn't say enough good things about you? How pretty you were, how nice you were, etcetera, etcetera."

"Get out!" I said, completely astonished. "I'll call you back as soon as I'm done."

I started to click over until I heard Char's voice again.

"Wait, I'm calling to find out if you want to go to brunch at Quimby's. You know on Saturdays they have their jazz fusion brunch and Boney James is supposed to be there this Saturday."

"What time?"

"Meet me there at one o'clock on the terrace. Stacey and Jaleesa are coming, too."

"Okay."

I told her okay but I didn't really feel like meeting Stacey and Jaleesa there. Jaleesa was somewhat ghetto and Stacey was, for lack of a better term, a dumb ass. (Harsh but the truth).

There was a whole story behind that statement.

I clicked back over to Mark.

"Hello?" I said.

"Hi, I'm still here."

"That was Charlize, and she wanted to go to brunch today."

I reached over the kitchen table and closed the window that I had left open all night. That could be why I was sick all the time.

"That's too bad; I wanted to ask you to brunch," he said, sounding defeated.

Hellllooooo, earth to Monica, earth to Monica? Wait, one more time. That was the same date we were on last night, right?!?!?!

"Maybe next time, but thanks for asking," I said.

"Can I call you tonight?" he asked.

This brotha was really trying. You had to give him credit for at least that.

"You can try but I may be out."

I looked at the clock. It was twelve-thirty.

"I gotta go. I'll talk to you later," I said.

"Bye."

I could've sworn he was trying to sound sexy.

Oh, please.

Lunch with Stacey and Jaleesa. Oh, goody. When exactly was the last time I talked to them? I couldn't even remember, but then it came back to me as clear as a sunny day.

It was when Char told me that Jaleesa's boyfriend was caught cheating on her a few times, and each one of those times she took his broke, tired, ignorant ass back. That did it for me on having any type of respect for her. It was a real shame, too. She was a computer programmer and made good money. I can't stand that. A woman who had her priorities straight but, when it came to men, they just became a complete mess.

They had been dating for about ten years and had three kids. How do you date for ten damn years? I still couldn't figure that out.

I filled Sydney's water bowl as I thought about that one.

F-that: if he hasn't married me after say, two years, then forget him. I also refused to have any kids by anyone before I got married. That just made it more difficult to leave if he didn't come through in those allotted two years.

I could still remember the first time her man Rakim was caught cheating on her. Notice I said *caught?* Chances were that it wasn't the first time he had done it. It had been the typical come-home-from-work-early story and *BAM!* There he was with their next-door neighbor. We all swore she was going to kick his butt out but she didn't. I couldn't even imagine what he had said to her in order to have her keep supporting him, but whatever it was, it had worked.

Of course, she had done all that talking about "Don't let him *ever* come around me and my kids again" and the "If I see his motherfuckin' ass on the street..." Blah, blah, blah, but, sure enough, four days later—not even a week—he was right back up in there. (And I mean that in more ways than one.) I mean dang, if it was all that, it was all that, but I couldn't see no dick being all that.

The worst part of it was that after she had done all that talkin', she knew she was wrong for taking his ass back, so she didn't tell us. She had hidden it from us for a good two weeks until Char had seen them together one night, and that's when she came clean.

The second time he had been caught, she got us again. She said the same bullshit about never taking him back and had even done the ol' "Waiting to Exhale" shit by burning up his clothes but, sure enough, after three days, I had spotted them all hugged up in Quimby's.

After that we just kind of rolled with the punches.

As I opened a can of tuna and put it in Sydney's bowl for her breakfast, I cringed at the thought of how ignorant one woman could be, especially when it came to a no-good man.

The third time, it was the same thing, but this time it had been this white girl two apartments down. She looked as though she was no more than sixteen years of age. This was the latest leverage Jaleesa would claim to have over him. She was now going to have him locked up for statutory rape.

Uh, huh. By this time we'd caught on to her game. She'd even gone as far as to call the police right in front of him and proceeded to ask the cop "general" questions regarding how to go about reporting statutory rape.

Nope, still wasn't buying it. That time it took almost a week for her to go back to him, a new record.

The last and final time of his indiscretions—and I say that with a grin on my face because even I didn't believe it was the final time, but it was the last time we caught him—he was caught in a compromising position with her little sister, who wasn't so little with her 38DDs.

We were all the lucky ones to witness this final episode.

I could remember it like it was yesterday and not a couple of months ago.

We'd all been out drinking at this bar on Main Street, and as we started to walk to our cars, there they were. They were coming out of a hotel and looking very cozy. We all just stopped in our tracks. It was like we all saw them at the same time, and the world just froze.

I looked over at Char before opening my mouth. I wondered if she'd seen what I'd just seen. Yup, she'd seen it because her mouth was just as open as mine, and she was thinking the same thing or at least I thought she was.

"Isn't that Rakim?" Char asked before anyone else had a chance to comment.

I just kind of looked at Jaleesa along with everyone else and waited for a response.

I thought Char was just trying to be bold by coming out and asking Jaleesa that dumb ass question, but as I had continued to look from Char to Jaleesa, I realized that Char didn't see Jaleesa's sister with him.

As she slowly realized it, I saw Char's face whiten to the shade of a ghost, and then she made this gasping noise.

No one had said anything else, but we all watched in silence to see the couple's next move.

Rakim hailed a taxi, both climbed into the back seat, and off they went.

Stacey was the first one to speak.

"So does this mean you guys are ready to go home, or do you want to hang out some more?"

Dummy.

No one said anything to her question, and we all just kind of proceeded back to our cars quietly and promised to catch up with each other later.

I hadn't seen or heard from anyone for the next few days until the following Saturday when Char called.

"Giiiiirl, have you heard the latest?"

Miss Gossip Queen herself.

"No, what happened?" I asked, feeling slightly guilty for even falling into her trap.

"I heard from Dynasty who heard from Toya...," she began.

"Who the hell is Toya?" I interrupted.

"You know Toya. She's Rakim's older cousin. Remember last year when we went to that picnic and there was that girl with the busted-out weave? They called her 'Tracks' because you could see the tracks from the weave sticking out through her hair. C'mon, you've got to remember her. We cracked on her for like a month after that."

"Oh, yeah, yeah," I said, not having any idea who she was. I just wanted her to continue with the story.

"Anyway, she found out that, that night we saw Rakim with Jaleesa's ho bag sister, Jaleesa threw his butt out!"

"And??" I said, not fazed by her story.

"Not only did she throw him out, but she made good on her threat by calling the police on his ass for that little tramp white girl he fucked like six months ago. It was triflin'. By the time the police got there, she had all his shit thrown out on the lawn and then turned the sprinklers on. *Then* I heard that somebody said he smacked her around a couple of times and the police took him downtown."

I highly doubted he smacked her around. He had a wussy thing about him. If anything, I think Jaleesa probably decked *him* a few times, but not vice versa.

"I was gonna call down there, but I felt weird. I mean, what would I say and how would I get information without sounding like I'm prying in her business?"

"Well, you don't because you *are* nosy and you *are* prying in her business. I say we go down there and talk to her in person."

I felt kind of guilty for being in the business, too, but if you really thought about it, Jaleesa wasn't really *my* friend. She was only a friend by association. If anything, Char should have felt like dirt because that's *her* girl, but I know she didn't.

When I finished talking myself out of feeling guilty, I ended up picking up Char, and then we rolled down to Jaleesa's, you know, to give her support in her time of need. Right?!?!

When we arrived, we saw what would've been humorous, but in this specific case it had actually been quite sad. In their yard sat a few pieces of clothing that remained from the night before. Evidently, that part was true.

To make matters worse, there were two dogs playing tug-of-war with what looked like a sock.

Okay, so it was a bit funny.

Charlize must've been thinking likewise because I heard her chuckle as she looked around and saw the same thing I did.

We pulled up the driveway and saw Jaleesa's black Mercedes, so we knew she was home.

"Well, let's go find out the deal," Char said.

I really felt as though I should feel guiltier than I did, but I didn't.

We knocked on the door, and there was no answer. We heard a TV so someone had to be home. We knocked again until we heard Jaleesa's voice.

"Who is it?" asked a voice from behind the door.

"Monica and Char!" I yelled through the heavy wooden door.

Jaleesa opened the door and stood there.

"Can we come in?" asked Char.

Jaleesa opened the door wider and walked back to the living room to continue watching TV.

We stepped into her house and shut the door behind us.

"So what's new?" Char asked.

There she went with those dumb ass questions again.

I, on the other hand, decided to just skip right to the point.

"How are you doing? I mean we haven't heard from you in a few days, and we were beginning to wonder."

"I'm fine," she said, not even looking at us. "You guys want a beer?"

Before we could answer she was off to the kitchen.

"*She's fine?*" Char questioned with a whisper. "*I don't think so!*"

"Could you knock off the dumb questions, please?" I told her. "What's new?" I mimicked.

I looked into the kitchen to make sure she wasn't coming.

"She knows the whole dang neighborhood knows, so don't act as though we were on Mars when everyone else was talking about it."

"I know, I know, but I just didn't know what to say."

I looked Char square in the face and said, "Didn't your mother ever tell you that if you can't say anything nice, then don't say anything at all? Well, the same thing goes for stupid ass things, too."

"I only have light beer. Is that okay?" yelled Jaleesa from the kitchen.

"That's fine," we said in unison.

The two stooges, at it again.

I decided to begin.

"What did he say when you confronted him?" I yelled into the kitchen.

Silence.

More silence.

"Nothin'," she said as she came back into the room with two beers in her hand. "It's done and over with. We talked it out and everything is fine."

I looked past her and into her apartment. It was a complete mess. I saw beer cans and empty bags of snacks sprawled out all over the floor. There were pizza boxes and dying plants everywhere. It really was a sordid sight.

When she said it was done and over with, I figured she was talking about the relationship, not the argument.

I looked at Char and she at me. It was time to play three stooges because I was about to take my two fingers and go straight for Jaleesa's eyes.

"Dammit, girl. I know you two didn't get back together...again. Please tell me that. *Please*," Char said, clasping her hands together as if she were praying.

"I don't see where it is any of your concern or business," Jaleesa said to both of us with much attitude. "I said everything is fine, and fine it is, and don't ask me anymore!"

This girl was a true dumb ass.

That was the last we talked about it.

That was about two months ago, and I haven't seen or hung out with her since, and now I have to go to brunch with her?

Well, I guess I have to see her sometime, so let's get it over with.

Chapter**2**

I decided to wear a pair of jeans and a black tank top to brunch with the girls.

I'd been working out for the past several months to release job tension (when I had a job, that is), and I had a tight, flat stomach, or as flat as it was gonna get.

I quickly brushed my hair and pulled it back in a ponytail and left.

I jumped into my Mustang, but as I began to pull off, I saw a note on my windshield. I got out the car and pulled off the note.

"I'm still waiting for you to call me," was all it said.

I started to smile as I immediately recognized the writing. This was my good ol' neighbor, Sam.

Sam was this Italian guy who kept asking me out. He was a little younger than me and drove this fly silver BMW, and I think he had some sort of computer job. I knew at night he worked as a bartender, but I figured that was just to meet chicks.

Sam had dark hair and a dark olive complexion. He was actually cute, but I didn't swing that way.

I looked up to Sam's apartment and there he was looking down at me grinning from ear to ear with that impeccable smile.

As he stood there waving at me, I smiled up at him and waved back. He then held up some sort of sign in the window, but I couldn't read it with the sun glare. I shaded my eyes with my hand and tried again to see what it said.

"I love you. Marry me today and have my children," it said.

Simple ass.

I started laughing and proceeded to get in my car. I beeped my horn as I pulled off and, from my rearview mirror, I saw him still in his window watching me.

Any other girl would've been lucky to have him. I just knew I wasn't the one, but you never know, maybe one day.

I pulled into the parking lot at Quimby's and it was packed. I heard the weather report state that it was going to be a hot ninety-two degrees and, with the humidity, it was going to feel a lot worse. Well, they weren't lying.

I didn't see Char's car but, then again, maybe I was missing it because there were so many cars in the parking lot.

I parked my car, started walking toward the restaurant and stopped dead in my tracks when I heard my name being called by a female voice.

"Monica, Monica sweetie," the voice said.

I looked behind me and there was Janice walking toward me.

Damn! This was the last person I was trying to run into.

Janice Beauvoir (now she knew that wasn't her last name) was the town loudmouth.

"Monica, hon," she said as she bounced toward me. "I haven't seen you in the longest. When Char told me you moved down, here I was speechless. I just knew we all were going to get together and hang out. What made you move here? I was talking to Marcy (who's Marcy?), and she said that you hated your job and that you just up and quit. Is that true? I know exactly how you feel. Sometimes I am ready to just walk out of my job at *The Law Firm* and be done with it."

She said "The Law Firm" as if it was the only law firm in the city. I guessed that made it sound more important.

We all knew she worked at "The Law Firm" as a secretary.

I didn't see anything wrong with being a secretary, but evidently she did. She continuously lied about it and called herself a paralegal, which we knew she wasn't. She even went as far as to say that she was some sort of lawyer in training. That must be hard to do *considering she didn't set foot in law school.* I don't know, maybe they started some sort of new program. Instead of going to law school, you could just work with a lawyer for X amount of years and *BAM!* one day you woke up and you were a lawyer. I think that's how it went for doctors now, too.

I was able to put on a forced smile.

"How are you doing?" I asked.

Damn, loaded question. Think, girl, think!

"I'm fine, but I just started this new aerobics class and my legs are killing me. You look good. Have you been working out, too?" she asked.

"I've been trying," I said.

Trying to stay interested in this conversation.

"Well, I guess you have, considering you have been out of work and probably don't have anything to do all day. That must be nice, but me, if I wasn't at *The Law Firm,* I don't know what I'd do. I'd probably be bored to tears."

Bored to tears? Gee, I wonder what that feels like?

"My man says that I'm just the type of person that has to work," she said, not skipping a beat. "I'm one of those career-minded women, you know. You'll have to meet him one day. We're all going to have to meet sometime in the not-so-distant future. He can probably introduce you to some of his friends at *The Practice.*"

Damn, doesn't this girl ever shut up? And what's up with "The Firm" and "The Practice?" Gimme a friggin' break.

I began to think of ways to get going and get the hell out of there, but no need, she provided me with an out.

"Listen, I have to meet my friends for lunch," she said, "but here's my card. Call me."

Before I could respond, she was waving her card in my face.

I smiled, took it, and proceeded on my way.

"Tell Char I said hi," she called after me.

I turned around and smiled again and waved buh-bye to her.

My face was literally hurting from all of the fake ass smiling.

I walked into Quimby's and immediately started looking around for a familiar face. I found no one so I proceeded to the terrace where we had agreed to meet. I looked at my watch and saw that it was twelve minutes after one.

You can always count on Char to be late, and usually it was no big deal when we met for lunch, but when we went out to a bar and I was there early and had to ward off all sharks, you could best believe I got pissed. I learned my lesson with Char. If we went someplace we were unfamiliar with, I needed to make sure that I was at least twenty minutes behind. (Just for the record, although I showed up twenty minutes late, I still had her beat by five minutes.)

I looked around once more for her, Stacey or Jaleesa and didn't see them. I didn't see *them*, but I'll tell you who I did see. Mark. My wonderful date from last night. He was standing there at the terrace bar laughing with some people.

Did I tell him that I was coming here? Think. I couldn't remember. I sincerely hoped not because if I did, then I would have to put him in the stalker category.

Then I remembered, I didn't. I did tell him we were going to brunch, but I never said where. Okay, he's good.

I still didn't see my friends, so I decided to walk up behind him and say hi.

"Excuse me, sir, but I noticed you from afar and decided I just had to say hello," I said to the back of his head in what I call my sexy voice.

He turned around and saw me and began to grin.

"Hey, what's going on?" he asked, taking a sip of his lemonade.

"Remember I told you that I was going to brunch? Well, this is our usual hangout on Saturday."

(Mental note: If he shows up "unexpectedly" next week, he's a stalker.)

"This is my first time here on a Saturday afternoon. It's cool. I like it," he said.

We stood there for a second just smiling at each other.

He looked nice in khaki shorts and a T-shirt.

I guess I didn't notice his chest and arms the previous night, but they damn sure looked good today.

"Mark?" a female voice behind him said. "Who's your friend?" she asked inquisitively.

"Monica, this is Tanya; Tanya, this is Monica," Mark said, still smiling at me.

Tanya stepped from around Mark to shake my hand.

"How do you do?" she said, sounding phony as hell.

"I do just fine and yourself?" I asked, sounding just as phony as she did. Two could play that game.

She smirked at my response.

Tanya, or Tunya as it should've been, looked to be a bit younger than Mark, and she was very thick. Five more pounds and she would've been just plain fat. She was also a lot shorter.

As Mark introduced me to the rest of his friends, she kept a sharp lookout, like a hawk waiting to swoop down on its prey.

It seemed as though this was some sort of couples' thing, but there were one too many females. I wondered who was the third wheel.

"This is a nice surprise," he stated, taking another sip of his lemonade.

I reached behind him to get a napkin from the bar to wipe the perspiration from my face. They really needed to turn the air conditioning up.

"I'm sorry, is this some sort of date thing or something? I didn't mean to intrude on anything. I just thought I would come and say hi since my friends aren't here yet."

"You aren't intruding," Mark said, clearing that up quick.

Miss Thang was *still* leering from behind him. Tell that to her.

Get a grip, sheesh.

I looked at my watch and saw that it was now one twenty-two.

Well, that's about Charlize time, so I made my excuse to leave.

"My friends should be here, so I should get going," I said, wiping the back of my neck with the napkin.

Damn, it was hot.

"Why don't you and your friends join us?" he asked.

This definitely must not be any type of date thing.

As Mark said that, girlie girl hovered directly behind him and gave me that why-don't-you-beat-it look.

"I'll ask them when I see them, (a lie) but I haven't seen them in a while, so they're probably just going to want to hang out, so if I don't catch up with you later, it was nice to see you again."

I said bye to the rest of his friends and purposely didn't even glance over in Tunya's direction.

"If you want, call me later. I should be home," I added for effect.

"Will do."

I grabbed one more napkin from behind him and turned to leave.

I wish I could've turned back around and seen Tunya's face, but that would've been too obvious.

Oh, well, obvious or not, I had to do it.

I turned around and looked directly in her face. Her glare was furious. Little did I know Mark was still looking, too, so I played it off and waved one last time.

I hoped that girl was getting the salad, I thought as I sauntered off.

I did one last walk around and saw Char with her back to me, sitting down with Stacey and Jaleesa. I started to walk over to them, and either Stacey or Jaleesa must have told her that I was coming because Char turned around and smiled and waved.

"Well, well, well, it's about time," she said.

"I *know* you ain't talking," I stated back to her. "Do you know I have been here for a good thirty minutes?"

"Only thirty minutes?" Stacey said. "You must be losing your edge, Charlize."

Thank you. I'm glad somebody else recognized.

"Yeah, you usually make us wait at least forty-five," Jaleesa added. "Girl, how are you doing?" Jaleesa turned her attention to me. "I haven't seen you in like forever. You have to tell me what's new with you."

"Yeah," added Stacey. "Like who are you seeing, who are you fucking, who you wanna fuck..."

We all started laughing.

I walked around the table to the only vacant chair that was directly in the sun. But of course.

"Leave it to you to be all crass 'n shit," I said to her.

I pulled out my chair and sat down.

"You know who I saw out in the parking lot?" I asked.

"Who?" Char and Stacey asked at the same time.

"Jinx!" They both yelled.

"Anyway," I ignored their immature game. "I saw Janice."

I waited for their reaction.

"Janice who?" Jaleesa asked.

"Janice, Janice," I said sounding kind of annoyed.

How could they not remember Janice? It was just like them to spend a good two hours talking about somebody and then forget their name.

"Ohhhhhhhhhh," Char said, finally realizing. "The one with all the boobs. You know, the secretary," Char offered when she saw that Stacey and Jaleesa still had no idea who I was talking about.

"Oh, c'mon, Jaleesa. The one that you called a hooker," Char said.

"Girl, I call everyone a hooker. You're gonna hafta be more specific than that."

"Okay, okay, how about the one that was dating that crackhead, Jimmy," I said, and they finally realized who the hell I was talking about.

Jeez, I forgot what I wanted to say.

The waiter came up and took our drink order.

"What's Ms. Crackhead up to now?" Jaleesa asked when the waiter left.

"According to her, she's supposed to be some sort of lawyer in training and works out and let's see what else, dating a guy I probably haven't met because they just started dating, yadda, yadda, yadda. There could be more, but I sort of zoned out after her telling me about some sort of face treatment she is considering, where they stick poison in your face to get rid of wrinkles, although she really doesn't feel the need because she has been using this new face cream..."

"Oh, aw right, we get it!" Char said. "That girl has always had a mouth on her."

"I thought that was *all* she had on her. That and those boobs, of course," Jaleesa said.

When the waiter came back with our juice, we ordered our food along with mimosas.

"Girl, you know you drink like a fish," Char said. "I can't keep up with yo' ass!"

"Oh, please! I seem to remember that it was you that was with me when we were hangin' out at the clubs and getting our dance on," I said.

"Remember the time we went home with those guys from Friday's?" Char took a swig of her juice. "They just knew they were Gatton' some and when they didn't, they sent us on our merry way and we had no idea where we were going?"

"I know, I know," I said laughing. "We eventually made it home around four-thirty in the morning after we stopped at the 7-Eleven drunk as shit and asked the cop for directions."

"And that's when your dumb ass asked the cop why he was there instead of Dunkin' Donuts getting his normal fill of donuts as cops usually do," Char said.

"Thank goodness he had a good sense of humor because we sho' nuff would've been in jail, and with my luck I would've had Big Bertha to room with," I said, reaching for my fork that had just fallen on the floor.

"Room with?" she asked. "What do you think jail is, the Hyatt?"

We all started laughing again.

"Ohhhh, yeah," began Char, "I found out from one of my co-workers that Schelling Inc. is hiring marketing managers for their overseas developmental something or other. I put your resume in. After all, you can't just sit around all day and do nothin'."

"You still ain't workin'?" Stacey asked.

I was really getting tired of everyone's interest in my employment.

"Let's see," I started with a sarcastic tone, "I've been out here a full month now and I'm not the president of my own company yet. Shame on me. I'd better get on the ball!"

Sometimes Stacey annoyed me, and this time it came out with my response.

"I was just saying that you didn't get any leads yet?" she said, trying to change her tone to a less caustic one.

Too late.

"No," I said, having decided to just end the conversation about my employment before she really got to me.

Hey, if I wanted to work at an accounting firm making $24,500 a year, I could do that, too. But I think I'll hold out for an even $26,000.

When our food came, we ate almost silently. While everyone else ordered their eggs, bacon, pancakes and fruit for Stacey because of her never-ending diet, I got my chicken fingers and fries with extra honey mustard.

Uh-oh, it has started already. Come to think of it, I didn't do my crunches today either. Oh, well, I'll start my diet next week.

When the bill finally came we all totaled up.

"Guys, I gotta go," I said as I got up from the table. "I have to pick up a few things at the store, so I'll catch up with you guys later."

I didn't want to tell them that I had to get myself together for a seven-thirty interview the following morning, and besides that, I had had enough of them and just wanted to leave.

"Okay, but do me a favor. Tomorrow night at around six-thirty, meet me at Jack's for happy hour," Char said.

"Happy hour?" Stacey asked. "Don't you have to have a job for that?" she said, laughing.

Evidently she must've been getting on everyone else's nerves, too, because no one else laughed at her sorry comment, but that didn't seem to faze her in the least.

Here's a note to self—stop hanging out with her.

"Jack's?" I said as I reached around the back of my chair for my purse. "I hate going there. Why would you wanna go there anyway? That's a hangout for couples."

Silence.

Then she smiled and it hit me.

"Ah, hell nah. Don't be tryin' to set me up again. I still haven't recovered from your last set-up," I said.

"It's not really a set-up. I met this guy and he wants to go out with his frat brother, or something, who's in town, so naturally he has to have a date," Char said.

"Frat brother? Shouldn't they be too old for that shit?" I asked.

Silence again.

"Exactly how old are they?" I sighed.

She smiled again.

"They're about twenty-four."

"Ah, hell nah," I said again. "Take Stacey."

Char knew good and well that she didn't wanna take big-mouth Stacey, so she scrambled with her excuse, and I enjoyed watching her scramble.

"Can't. His boy described the type of girl he's attracted to and guess what, he described you to the T."

That's the best she could come up with?

"You might as well go," Jaleesa said. "You ain't got shit else to do. I'd go my damn self. I love me some island men."

Island men?

"How do you know they're from the island and what island?" I asked.

"Char already told me about them, and they sound cute," Jaleesa said, adjusting her chair. "They're from the Bahamas."

"Do they even have fraternities in the Bahamas?" I asked.

"I lied. They're not frat brothers; they're just buddies," Char said.

Why would she lie about that? If she lied about that she could lie about anything regarding them.

"How in the hell did you meet guys from an island anyway?" I asked.

The girl could really get around.

"Just go and I'll fill you in on all the details later. Dang! Meet me at Jack's at six-thirty."

"Fine," I said, placing the money for my food on the table. "Call me tomorrow morning after eleven and we'll see."

"Why after eleven?" she asked nosily.

"Just call me tomorrow. Peace out, folks." With that, I was ghost.

As I walked to the parking lot of Quimby's, I spotted my car and, at the same time, heard my name being called. I turned around to see Mark running toward me waving.

"Hey. So it's okay to call you this week?" he asked when he reached me.

"If you want to?" I was fidgeting in my purse for my car keys that were inevitably at the very bottom.

That may have sounded a bit callous, but the truth was I didn't care one way or the other. Personally, I am really too old for that will-he-or-won't-he-call-me-crap.

"Okay then," he said, nodding.

I looked past him and saw Tanya glaring from the restaurant entrance.

"You might need to get permission from her first," I said, motioning toward the entrance.

"Who?" he asked, turning around to see who I was talking about. "Please. I probably won't even see her after today. I'm doing this as a favor to a friend."

"I hear ya," I said and turned and got into my car.

I put the top down and started the car. I decided to drive in the direction of the entrance of the restaurant where Hawkeye Hippo was standing. I don't know what made me do it, but I did.

Mark had just reached Tanya, and they were both standing there at the front. I beeped my horn, and they both turned around.

"Don't forget to call this week," I said without stopping the car.

I looked through my rearview mirror and saw her fussin' at him.

Sometimes I just hated me, and this definitely wasn't one of those times. *Ha.*

Chapter3

By the time I finished running my errands and visiting my sister in Bowie, it was almost six o'clock, and the sun was still beating hard.

I reached my apartment complex in time to see my neighbor Sam get into his silver bullet with this cute little brunette girl.

I waved and kept rolling.

Damn, I had only turned the guy down half a dozen times, and he was already cheating on me.

I got upstairs, opened the door to my apartment and banged the door right into Sydney.

"Move, Cat!"

I don't know why she insisted on lying there right in front of the door.

She cut her eyes at me (no, I'm serious, I think she can do that) and went into the bedroom and jumped up right on my pillow. The little shit probably pissed somewhere and I'd never find it. It would take someone coming over and telling me that my place smelled like cat piss for me to ever realize it. I was completely immune by now.

I checked to see if I had messages and there were none. I went into the kitchen and opened the door of the refrigerator and closed it. I'd eaten too much already. I'd had the chicken fingers, and then I'd gone over to my sister's house and had some cookies.

Okay, okay, diet started tomorrow. (If I had a dollar for every time I said that...)

Riiiiiiiiiiing. My phone had the weirdest ring. It sounded like one of those phones I used to use when I worked as a telemarketer in college. I hated that job.

I picked it up without looking at the caller ID. I couldn't tell you why I even had that thing. Most of the time, I didn't look at it. It ruined the element of surprise. Of course, when the solicitors called and I picked up the phone without looking at the caller ID, I'd get pissed and always vowed to look at it from then on, but that never lasted.

"Hello?"

Of course, it was a solicitor.

The girl on the other end started in on a rehearsed speech about free minutes.

Now, I understood that telemarketers had a job to do just like everyone else, so I tried to be as nice as possible and cut her off in the middle of her written spiel from section four, paragraph seven of the employee handbook, instead of letting her go through the whole thing and *then* telling her no.

Well, she wasn't having it. She was a black girl. I don't care what anyone says, sometimes you can just tell when someone is a brotha or a sista, and this girl was definitely a sista.

All I said was, "No, thank you, but thanks for calling anyway," and girlfriend went off.

"Why not?" she said with an attitude as she cracked her damn gum in my ear. "I saw your bill and you could really do with free minutes."

Was this a joke?

"With a bill like that, you must be calling somebody in Guam. I'm tryin' to hook you up," she continued.

(Now tell me that wasn't a sista.)

"Thanks, but no thanks," I said again.

"Fine, but it's your loss!" And then she hung up on *me*.

I just chalked it up to her having a bad day and shrugged it off.

Then I thought about it. Why the hell was she all in my callin' business and how the hell did she see my bill in the first place? I didn't even know where she was calling from, so I couldn't call back and complain.

My phone rang again.

Please don't be the solicitor from hell again.

I checked the caller ID this time—duh—and it was Char.

"Where the hell were you? I called you all afternoon and there was no answer."

"Damn, bitch," I answered back, "What are you? My man?"

I walked into the bedroom and took off my shoes.

"If you need to know, I was running errands and went to Sharee's house," I said, opening the refrigerator for like the tenth time hoping to find something different in there that wasn't there the last nine times.

"When does your sister plan on having kids? She's like forty now," Char said.

"First of all, she's not forty, and why you all in it? Mind yours."

"Anyway," she continued, "I talked to Broadus and he and his buddy are going to meet us at eight o'clock at Jack's tomorrow night."

"Eight o'clock. Damn you. I thought we were going to happy hour? What happened to that?" I asked.

I wanted to get this over with as soon as possible.

"He said he has some other things to do first and then they'll meet up with us. I say we get there about seven and get a glass of wine beforehand. I know how evil you get when you don't want to be somewhere...on second thought, maybe, you need two glasses."

"Weren't you supposed to call me *tomorrow* night anyway?" I asked reaching for the towel to clean up the water I had just spilled all over my kitchen floor.

"Yeah, but since Broadus just called, I thought I'd call you now and let you know the 411 instead of keeping you in suspense."

"Speaking of suspense, what does this fool look like?"

I was really curious now.

She was silent for a moment and I thought I heard her take a sip of something.

"Which one, mine or yours?"

She said that like I actually gave a damn what her man looked like. But then again...

"Both," I said.

"Well, mine is about five feet nine and he's okay looking, but he's really nice. He's funny as hell, and we had a great time when we first met."

"That reminds me, you never did tell me where you met him," I said.

"I met him on vacation when I went with this girl from work. He's only here for a short time, so be nice please."

"A short time?" I asked.

What was up with that?

"They both live in the Bahamas and are going back next week. Yours just came up here to get him, and then they're both leaving together, so you don't have to worry about him calling you."

So now he's mine?

"So what about mine?" I asked using her same expression.

"Your what?" she said, definitely taking a sip of something. Alcoholic beverage, no doubt.

"What does my guy look like?"

"I don't know, I've only seen him once, and I don't really remember. I think he was cute though," she said.

Great, can't wait to meet Frankenstein.

"Ohhhhh, I almost forgot to tell you," I said. "Mark asked if he could call me next week."

"Well, what did you say?"

"I told him that's fine."

"I thought you didn't like him?"

"I never said that," I said defensively. "We just had a bad date."

"So what, you want a repeat performance?" she asked.

"Nah, I think he knows better. But listen, what's up with Tanya?" I asked, changing the subject from him to her.

"Who dat?" Char asked.

"The hoochie he was with at brunch today."

"Rrrrrrrr," Char said, making that God-awful catfight noise. "Listen to you. I didn't even know he was there today. I'll find out and get back to you on that one. Just don't forget about tomorrow. Do you want me to pick you up?" she asked.

"Yeah, bring your raggedy Neon over here and pick my ass up," I said, laughing. "And come at six-thirty so we can get there by seven."

"Bet! Catch you tomorrow," she said and hung up.

I opened the refrigerator door once more.

Broadus?

I spent the rest of the night getting my resume together on the computer and sipping a glass of wine.

I put on my favorite Jamiroquai CD and took it into the night until I went to bed. My phone rang about a half-hour later. Since it was dark, I couldn't see the caller ID, so I just picked it up. (At least I made the attempt this time.) I *was* able to see that it was eleven-thirty at night though.

Who was calling me this late?

I picked it up and whomever it was hung up. I guess I missed it.

I lay back down and my phone rang again, no more than two minutes later.

"Hellooooo?" I was more annoyed this time.

They hung up again, but this time there was a pause, so the person on the other end knew I had picked it up.

What the...???

Chapter4

I opened my eyes the next morning at five-thirty. This gave me about an hour to get ready and leave out around six-thirty. I decided to check the caller ID to see if my crank-calling friend had left a trail, but of course, they hadn't. The ID read "ANONYMOUS." That could be anyone.

I made a note to myself to get anonymous numbers blocked.

The place where I had the interview was only twenty minutes away. I had plenty of time.

I really should get an alarm clock one day, but I've always had this sort of internal alarm clock inside of me. I told myself what time I wanted to wake up in the morning and *"BAM!"* I was up the next morning, right on time. I could come in from partying at two o'clock in the morning and still be able to get my butt up on time the next day. Although there were times I misjudged and woke up twenty minutes early or twenty minutes late. Overall, I had it timed pretty well.

After I showered, I put on my best navy blue suit. It was perfect. It was somewhat form-fitting, but the skirt was past my knees. This covered both bases. If it were a man interviewing me, I could be cute with the tightness and if it were a woman, I could look professional and exude confidence with the length. First impressions are everything in the business world nowadays. Oh, yeah, and there was always the all-important resume. That could help, too.

I finished getting dressed, and it was already six forty-five. Damn, I was late, and I didn't even have any of that, lemme-try-this-on-lemme try-that-on. What-do-you-think-of-these-shoes? No-wait-I-gotta-change-I-don't-like-this outfit-crap. No biggin, I could always make up time on the road and be right on schedule again.

When I got to the parking lot, I realized I had forgotten my dang keys. *Damn!* Now I would have to run back in, find them and come back out.

When I got back to my front door, I opened it up, knocked kitty in the head and began my random search. Each minute it took me to find my keys, I was getting more and more pissed off. I must've said every four-letter word twice over.

I finally found my keys under the couch (how they got there I'll never know) and rolled out again. Now I would have to rush because it was seven-fifteen and my interview was at seven-thirty and I still had a twenty-minute ride.

As I got into my car and pulled off, I realized that rush hour started at seven in Maryland and, of course, there was that inevitable non-working stoplight up ahead, so each car had to take its time inching out into the death-by-design intersection.

Could it get any better?

Well, I could've done one of two things. I could've gotten all worked up and sat in the car cussing up a storm and honking my horn at every idiot on the road, or I could've just turned up the radio and dealt. I chose the latter. I was late anyway. Great impression. *Damn, damn and damn again!*

I pulled up to the parking garage right outside the office building and naturally there were no vacant spaces. Every office building I'd been to had the same issue. Not enough parking. I drove down the street and pulled my car into another lot. I drove round and round the parking garage until I found this teenie-weenie parking spot on the top level. I carefully pulled in and thanked the stars that I would more than likely be leaving before the two cars I pulled in between. There was no way I was going to be able to get out of that spot without dinging one of those cars.

Better them than me, I always said.

That was one thing about Maryland. Everything had damn pay parking. I could understand the city, but even the suburbs had pay parking. Everyone was always trying to squelch money from you.

I walked into the office building and did my customary quick assessment. There were a few well-dressed people already waiting for the elevator. All of them white, except for this one little black lady. I started to smile as I looked at her. She was cute with her handbag and glasses hanging off the end of her nose. I wondered where she was going. I looked at the directory and couldn't place her. There was an accounting firm, nope, a web design company, nope. Oh, well.

I found my destination on the seventh floor. I hopped in the elevator and up I went. I felt someone looking at me. As I turned to my left, I saw a man staring directly in my face. I smiled and said, "Good morning," and turned back around. I knew he was still staring at me.

Four, five,—c'mon, seven, hurry up—six, seven. Bing!

I stepped off the elevator and couldn't believe what I saw. This floor was nothing like the lobby. The lobby had fresh flowers, marble floors, and mirrors on the ceiling. The seventh floor was—for lack of a better word— jacked! I looked around expecting to see a scaffold and some painters around. At least then there would be an excuse.

I walked to Suite 714, opened the door and met a young secretary sitting at the front desk. She couldn't have been any more than eighteen.

"Good morning," she said all cheery. "Welcome to Schelling, Inc. How can we help you today?"

"I have an interview with Ms. Leslie Gordon for the marketing position," I said.

"One moment, please," she said, without wiping that smile off her face. I was talkin' serious teeth.

She got on the phone and dialed like eight numbers. What was all that about?

"Uh-huh, okay, uh-huh, yes, she is," she said to the receiver, with that smile still on her face. I was getting a headache just looking at her.

I wondered what in the hell was all the talking about. *Just tell her I'm here.*

I imagined the person on the other end telling her that her tiny apartment she rented in downtown D.C. just burned down.

"Uh-huh, yes, okay."

And that her dog she had for fourteen years was just struck by a car.

"Yes, ma'am, okay, uh-huh."

She hung up the phone and told me to have a seat and that they would be right with me.

They? I had assumed it would just be Leslie Gordon.

I picked up a magazine and started reading about Cher's diet secrets. When I finished that article, I looked at my watch and it was seven fifty-five.

I then picked up a *Home and Garden* magazine and read up on kitchen designs.

When I checked my watch again, it was ten minutes after eight.

See, now they were trippin' up in here.

Just as I was about to give them another five minutes, a *really* young black woman walked out of one of the offices and toward the receptionist's desk. I figured she must work there or something. She walked straight toward me.

I smiled and looked around.

Why was this young black woman walking straight at me?

I looked again and she was extending her hand.

"Good morning, uh...Miss, um, I'm sorry. Your name again?"

I began to tell her but she cut me off.

"Never mind, I have your file in my office. You can follow me," she said as she turned and walked off.

I guess that was my cue to follow, so I did. As we were walking down the hall, she introduced herself.

"I'm Ms. Gordon. I believe I spoke to you on the phone."

Correct me if I was wrong, but I was now getting vibes of a greater than thou complex from her. I hated to admit it, but I have had bad experiences interviewing with black females, but I was trying not to carry those experiences in this interview. I needed to be open-minded and just see how it went.

"Did you have any problems getting here?" she asked without turning around.

"None at all. I knew where the place was."

"Oh," she said, reaching into her pocket and pulling out a pen. "I was just wondering because you were slightly late."

I apologized for that.

She marked something on a file she was carrying. I think she was giving me a demerit.

"Actually I was early, but I lost my keys and then I underestimated the traffic. In Philadelphia, where I am originally from, traffic isn't nearly..."

"Uh-huh," she said, cutting me off again. (Oh, boy, I can't wait for this interview to kick off—speaking of kick off...)

She did have a point though. Regardless of the circumstances, I was late.

"So," I began trying to make conversation. "How long has this company been in existence?"

I was going to be as professional as she *thought* she was being and just take it from there.

"For a few years now." She smiled, showing off the fact that she was obviously a smoker.

Who did this woman remind me of?

She led me to a tiny office with no windows that barely fit a desk and chair. From how hoity-toity she was acting, I imagined her having one of those executive offices with the couch and the big picture windows.

"Have a seat," she offered, and I sat, almost bustin' my butt on that little ass chair that was dang near on the ground.

She walked behind me and shut the door.

Why did this seem like an interrogation? Why did I also think that she WANTED it to seem like that?

I was waiting for her to pull out a bright light to shine in my face while she asked questions.

She went around and sat at her desk.

She really reminded me of someone but I couldn't place it. *Who was it?*

She pulled her chair in and straightened some things on her desk, and she did all this without saying a word, probably some sort of intimidation tactic. I grinned at the effort.

I was thoroughly amused by all of this because, by now, I had already decided that I definitely did not want that job but to use the interview as an experience to take with me to my next job interview. And believe you me, there would be another interview.

Stacey! That's who she reminded me of. They both had that superior attitude, which led me to believe that she didn't have shit either, but loved acting like she did.

I was so busy with my thoughts that I didn't even hear her question.

"I'm sorry, I didn't hear your question," I said as politely as I could muster.

She opened her top desk drawer and pulled out a tissue and proceeded to wipe down the phone handset on her desk.

"I *asked* how you heard about the position and why do you think you are qualified for this type of work," she said.

Well, from what I heard about the position it is a remedial one that I am sure you yourself started out in, but by acting high sidity, you were able to muster up a "promotion" with no salary increase, but hey, at least you have a great title. My main objective was to take this mediocre position and do such an excellent job, as I know I could, and eventually take your job. That's what you think, isn't it?

Okay, no more wasting my time.

"You know Ms., uh, I'm sorry I forgot your name," I began. (That felt good.)

Before she could interject, I cut *her* off.

"I apologize for wasting your time, *and mine*, but I do feel like I'm overqualified for this position. I mainly came here to see what cards would be put onto the table, but now that I'm here, I can see that an offer of any sort would not be lucrative in my career goals," I said, standing up out of Papa Smurf's chair.

"Thank you for your time and you have a great day," I said and turned and walked out of her office.

I walked down the hall and past the receptionist. I couldn't help smiling to myself. I must've made an impact because when I reached the receptionist's desk, the teenybopper was still on the phone, only this time without the smile. She looked at me and then looked quickly away as if she were already talking on the phone about me, which I knew she was.

"You have a great day," I said to her.

She looked up at me as if she didn't know what to do and just half-smiled and looked down while still on the phone.

I really wanted to tell her to tell Ms. Uppity I said hello because I knew that's who she was talking to.

I continued out through the doors and toward the elevators.

My black sisters. Why must it be like this?

Chapter 5

"How was your interview?" Char asked while trying to get the bartender's attention.

"The interview sucked and wait a minute, how did you know I had an interview?"

"Your big-mouth sister told me," she said. "I called over her house this morning trying to catch up with you."

I didn't know why I decided to go ahead and meet up with her at Jack's as planned. It was only seven-fifteen, and we were seated at the bar and our dinner reservations were changed to eight-fifteen.

I was almost late trying to figure out what to wear, but as usual, I made it on time. I didn't know what was going on; I never used to be on CPT.

The bartender came over to us and Char ordered another drink. She then directed her attention back to me, looking me up and down.

"Why didn't you put something sexy on?" she asked.

"By sexy, do you mean like what you have on?" I said as I looked at her outfit.

Tonight she was full hoochie from head to toe. She had put up her hair and wore this tight, tight, tight, and did I say tight, dress that was low-cut. On a normal day she didn't really have any cleavage, but tonight she had plenty by way of falsies.

I decided against saying a smart-ass comment regarding her newfound tits, so I just left it alone.

"I hope you don't expect me to pay for young buck," I said, cutting my eyes at her.

"Girl, please," she said. "If that were the case, I wouldn't be going out with them, much less you."

"So tell me again how you met him," I asked curiously.

She took a drag of her cigarette.

"When I went to the Bahamas a couple of weeks ago, I met Broadus," she began. "It was strictly by chance. Denise, the girl I went with, tried hooking up with Cornelius, but it seemed like he wasn't interested."

"Eweeee," I said, turning up my nose. "My date? Don't be givin' me somebody else's leftovers. They probably did it, too," I said.

She took another drag of her cigarette. She was one of those smokers who smoked only when she drank. Translation: she smoked all the time.

"I don't think so, but she did offer."

"Why not? I've heard stories of island men just preying on unsuspecting American women," I said.

"Yeah, okay. First of all, most of these American women are not unsuspecting, and more times than not, they go over there looking for it themselves."

"Tru dat, tru dat," I admitted.

"Besides, Cornelius isn't like that. He's actually a nice guy, and he's cute, too, if I remember correctly."

She paused and looked up to the ceiling as if recalling.

"He was a little square for my taste though. He was quiet and reserved and looked disinterested in being there."

"Like he was dragged there by his friend. Gee, I wonder what that feels like?" I said sarcastically.

"Anyway," she said, rolling her eyes. "They really are cool."

Yeah, okay.

"If they're anything like Frick and Frack we went out with a few months back, then you might as well count me out now," I said, taking a drink of my vodka martini.

The guys I referred to as Frick and Frack were two duds that Char met one night, and as my luck would have it, she decided to bring me in on it to share in the same misery. They were accountants, mutants, mutant-accountants, whatever. I just remember them being boring as hell, and at some point during the date I even thought they were gay, and with each other at that. That could've quite possibly been the worst date of my life.

"Yeah, and remember he even had the nerve to call you the next night for another date?" Char asked.

"Thank goodness for caller ID," I said, nodding. "It was just pure luck that I happened to actually look at it that time. I guess God had pity on me."

"Did you ever talk to him again?"

"He never reached me."

I reached over the bar for another stirrer.

"Wait, actually he did once. It was one of those times where I didn't look at the caller ID and, as I picked it up and said hello, I looked down to see his name and number, but it was too late."

"I told you about that," she said, laughing.

"It didn't matter because before I even said hello, I had my lie together. He got out maybe two words before I gave him the ol' I-was-just-walking-out-the-door-and-I'll-call-him-back line."

"No, you didn't!"

"Yes, I did, and he fell for it hook, line and sinker. He had the nerve to try to give me his number to call his ass back, but I was quicker. I told him I'd call him back and hung the fuck up. For some odd reason he never called again. Go figure."

Char almost choked on her drink from laughter.

"I see why you don't have a man. Keep acting up like that; you'll never get one."

This coming from a woman who may get 'em but she sure enough doesn't keep 'em.

We were on our second drink when I checked the clock. It was seven fifty-five. Good, we still had more time.

"Hey, Monica, how are you doing?"

I turned around to see Mark standing there looking all cute. This time he had on a navy suit with a deep red tie and looked as impeccable as usual. This man could really dress. This was like my fifth time running into him. I couldn't believe we hung out at the same spots and had never met each other before.

"What are you guys doing here?" he said, smiling at me.

"What's up, Mark?" Char said. "I guess you didn't see *me*, huh?"

He said a quick "hello" to her and then turned his attention back to me.

"I'm meeting a few people for dinner tonight," he said.

Damn, he even smelled good, too.

"You ladies look nice tonight," he said, looking from me to Char.

He then turned back to me.

"I'm glad I caught up with you," he said, still smiling at me. "I tried calling you this past weekend." (I knew this but I didn't feel like picking up.) "Would you like to go to dinner tomorrow night?" he asked. "I have to go out of town the latter part of this week, so I'd like to try to catch up to you tomorrow before I have to go."

I could feel Char grinning next to me, which is precisely why I didn't even bother to turn to look in her direction.

"That sounds good to me. I probably won't be home until late tonight, so try calling me sometime tomorrow afternoon," I said.

"Why don't we just say I'll pick you up at seven tomorrow night, so just be ready."

Oh, no, he didn't. Set it up while he had me in case he couldn't get in touch with me later.

I wished I had a snazzy comeback for that one so I would be in control, but nope. Instead, I said, "Sounds good. I'll be ready."

Ooooooh, good comeback. Control lost.

"I'll see you guys later," he said, still smiling at me.

I followed him with my eyes to see where he was going. He went to a table with several people, male and female, but guess who was there? Tanya. Evidently she didn't see him over by us because she sure enough would've been glaring at me trying to turn me into stone.

"Girl, I think he actually likes you," Char said.

"Yeah, okay," I said sarcastically. "You know how men get with a new toy. He probably acts like that with all new females he tries to conquer," I said, looking over at his table again.

He was cute. Looking at him now, I was ready to be his toy, and he could play with me all night long.

"I don't think so," Char began.

"And how, pray tell, do you know this, missy?" I asked curiously.

Char grinned that grin like she had something to tell me.

"Okay, promise me you won't get mad if I tell you something?"

Oh, Lawdy, here it comes. All I could think of was that song by the Gap Band, "You Dropped a Bomb on Me."

"What?" I said, cocking my head to the side in disgust.

Oh, *now* she had something to tell me about him after sending me out on a date with him.

"Lemme guess, serial killer? How about child molester? He has six toes? No wait, he's a bigamist and has twenty-four kids? Am I getting close? Whaaaaat?"

"You done?" she asked, stirring her drink with a straw. "It's nothing at all like that. I know he really likes you because I tried fixing him up with Jaleesa before."

She stirred a little faster.

"You're kidding?" I said. "When?"

"Girl, this was like two years ago when she and her deadbeat man were broken up. Mark told me he had no interest in her, so it never progressed."

"So what all happened?" I asked, "And why didn't Jaleesa ever tell me before?"

"Jaleesa didn't know that I fixed you up with him. It's none of her business. Jaleesa is cool and all, but he just didn't like her. There was no attraction there. I think he thought she was too unrefined for his taste."

I wasn't sure what to make of this newfound information.

"Calm down, it was just one date," she said when she realized that I was still in shock.

The bartender came back and asked us if we wanted another round.

"So, why me then?" I asked after ordering another martini.

"He had seen you at our company picnic when you were dating Kenny, Kenyon, whatever his name was, and asked me about you then. I told him you and dude were serious and that was the end of that. Besides, you were living in Philly at the time."

"Why are you steady trying to fix me up with these leftovers, first Mark and now this island guy? This is it and I mean it," I said.

"Are you mad at me for not telling you?" Char was trying to give me her standard pathetic look.

"No, but I'm telling you now, this is it."

"Yeah, yeah, whatever. Besides, this doesn't count as a fix-up because we're just hanging out until they go back to the Bahamas next week, so I still owe you one," she said, winking at me.

"Keep dreamin'."

Just then, two guys walked up on the side of Char.

"Broaaaadus!" she screamed and gave him a big hug. "What's up?"

"Nothin' much, just couldn't wait to see you," he said in a sexy island accent.

"I want you to meet my girl, Monica," she said, touching my shoulder. Broadus walked over and gave me a hug.

"Nice to finally meet you. I've heard so much about you."

Liar.

Broadus was a cute little guy. He had brown skin and, as expected, I was taller than him. Not at all like I pictured, but nonetheless, his face was still cute. I could tell he was a big beer drinker, a *very* big beer drinker. Although he was small he had a round mid-section.

"And this is my boy, Nealy-mon," Broadus said.

Out steps this gorgeous man. Where do I begin to describe him? He was about six feet one, and the first thing I noticed was that he had very broad shoulders. (I have a thing about broad shoulders.) He had a slim build, but it wasn't by any means skinny. His face was chiseled and he had a slight mustache with these cute sideburns that seemed to match his face perfectly. If I had to say he looked like someone famous, I would say he looked like the singer Ginuwine minus the Jheri-Curl.

I had never been attracted to someone so much at first sight. I couldn't believe it.

"Good evening," he said in the same accent as his buddy.

Char elbowed me. She was shocked by his looks, too, and she had seen him before.

"Well, do you guys want to sit at the bar, or are you ready to get a table?" Broadus asked.

"Our reservations aren't until eight-fifteen, so we have another ten minutes to kill. Have a seat and we'll get some more drinks," Char said.

Broadus sat next to Char. Cornelius sat beside me.

"So Broadus," I began, "Char gave me her *vague* story on how she met you, so why don't you give me your version," I asked and grinned at the prospect of getting juicy information.

I somehow got the impression that Char didn't tell me everything and probably wouldn't, so therefore I had to go to a different source.

Broadus began to smile. He had a nice smile.

"I met her while she was on vacation with her girlfriend, and we went out to a restaurant and then dancing, and that was it."

"That was it, huh?" Cornelius said.

I looked toward him now.

"What do you know about the situation? Maybe I can get a straight answer out of you," I said, smiling at Cornelius.

Cornelius started smiling and, my goodness, he had a beautiful smile. One of his front teeth kind of stuck out, but not obviously. I was thinking it was some sort of childhood accident.

"I'm gonna plead the fifth on this one. You guys are just gonna hafta sort this out on your own." With that said, we all started laughing.

The bartender came up to us and we continued to order more drinks. Char had her usual, but this time I decided on vodka and cranberry juice. I noticed that Cornelius was drinking beer and Broadus had rum and Coke.

When our table was ready, the hostess came over to us and directed us to our seats. We had to pass Mark and his party and I could feel his eyes on me. I could also feel Tanya's eyes on me, or should I say seeing *through* me.

As we passed the table, I politely looked over toward Mark and gave him a smile, but he kept staring at me intently, which I thought was kind of weird considering he had a date with him.

When we finally reached our table, we were in full view of Mark's table. Sure enough, he was *still* looking.

Since our table was a cozy booth, Cornelius and I sat on one side and Broadus and Char sat on the other.

We spent the whole time having great conversation amongst all of us. Broadus was really nice and had a great sense of humor, whereas Cornelius was more cool and laid-back.

This gave him a sexy quality. I also noticed that when we finished our drinks, Broadus asked if we wanted more, but when they came, it was Cornelius who paid. When those drinks were finished, Cornelius offered us more drinks, and when *they* came, he paid again. If I remembered correctly, I don't think Broadus paid for one set of drinks.

Throughout our conversations, I found out that Broadus was twenty-nine and a driver for one of the hotel resorts in the Bahamas; Cornelius was twenty-four and a waiter. He'd also just started going back to school for computers.

So he had goals. That was good. Of course, at this point, he could've told me that he was a bum living on the streets and I would've just said that he was an outdoorsman.

When the bill was laid down in the middle of the table, I was prepared to pay. I didn't mind, either, because I had such a great time and was thankful for it.

"Don't worry about the bill; we got this," Cornelius said as he instructed the waiter to give it to him.

I looked at Broadus to see his reaction and he just had a blank expression on his face and gulped down the rest of his drink.

Something told me that Cornelius would be paying this bill himself, so I stepped up to the plate. I grabbed the bill out of his hands.

"No, really, you guys don't have to. You're here on vacation and we'd like to treat you guys," I said. (I wish you could've seen Char's face. I was definitely going to hear about this one later.)

Cornelius grabbed the bill back from me and looked me dead in the face. "Let us thank you for your hospitality by paying the bill." Then he paused. *"Please."*

That was all she wrote. I was in love.

"If you want to, you can buy drinks later," he said.

I didn't realize that I was still holding on to the bill so I let it go.

This guy was good-looking *and* diplomatic. *Watch out now!*

Sounded good to me. Did that mean he would like to spend more time with me? I wondered.

Char and I got up from the booth and went to the front of the restaurant to wait for them.

I passed Mark's table and it was empty except for glasses and plates. I didn't even see him leave, but when we got to the front entrance I saw his whole party walking out the door with him being last. He turned around and spotted me and came back.

"Hey, ladies. How was your dinner? You looked like you were having a good time," he said, looking only at me again.

"I had a great time," Char said facetiously, upon realizing he wasn't even looking at her. "I gotta go to the ladies room. I'll be back."

She disappeared around the corner.

"Yeah, dinner was good. I had a chicken caesar salad that was delicious," I said, smiling-slash-flirting.

He took a step toward me and smiled generously.

"That's good, that's good," he said, not really concerned about my damn salad.

I took a seat at the front bar, and I peeked over his shoulder to see if I could see his friends.

"Your party is probably waiting for you so you'd better go." I was getting slightly uncomfortable with him being so close to my face.

"Are we still on for tomorrow night?" he asked.

I didn't know if he was really asking that question just to have something to say because he knew I was getting uncomfortable, or if he really thought that things might have changed in one hour.

"Yup," I said. "At seven."

Just then Tanya came back in the front door, checking around for Mark no doubt.

"Well, your friend is back looking for you so you'd better go."

He rolled his eyes.

"Okay, then, see you mañana."

What *was* the deal between them?

"Bye," I said, and he turned around and walked toward the front to where she was standing.

By this time, she had spotted us and was glaring yet again.

Pathetic.

"Was that a friend of yours?" Cornelius asked, coming up behind me.

I turned around, startled.

"Uh-huh," I said, leaving it at that.

"So are you ready to go?" he asked.

He pulled out the chair I was sitting in and helped me up.

"Broadus and Charlize are going to another bar. If you don't wanna go, we could go someplace else," he said, still holding on to my hand.

I wondered if it was Broadus or Cornelius that requested this. Then again, it could've been Char and her fast ass. Either way, it didn't matter to me. I really had a good time that night and I wanted to get to know him better, even if he was only going to be around for another week or so, so I opted for the coffeehouse.

Since Char picked me up, Cornelius and I took the rental car they had and Char drove herself and Broadus to wherever they went.

"Do you know where you're going?" I asked once we were in the car.

"No, I was kind of relying on you guiding me to where you want to go."

"You know what?" I asked. "How do you feel about Dave and Busters?"

"Dave and *who?*"

"Dave and Busters," I repeated. "You can play video games, play pool, drink, eat, etcetera…"

"Let's go then," he said and off we went.

When we got there, not only was the line out the door and around the corner, but they were charging, too.

"I forgot. I think after ten o'clock they start charging," I told him.

It was eleven-thirty.

"This time, I'm paying," I offered and pulled out the money before he could say anything.

When we finally got in, it was even more crowded. People were everywhere.

"Do you play pool?" he asked, spotting a pool table.

"Not really," I lied.

I used to play pool all the time in college but, then again, that was a *loooooooong* time ago and I didn't want to oversell myself.

For being his first time there, he seemed to know his way around pretty well. Confidence. I liked that. It was nice to have a guy take charge and he received extra points because he was not even from this country. You go, boy.

I watched him walk over to the pool table and what a nice sight it was. He had on a pair of jeans and a T-shirt that fit nicely over his shoulders. The best part was his ass. It was perfect. It fit his body perfectly. I wondered if he had hair on his butt. That would definitely be minus a few points. That's a big no-no.

How was I sitting there seriously checking out this young buck who didn't even live in this country?

He came back and told me the wait for a pool table was forty-five minutes. Damn!

"We can wait at the bar if you want to," he offered.

He grabbed my hand and directed me to the bar.

When we got there, there was a couple getting up from a tiny round table directly next to the bar. We sat there. It was noisy but cozy. The room was dark and there were people everywhere around us, some smoking, some on first dates, (you can just tell sometimes) some drunk, some getting drunk. People just everywhere.

"So what did you think of tonight?" he asked boldly.

Wow, I liked that, too. At this point there really wasn't anything I *didn't* like about him.

"I had a great time," I said. I hoped I didn't sound overly eager.

Oh, yeah, who cared? He was leaving anyway.

"I *really* had a good time," he said. "I've only been to the States a couple of times, and this by far has been the best time yet."

He sounded so cute every time he talked. His accent reminded me of waves crashing against the rocks in some beautiful, sunny island countryside.

The waiter came over and we ordered more drinks.

"You know we have been drinking all night?" I said to him.

"I know," he added. "This is going to be my last one."

"Yeah, sure, me, too," I said, laughing.

He called the waiter back to our table and ordered appetizers for us.

"If we're going to drink, we'd better keep our stomachs full."

We spent two hours sitting at the table talking. We missed our turn at the pool table, but it didn't matter. I just liked talking. I found out so much about him. His father died when he was younger and his parents were never married. His mom had cancer but was in remission. Back in the Bahamas he lived with his mom in order to take care of her. He had several brothers and sisters, some of which his mom had adopted. He liked to be called Neal and never really went by the name Cornelius. Too bad because I liked it. He wanted to own his own restaurant someday. He was a real thinker, too. He had a lot to say but he also listened to everything I said with intense interest. He would sometimes remind me that I had already told him something, but not in an arrogant way. He really was sweet. His heart was huge, and I could tell all this just from talking to him for a couple of hours.

"I really would like to see you again," he said. "I can't tell you how much fun this has been tonight." He got silent and took another sip of his drink. "Is it possible to call you and hang out with you before I go back home?"

Well, duh?!?!

"Of course." I punched his shoulder.

When he said "go home," my heart sunk a bit.

Why was that?

We left and he took me home. We joked the whole time in the car. He really was funny as hell.

When we got to my apartment building, we sat there for a moment outside in the parking lot.

"Well, call me when you are ready to hang out again," I said.

"How about tomorrow night?" he asked.

I was about to say "yes" when I remembered Mark.

"I can't," I said. "I have a prior engagement. How about Wednesday?"

"Sounds good. I'll call you."

He leaned over and kissed me smack on the lips. His kiss was so soft and sweet. It sent tingles down my spine.

He pulled away and just looked at me, waiting for me to say something. *What could I say?*

He leaned over and kissed me again. It was wonderful. This time it was longer and softer and he didn't try to push it with tongue.

There went the tingles again, but this time it wasn't down my spine.

I said goodnight to him one last time and started to get out of the car, but something stopped me, and I turned back to face him.

What the hell?

"Do you want to come in? I have some wine and we could just chill. I mean, if you want to and you know, if Broadus doesn't need the car, I mean only if you want to...It's really no big deal if you're tired and want to go home, but I just thought you might want to come in and we could just chill and if not, that's okay also."

Damn! I was mumbling again.

"Okay." He was laughing at me.

He parked in one of the vacant parking spots. We proceeded to my apartment.

"It's quiet," he said, while looking around the complex. "I like that."

"Yeah, it's quiet now because Bebe's kids in apartment 1C are sleeping," I said, laughing.

He started to laugh.

As I said the joke, I realized he probably didn't even know who Bebe's kids were. He still got the main idea.

"I had a good time tonight," he said.

"Just good?" I asked in jest. "What do I have to do to get you to have a great time—run around in my underwear?"

"Hey, now that's a thought," he said in that island accent.

Don't test me.

When we got to the door, I opened it up slowly and, as usual, knocked Sydney in the head.

"What was that?" he asked upon hearing the bumping noise.

"That's my cat."

"Is he okay?"

"*She's* fine. I open the door slowly so I don't hit her too hard with it, but she insists on sitting at the front door waiting for me every time I go out," I said, turning on the light.

Neal reached down and scooped her up. Wow, she never let anyone pick her up. Not even me sometimes.

"What's her name?"

"Her name's Sydney, but I just call her 'Kitty' all the time."

I offered him a seat and went to the kitchen.

"Did you want something to drink?" I yelled, peeking from the kitchen.

Sydney had jumped up on his lap and was resting comfortably. *I wished that were me.*

"Do you have orange juice, pineapple juice, rum and grenadine?"

I opened up my refrigerator and saw that I had the requested ingredients, but for what I didn't know.

"You'll have to use O.J. from frozen concentrate."

"That's cool," he said, coming into the kitchen.

He grabbed my waist and moved me aside.

"I'm going to make you the best Bahama Mama you've ever had."

"Actually, this would be my *only* Bahama Mama," I said, correcting him.

I watched him move from the refrigerator to the blender to the sink and back to the refrigerator. It was the cutest sight I'd ever seen. He reached into the pantry and found the apron I never used hanging on the door.

"Just what I need to make a masterpiece." He grabbed it from the hook and put it on.

I went up to him to help him tie it in the back. I was close enough to smell his cologne and it smelled heavenly. I wanted to ask him what it was, but I didn't, so I just slowly inhaled it.

When he finished making the Mamas, he handed a full glass to me, and I took a taste. It was a delicious frozen tropical drink.

"You're really not supposed to serve these without umbrellas," he said, taking a sip.

"That's okay. It just so happens that I have some in the cabinet."

He looked astonished.

"Really?"

"Nope, I was kidding."

"I knew you were lying." He lunged for me.

I jumped back from his grasp and ran into the living room spilling splashes of my drink all over the place, with him following close behind. When we reached the living room, I plopped down on the couch with my cat jumping up next to me.

"What do you want to do now?" I asked with him now standing directly over me.

He sat down next to me and put his drink down on the table. I could feel it was coming, and I was right. He leaned in to me and kissed me. He pulled back, waited for my reaction, and then leaned in to kiss me again.

I wanted to sleep with him but, then again, I didn't want to. What I meant was that my body wanted him, but I didn't want to ruin our "thing" we had going on. Whatever that was. The more he kissed me, the more I wanted it. When he pulled back the last and final time, he looked at me and waited for a response.

Verbally, I had none.

"Maybe I should go." He seemed to sense my discomfort.

"No!" I said, surprising myself as to how loud and urgent that came out. "I want this to happen as much as you do, but I don't know, I feel so comfortable with you and I don't want sex to ruin that. Besides, you're in town for a few more days. Who knows what will happen." I winked and tried to make light of a situation that was way too uncomfortable.

He kissed my cheek softly.

I knew then that he was okay with it. I even think he felt relieved, as I did.

For the rest of the night, we talked and played UNO until we fell asleep on the couch. I learned more about him in that one night than I had about all of my boyfriends combined.

Chapter 6

The phone rang the next morning at six-thirty and I knew exactly who it was. Char was trying to track me down again. Doesn't she ever give up? I thought about not answering the phone, but then again she might call and harass my sister for a second time, so I looked at the caller ID to be sure it was her. It was.

"Don't you have to get ready for work?" I said when I picked up the phone.

"Yeah, yeah. I just couldn't wait to tell you about my night last night and then you can tell me about yours, you ho."

I walked out to my living room and took a seat. Something told me this was going to be an interesting story.

"I stayed with Broadus all night in their room and, lo and behold, Mr. Cornelius didn't come back to the room. Gee, I wonder where he was," she said.

"Wait a minute now, *you* stayed with Broadus all night your damn self, so now who's a ho?" I countered back.

"Girl, thank goodness he didn't come back cuz we did it all night and it was all that. It was much better than the first time. The first time in the Bahamas kinda sucked because he was afraid his girlfriend was gonna come home."

The first time? Girlfriend?

"You gave it up to some guy from another country you didn't even know on the first date?" I asked. "Did you even *have* a date and not to mention, he had a girlfriend and you knew it! I knew something happened while you were down there."

Char started laughing. "I thought I told you," she said coyly.

Kitty jumped up on my lap and began to purr.

"Now you know you didn't tell me shit, and you need to quit with your triflin' ass."

"Hold up! Just hold up for one friggin' cotton-pickin' minute," she said. "Remember now, your man didn't come home last night, so explain that!"

I brushed Kitty off my lap and went to the kitchen to get her food. That's all she wanted anyway.

"Neal stayed here last night and left early this morning, but we didn't have sex. We had a great time just talking and getting to know one another."

(Now even I wouldn't believe that shit if someone told me that, but it was true.)

"C'mon now," she began. "What part of that story do you really expect me to believe? (See, I told you.) I'm just sensing some denial here."

Now she was trying to turn this on me, and I wouldn't allow her.

"If it makes you feel better to think that I was stank, too, then go ahead and think that we fucked each other's brains out. Is that cool for you?"

"Whatever you say," she said. "I gotta get ready for work, so I'll call you this afternoon."

"Do you ever actually *work* at this job of yours? I just can't figure out how you can call me midday and then talk for an hour straight and get paid for it. They hiring over there? Hook a sista up," I said, kidding.

"Let me know when you get serious because they are hiring more customer service reps," she said, laughing. "With your degree and your grad school, I could probably get you in on minimum."

Funny girl she was. Real funny.

I did do customer service all through college and even when I got out of college. That was my first job out of college as a matter of fact. I made like twenty a year and you couldn't tell me nuthin'.

"Bye," I said and hung up on her.

I couldn't even imagine doing customer service again. I did have a lot of experience though. I remembered those days well.

I had a CR job at a huge East Coast healthcare company. I hated that job with a passion, but I was good at it. I had to take calls from usually irate companies asking why a bill wasn't paid for one of their employees. I didn't decline the bills, but it was my job to look it up in their archaic system and tell them that a bill didn't get paid because, although their arm was falling off and they had lost twenty pints of blood, they were supposed to contact their primary care physician first, and they had not done that. Did I say I hated that job? Half the time I sided with the poor schmucks on the phone because I knew all about these health care companies. An individual paid out all this money a month to have health care coverage, but when it came time to actually utilize it for an emergency, the company all of a sudden got cheap and never wanted to pay out. It was up to me to tell the poor sucker on the phone that while he was paying fifty billion dollars a year for him and his family to have this so-called medical coverage, our company wasn't paying the thirty-dollar doctor bill because they had not contacted their primary care physician in an appropriate manner, arm falling off or not. Needless to say, that position lasted one year.

MALE BREAKDOWN

In the midst of my drama-filled corporate career, I met men that I fell in love with, men who fell in love with me and just bizarre men in general. The first guy was Kenny. He was everything I was looking for. He was dark-skinned, tall and actually had a six-pack that I loved to touch. I had never dated a guy with a real six-pack. I had only seen them in magazines or on TV. I *love-ded* me some Kenny. He was from Baltimore, and we had gone to college together and dated a bit, but it wasn't until later that we got involved. To this day, he thinks that he was my first sexual experience, but that's another story for another day. Of course I let him think that. (Wink, wink). Hey, I never told him he was. I had one other guy before him but, to this day, he still thinks he was my first. He ended up moving to Philly, and we started dating again, this time exclusively...or so *I* thought anyway. I was twenty-one, had just started working at the company, and you couldn't tell me anything about life. We had only dated casually in college. In other words, we pretty much just had sex. Okay, okay, confession time. The reason we only "dated casually" in college was all him and not me. Like I said, I loved me some him, but apparently he loved him some her, her and her. The sign should've been when he told me that he didn't want to get tied down with any one girl. Ladies, if anyone says that to you, you aren't the one. Roll on out as quickly and quietly as possible. Trust me on this one. It's like a Band-Aid: just pull that sucker off quickly and get on with life.

He broke my heart, but then when I met up with him after college and felt I had grown some, he came back into my life and reduced me to that college girl idiot I was before, and again he took no prisoners. I can't lie. It hurt just as much the second time as it did the first. At least I can say that when he came back for a third helping, I finally wised up.

My mom used to tell me to wise up all the time when I was being stupid regarding men. This time I actually took her advice (for once). So all in all, he got two burns in on me but that was it.

After him, there were a string of guys. Some of whom I slept with and some of whom I didn't.

Then I dated a broke-down guy with a kid that couldn't afford twenty dollars a week in child support. I'm not kidding, I mean that literally. He was brizzzzzzoke big time. The baby's momma took out a court order on him for child support. His mom was an ex-crackhead. He lived in a house with a brother, a sister, her two kids, his mother, his grandfather and a shit-load of roaches, and none of them worked, including the roaches. I'm talking generations of welfare, and don't get me started on that one. That was back in my trying-not-to-be-a-snob day but, looking back, I could've and should've been a little more discriminatory. To show you where I'm coming from, I used to attempt to spend the night in his house but had to sleep with the lights on so the roaches wouldn't get me. After awhile, they just stopped caring and came out in the light anyway. That's when spending nights ceased.

They even had roaches in their refrigerator. For the life of me, I couldn't figure out how they got up in there. Still can't.

I knew I was in trouble when we used to get up in the morning and before putting on his sneakers, he turned them upside-down and shook them out (yuck).

Then there was the next brother man I had met at one of those Young Urban Black Professional hangouts. I don't think I need to tell you about those things. They were just hoochies and playas dressed up in suits...and half of those suits were red, yellow and purple.

Anyway, we danced and we had a good time. The tip-off on that one should've been when I saw him later in the evening talking to three, count 'em, three other women.

That's just the ones I saw.

We had an off-and-on "relationship" for two years, mostly on for me and off for him. Mind you, hindsight is twenty-twenty and in this relationship, I couldn't see a single sign, even if it was a purple neon sign on a billboard in Times Square.

For the first year, I used to go visit him on Saturday morning and leave Sunday evening. We had a ball. He had his own house, took me to dinner and lunch, and we even worked out together. We did things like playing basketball and taking his dog for a walk in the park. It was great *in the beginning.*

Tip-off one: When you first walk into the house and the first thing you see is a hot tub in the living room.

There was no furniture or anything, just a hot tub. At the time I wasn't complaining because after our workouts I got my relax on but, think about it, a hot tub in lieu of furniture? (Think purple neon sign.)

Tip-off two: I used to go over there on Saturday, but when I had tickets for a show on Friday and attempted to ask him, I got the big shoot-down. I *never* saw him on Friday nights. When I confronted him about that, he said he just liked to hang out at home on Friday nights and relax.

(Uh-huh, I think that sign is about flashing now.)

Tip-off three: When you are over there all weekend (meaning only Saturday and Sunday because Fridays were out, remember?) and his phone *never* rings. So you think maybe no one calls him. You have him all to yourself. (Flashing sign now has sirens and fireworks.)

So when I went to use his phone, I noticed he turned the ringer off, but I still heard the clicks of the answering machine. When I "innocently" asked him about that, the excuse I got on that one was that he didn't want the phone to disturb our time together. (I don't even have a comment for that one.) This would be the part where he thinks I have "jackass" printed on my forehead. He had an answer for everything. They usually did. When I kept hearing the clicks of the answering machine, he eventually went as far as to completely unplug the phone. I mean, that jack was out of the wall. No lie. That, too, began to be a *slight* tip-off for me.

Toward the end of the relationship, I got the code to his answering machine (don't ask) and listened and surprise, surprise, I heard not one but *various* women on his answering machine thanking him for a "good time."

I would say that was tip-off four.

Then there was the pornography addiction.

One time I found what must have been his collection of like one hundred porno videos, just stacked up in the corner of his bedroom like what. The really scary part was the name of these porno videos. They were like "Wrinkled Pussies," "Suck My Cock" and "Half-man, Half-woman Sex Tapes."

When I found the tapes, I guess he thought it was okay to come out in the open because it became a real habit for him to take me to dinner and then off to the nasty X-rated video store for his nightly fix.

The real pathetic part (as if it wasn't all pathetic) was that he tried to coax me to get a membership at this one sleazy video store because he messed up his membership by not returning a boat-load of videos.

That would be tip-offs five, six, seven *and* eight, folks.

And then there was his gun collection, and after all this, our relationship eventually broke up, but it wasn't due to any of the above. That added to the problems, but the reason was because he didn't want to get married and told me throughout our relationship.

Is it that bad out there?!?!?! (rhetorical question because I already knew the answer).

Chapter 7

The one thing to do all day when you don't have a job is to find something to do all day.

I went to the gym, I read, I wrote (I was writing a novel I hoped to finish one day) and then I decided to go to the mall and pick up some things. Macy's was having a sale, and I wanted to take full advantage of it.

When I got to the mall, I went directly to Macy's and immediately started looking around the perfume counter. I could've used a new scent but there was nothing I really liked.

"Do you need any help?" the sales lady asked for the third time.

I said "no" and brushed her off...again.

I hated that. When I needed help, I'd ask your commission-based-salary-ass for help.

I sauntered over to the men's department and started looking around. I don't know why I went there. I just knew that I had Cornelius on my mind and if I happened to find something, maybe I would purchase it and send it to him after he left.

I ended up at the cologne counter to see if I could find that scent he was wearing the previous night. It had this distinctive smell and was intoxicating. It was probably Tommy cologne. I had heard that was big in the islands.

"Can I help you?" said a man from behind the counter.

I looked up and saw this fifty-year-old black man smiling at me.

I told him, "No thank you. I'm just looking."

"If there is anything I can do for you," he said, spitting through his teeth. "Just let me know."

This time I noticed that his smile was not so much friendly as it was the I'm-trying-to-pick-you-up-smile-regardless-of-my-age-or-my-looks look. This man had to be no more than one hundred pounds and had this hideous gold tooth right smack in the front. Not like you could tell next to all his yellow teeth.

"I specialize in the needs of a woman for her man in this department, so I'd be able to help you with *anything* you need," he said, winking.

Just stop it. Please.

"Is this a gift for your man?" he said, breathing directly in my face.

Evidently, my look of disgust didn't deter him but even worse, he had alcohol on his breath, and I was able to get a good whiff of it with him in my face like he was. It was friggin' eleven in the morning and this man smelled like a brewery.

"I'm just looking," I said, wiping off the spittle that had landed directly on my lower lip, compliments of the sales guy.

At that point, if I had a surgical knife I would've considered cutting off my lower lip and then my nose, so I wouldn't have to smell his breath.

I noticed some people standing on the other side of the counter and wondered why he wasn't harassing them.

There were two young black women on the other side that he could harass. Why didn't he give me a break and bother them?

I really didn't pay much attention to the people on the other side until their voices started getting louder. All I heard was, "She thinks she's cute," and the word "bitch" a few times out of the two girls' mouths.

When I looked up, I saw that it was Tanya and one of her friends looking at me. They just stared.

They both started walking over to my side of the counter on opposite sides of me. Now I *knew* she wasn't going to try any shit in the store because if she was, I was ready.

Her friend stopped midway, but she kept coming until she was directly next to me. I had no idea that this girl looked so young. She couldn't have been over twenty-two and had makeup caked all over her face.

She bumped me slightly, took a step back, and said, "Ohhhhh, excuse me. I didn't see you there."

I looked over to her friend, who I heard laughing.

I ignored her until she bumped me again.

You have got to be kidding. Tell me I wasn't about to scrap in a department store with this girl?

"Do you have an inner ear problem that would prohibit you from standing up straight?" I asked. "If so, I've got a doctor friend that could hook that up. He could probably take care of some of your other problems, too," I said, looking down at her body.

The girl really could've done with some liposuction on those hips.

She looked shocked that I had actually said something.

She took another step closer to me and was now in my space.

"No, I don't have a problem, but you do," she said, looking up at me.

This little troll really had guts.

"You need to check yourself with Mark. We've been dating for a while now and I'm not about to let some bitch come up in here and mess up *my* good thing," she said, looking me up and down.

This gnome had better be glad that I wasn't Cleo from *Set It Off,* because if I were, it would've been on.

"Look," I began. "You do what you gotta do, but just stay outta mine. I have no time to be running behind some man and you need not either."

I turned and walked out. I didn't hear any laughing behind me after that. *Now what, Bitch?*

After the minimal shopping I had done due to National Psychos Day, I went to visit my cutie neighbor, Sam. I knew he did part-time work as a bartender, but I wasn't sure what he did during the days. I only knew he owned some new tech company, but that was it. I took a chance and went for a visit anyway. Surprisingly, he was home.

"Do you have any interviews lined up?" Sam asked. "You know, we have barmaid positions open at my bar. What do you think?" he said, winking at me.

Everybody was just so damn funny.

"I think not," I said, taking a bite of the banana bread he had just baked. "Besides, it may not be good for us to work together, you know, with our raw animal attraction to each other."

"You think I'm kidding all the time," he said, ironing his pants. "I really do find you attractive and think you find me attractive. Unfortunately, you have this hang-up with color that's prohibiting us from getting together."

I took another bite of the bread, not knowing what to say.

"Am I right or am I right?" he asked.

I could see that he was dead serious but I really wasn't interested like that. I had often wondered what it would be like to date him. I mean, c'mon, he was a good-looking Italian guy, but again I say, I just really didn't have that kind of interest.

"Sam, I've seen you go out with beautiful women. What do you want with me?"

That really sounded like I was fishing for a compliment, and maybe I was, so what?

He looked at me and then went back to what he was ironing.

"You're every bit as beautiful as those other girls, even moreso (bingo). Not to mention, you have a great personality. You're funny, athletic and very smart. Actually, I could use someone like you to handle some of the aspects of my flourishing business."

Now this sounded like a set-up to me.

"Let me know when and how much, and I just might take you up on that deal," I said kidding.

He put the hot iron face-down on his pants.

"I'm serious here. I now have office space that I have rented out and have fourteen employees. I don't know the first thing about benefits and all that other human resources crap."

"Uh, Sam...," I said, looking at the now smoking iron. "You might want to pick up that iron."

"Oh, shit. Thanks," he said, turning the iron off and placing it to the side.

"Now, back to what I was saying. I could use you at my company with your HR expertise."

"What makes you think that I have HR expertise?" I said, taking a sip of milk.

"I *know* you do. You told me that you studied it in college and that you did some work in that field for a year while you were in college. Remember?"

Oh, yeah, I did tell him that.

"Since the company is small, I can only start you out at, say $50K, but by next year you could be making upwards of $80K and so on. Trust me. I know this." He came from around the ironing board. "I have to go to work but if you have time later on this week, we could discuss it further."

This could actually have been something, so I made dinner plans with Sam for sometime the following week. I really wanted to find out just how legitimate his offer was.

~❤~

It was five o'clock by the time I returned home from running my errands and visiting Sam. I checked my messages and there were three. Neal called me just wanting to say "hello." How sweet. Mark called to remind me that he was going to arrive at seven-thirty. *I thought I said seven?*

And then Char called as promised. Of course she was pissed that I wasn't home and couldn't flap her yap all day long. She actually had to work at work. Go figure.

"Did I not tell you I was calling you this afternoon, ho?" her message said. "You'd better have your ass home when I call back."

That was nice.

I checked my caller ID and sure enough there were at least six other calls from her.

Great, now I'd have to hear her mouth about not being home and where was I, and what I was doing and why it took so long for me to call back.

I called Neal back and left a message at the front desk because there was no answer in his room. I really didn't expect him to be there because he was only going to be in town for another four days. I figured that he wanted to sightsee as much as possible.

I really did have a great time with him. Let's see, if he were older, lived in the States, finished school, etc., etc...I could actually get with him.

Even though he was younger in age, he was more mature than any of the older guys I dated, especially porn man.

Maybe Sam was right; I was too hung-up on the physical attributes of a man.

In any case, Neal was from another country and was going to be leaving soon anyway, so I guess it didn't really matter.

I had been thinking about him all day and hadn't even realized it. When I went to the mall to buy a new dress, I subconsciously thought about whether or not he would like it.

When I bought a hot dog from one of the vendors, I thought about whether or not they ate hot dogs in the Bahamas.

I just hoped that I could hook up with him before he went back.

Chances looked good but you never knew.

Then the phone rang and interrupted my thoughts. I looked at the caller ID (I'm getting used to this now) and it was Mark. I picked up.

"Hello?"

"Hey," he said. "It's Mark." (He didn't know I had caller ID, and for now I wanted to keep it that way.)

"Did you get my message earlier?" he asked.

"Just got it, so what's up?"

"I'm going to be a little late, so I'll pick you up at eight-thirty instead. Is that okay with you?"

I plopped down on the couch and put my feet up on the coffee table.

"Okay by me," I said.

Good, that gave me more time to get ready. That also gave me time to get a short workout in. (And I did mean short seeing as my diet hadn't officially started yet.)

After I finished the workout, I jumped into the shower and washed my hair.

Dang, Char must've been mad because she would've called. I'd give her time to get over it and then I'd call her the next day.

When I stepped out of the shower, I went to my bedroom to get ready. Just then I saw Sydney jump down from my bed. That little bitch was lying on my new black dress I had just laid out. I was gonna kill her!

I looked at the damage and it wasn't anything a lint brush couldn't fix. She was dead meat! I should've known better. Every time I got something new and put it down for a few minutes, she found it and laid all over it. Every friggin' time.

No treats for her!

I thought I was going to wear the other new dress I'd bought the previous week but decided against it because I wanted to save it for Neal when I saw him again.

There I went again, thinking about him (see, I told you.)

Maybe I wouldn't wear that dress. I knew we were going to dinner and Mark was one to shell out cash. I needed something a little less casual, so I decided on a long, straight skirt and a backless shirt. Since my boobs aren't humongous, I could get away with no bra but could still fill the top out nicely.

I thought I would wear my hair up, so I plugged in the curling iron and prepared to do battle. I had to be careful not to sweat too much while curling my hair. I also had to be careful not to burn my forehead, which I usually did and then tried to cover it up with foundation or comb my bangs over. I didn't feel like having the hassle of trying to hide my forehead all night and wondering if he had seen my battle scar.

At eight thirty-five, my doorbell rang and there was Mark looking real good. He had on a black suit and a black tie with splashes of color. When I opened the door, his eyes lit up and I knew he was impressed with my choice.

Fellas, ladies know when you think they look good. You don't have to say a word. Your expression tells all. Remember that.

Thank goodness for the sit-ups I had done earlier because the top was cut short and showed my stomach. No six-pack yet but it was getting there.

"You look beautiful," he said with his eyes roaming all over my body.

"Thank you. You look nice yourself." I returned the compliment with a little more tact.

I noticed he had flowers behind his back.

"These are for you," he said and whipped them out.

The roses were beautiful but predictable. I thanked him for them and we were on our way. He led me to his car, and to my surprise, he drove a nice black Range Rover with gray leather interior.

I had never seen his car. Our first date, we met each other, and I had ended up leaving early to get my drink on, and at brunch we had arrived and left at separate times.

We ended up going to the jazz restaurant that I loved in the city. They had live bands there that played all night.

When we walked in, I saw that it wasn't crowded at all. I didn't expect it to be, considering it was Tuesday night.

The maitre d' showed us to our table, and as we walked to it, Mark grabbed my hand. Just the way Neal had done the previous night. Once we got to the table, I scooted in on one end and he on the other so that we met at the center of the booth. It was one of those booths in the corner with one of those contained scented candles that smelled like flowers.

It really was romantic.

"So Monica, you looked good last night. I couldn't keep my eyes off you," he said, smiling at me.

I wasn't stupid. I knew eventually he would fish for information regarding my date with Neal.

"Thank you. But how do I look tonight?"

Gotcha!

"You look very good tonight, too," he said.

He paused for a moment to look around the club but, in reality, I knew he was just trying to think of a way to bring up the topic of the previous night again.

"You looked as though you were having a good time last night," he said. Did I call it or did I call it?

"Who was dude you were with?"

No getting around that question.

Now I *know* he wasn't trying to feel threatened by Neal. Now that was funny.

I decided to play the game with him.

"Char set me up with him. Real nice guy and had a sexy accent, too. He's from the islands."

This was fun.

I glanced at his face and he appeared shot down.

Real fun.

I decided to let him off the hook and finished the story.

"Char met them on vacation in the Bahamas, and they're just here for the week."

"Ohhhh," he said, playing it cool.

Just then the waiter came and took our order.

We snacked on the bread that was on the table and took in the atmosphere in silence. I looked around the club and it was nice. I would've made the stage a little bigger though.

"So how's the job hunting going?" he asked, breaking the silence.

Instead of getting into it, I just said, "Fine."

Remember, this is the same guy that on our first date pretty much called me an idiot for leaving one job before obtaining another without knowing me, or my situation.

I decided on a bold move. I changed the subject to Tanya and asked him what the deal was.

He looked down and fixed his napkin on his lap.

"Are you jealous or something?" he said.

Ah, the ol' elude-the-question tactic.

"Not at all; just curious. I'll admit to that. She seems to be out with you a lot, and every time she sees me, she gives me that I-want-to-kill-you-in-your-sleep look."

He laughed. He had this deep, rich laugh. A cross between Barry White and Santa Claus.

"We're just friends."

That told me absolutely nothing because for a man, the word "friend" had such a broad meaning. Could it be the fucking friend, or how about the just hanging-out friend, or the she's-only-a-friend-when-I need-to-borrow-money friend. Which was it?

"She worked at my firm and we started to hang out." He started explaining when he realized that I wasn't buying his friend explanation. "She's a real nice girl but she just gets a little clingy sometimes."

I took a sip of wine, preparing myself for the rest of the explanation.

"That might be due to the fact that she's only twenty-three and still has some growing to do, but all in all she's cool. That reminds me, if you don't mind me asking, how old are *you?*"

Sheesh, that came from nowhere.

Evidently, he didn't want to talk about that subject anymore, so I bit and let him change the subject.

"The million dollar question," I said. "Well, how old do you think I am?"

He looked me up and down.

"I can't figure out why women just can't give their age. Why women are sensitive about their age and weight I'll never know," he said.

"Just shut up and guess," I said teasingly, grabbing another piece of bread.

"Well, Charlize never told me, but I'll guess you're about twenty-five."

I started to smile.

"Nope."

"Twenty-six?"

"Nope."

"Damn, how old are you then?" he asked.

"I'm twenty-nine," I said proudly.

"Okay, you look good for twenty-nine."

What in the hell was twenty-nine supposed to look like?

"How old are *you?*" I asked the question back.

"I'm thirty-five. Do I look it?"

Actually he did, but in a good way. He was sure about himself and you could tell he had been around the block—so to speak—but I opted for the safe answer just in case, because deep down inside, men were just like women when it came to aging. They wanted to be told that they looked good for their age and that we thought they were younger than they actually were.

"Not at all. I would've guessed twenty-seven," I lied.

Throughout dinner we had a nice conversation and filled up on wine and bread. This was really an improvement over the first date we had, *big time.*

Mark was everything I was looking for in a man—wasn't he? He had a good job, a great job as a matter of fact, in computers, and was the "right" age. He also had style and taste, but there was that something missing. It wasn't the physical attraction thing because I was very much attracted to him. I couldn't call it, but I just wasn't getting that "this is my man" feeling. I could tell that he really enjoyed our conversations, too, and I knew he was interested by the way he leaned in to me to talk and by the way he listened when I spoke, but it just wasn't there. Not right then anyway. *What was it?*

It was ten-thirty when I finally looked at my watch. I thought we had better go. Besides, I wanted to get home to check my messages in case anyone had called.

Anyone or Neal?

Here we go again! My mind had yet again drifted to Neal as it had been doing all night long.

When the waiter brought the food, I wondered if he was back at the hotel or not. When dessert came, I wondered whether or not he had tried to call me.

This little young buck affected me more than I cared to admit.

I had to quickly get my mind back to this attractive man sitting next to me.

After dessert, we (or should I say I) decided it was time to go home. After paying the bill, we got up from the table to leave.

"Is there something else you wanted to do?" he asked hopefully.

"No, that's okay. I'm kind of tired, so I guess I'll just go home and go to bed."

"Well, I really had a good time and hope we can do this again."

When I nodded and didn't say anything, he pressed it further.

"Is that okay by you?"

I reassured him that I would enjoy hanging out with him again.

"Just let me know," I said, stroking his ego.

He drove me home and walked me to my apartment door.

Oh, please don't let him attempt to come in.

"Well, I'll give you a call when I get back in town."

He leaned in and kissed me softly on the lips. His kiss was delicious. He had thick, soft, sexy lips. Neal's lips had been better, but he was definitely in the running.

"Goodnight, Mark."

"Goodnight," he said.

I turned and went into my apartment and immediately checked my answering machine to see if I had any messages.

I had none. (Shit!)

My caller ID said that even though I had no messages, someone had called. I flipped through and saw Char's number four times. I guessed she wasn't mad anymore. Then there was a number I didn't recognize. Maybe it was Neal, maybe it wasn't. I was too tired to figure it out, so I just called it a night and went to bed.

Chapter8

The next couple of days went by quickly. I pretty much did the same thing every day. I got up early to go jogging and then came home and showered. Midday I would go to the gym and work out and then visit Char at her job and go to lunch with her. I had another interview for another position I was overqualified for, so I didn't even bother sending the usual thank you card to the interviewer. I was really anxious to see what Sam had to say about the position he was offering. It had been almost a month since I had been out of work, and although I was financially okay, I was getting bored of doing nothing. I was ready to get back into the game.

At lunch one day with Char, I asked her if she had heard from Broadus. She said she had a couple of times but they hadn't gone out anymore. Then I led into the real question I wanted to know—had she heard anything regarding Cornelius. I hadn't heard from him since the time he tried to call me and I wasn't home. He didn't leave his number for me to call, so I figured he would call back, but no such luck. He hadn't even called and hung up without leaving a message because my caller ID had said so. What was up with that?

"Broadus told me that Cornelius wanted to hang out with you, but he couldn't get in touch with you earlier this week," she told me over burgers, fries, and chicken fingers at Quimby's. I figured I'd start the diet next week. Between looking for a job and Neal, I was too overwrought to diet.

"That was earlier this week and he hasn't called since," I said, taking a bite of one of my fries. "I take it we're not going out anymore before they leave?"

As I said it, I got that tightening feeling in my stomach again. It felt like someone had my stomach in their hands and was just wringing it like you would a wet T-shirt. I'm not sure if I had that feeling because I misjudged our evening together or was it that I really liked him and I wanted to see him again.

"I dunno." Char didn't look up from her burger.

"That's a shame," I said, now more angry than upset.

Char finally looked up from her plate suspiciously.

"You guys *must've* done it that night because you sure are sweating him something bad."

She shoveled in another bite of her burger and waited for my reply, but when I said nothing, she pushed on.

"Looks like little young 'un got to you, didn't he? I mean damn, he was cute and all, but damn! Get some dignity about yourself," she said, laughing. "I'll tell Broadus to tell him to call you."

"You'd better not," I said quickly. "If he doesn't want to call, then he doesn't want to call. Nobody has to tell him to do anything."

She started laughing, which annoyed me even more. I knew how ridiculous I was sounding but I didn't need her facetious attitude for the added insult to my painful injury.

When we finished lunch, I went directly home to check my messages. I saw that I had one message on my machine. Maybe I was worrying for nothing. Maybe the message was him calling me, apologizing for *not* calling me. I laughed at myself for being so uptight over this guy. I pressed the "message" button and was immediately shot down.

"*Good afternoon. This call is for Monica. This is Alice Smith of Jordan Pharmaceuticals. You interviewed with me today for the marketing associate position, and I am pleased to inform you that we would like to extend an offer...*"

I clicked the answering machine off.

Thanks but no thanks.

Chapter 9

It was Friday evening. Sam and I decided to go to Friday's for dinner. (I really was the most eatingoutinest, always drinkingest person I knew).

I'll *really* start the diet tomorrow, I promised.

It was a social dinner with business mixed in. He saw it as social and I saw it as business. I didn't know about him, but I was trying to get my work on.

"I just got back from a conference in Atlanta. You wouldn't believe the hotties down there, and the women just love them some white boys," he said. "The conference was over every day by three-thirty and every night, some of the other attendees and I went out from three-thirty in the afternoon until four in the morning and had to get up again for the conference. The clubs down there were slammin'."

"That's all fine and nice, but did you learn anything? You know, the reason you went down there?" I said, laughing at him trying to talk Ebonics.

He got serious.

"Actually, I learned a lot and if you're willing to trust me, I'd like to bring you on board. I'll have my lawyer draw up an offer letter. If it's to your liking, I'd like for you to start on Monday." He didn't skip a beat.

I thought for a moment about what he'd just said.

"Sam, I'm serious here. I'm looking for a serious job, with serious money. I hope you aren't just offering me a job to get next to me," I said.

"I don't play when it comes to my money. I need somebody who has some know-how. If anything, us working together would stop me from harassing you because I don't mix business and pleasure," he said, punching my shoulder.

That was real convincing.

"Most of the time I wouldn't be there anyway. That's why I need someone like you to run things and keep it straight. Like I've said before, you're a smart woman, and my business won't fail. I guarantee it."

He pushed his plate aside, reached for his briefcase from under the table and pulled out some pamphlets.

"I have literature I want to show you regarding my company. Take a look at it, and if you have any questions, let me know. I'm going to have my lawyer draw up the offer letter and get it to you on Sunday. I'd prefer you sign it after reading it Sunday evening so we can start you on Monday. That's when the new employees will all be starting. I'll be giving a new-hire orientation Monday morning at eight a.m. sharp, and the hours will be technically from eight to five, but since you'll be part of the management staff, we'll need you as we need you. I'll issue you a pager that my company will pay for. Plus, I'm putting you in charge of ten out of the fourteen employees that will be in this office. This includes the IT staff, and the data entry specialists."

Wow, this was a lot to take in.

"Eventually, I want you to run this office. I want you to hold the weekly staff meetings that we'll be having. In the future I want you to be in charge of the new-hire orientations, *and* you'll be in charge of dealing with anything HR, like benefits, offer letters, termination letters, etc...."

I took a sip of soda, taking it all in.

"Does this sound like something you'd be interested in?"

He was really serious.

"It really does," I said to him. "I know I'm ready for this. I have supervisory experience, I have HR experience, and I can learn anything I need to learn."

He started laughing at me.

"What?" I said, trying to figure out what he was laughing about.

"This isn't an interview. You don't have to sell yourself. I *want* you for this position."

"I know, Sam." I was laughing at myself. "This sounds like a position that I've been waiting for. There's just one question though."

"What's that?"

"Where the hell is the office located? I may need to know where I'm going if I'm going to work there."

He started laughing again.

"That's the best part. It's ten minutes from our apartment complex."

With Maryland traffic, that meant it was at least twenty-five minutes from our complex.

"I really want to do this, but I do have one condition," I said.

"Anything."

"All you need to do is show me the ropes and then give me total autonomy. The way you told me to trust you, I'm asking you to trust me. I can do this. I don't need and don't want someone hovering over me all day and all night; especially since we live in the same apartment complex."

He nodded. "Deal. If I have a problem with the way you're running things, I'll say something, but we'll work together."

We finished our lunch, had a few drinks at the bar and hung out having a good time until one o'clock in the morning. I figured it was okay one last time, considering it wouldn't be happening again because I wouldn't hang out with the boss.

~❤~

"Your apartment could use some fixing up," Stacey said. "It looks all beat down."

It was Saturday afternoon and I had met up with Char, Jaleesa and Stacey at Char's apartment. We were going to go rollerblading, but when we finally got together it had started raining so we just sat in Char's living room trying to figure out what to do.

"I know *you're* not talking," Char said back. "This coming from someone who lives in a one-bedroom with a roommate because she can't afford a two."

We all started laughing.

It wasn't the fact that Stacey lived in a one-bedroom apartment; it was the fact that she had a roommate in that one bedroom apartment. The apartment was located in high-end Chevy Chase and was *real* nice, but why you would get a ritzy one-bedroom with a roommate instead of a nice comfortable two-bedroom was just something I couldn't fathom.

Staying true to herself, Stacey changed the topic of the conversation to me. I wouldn't have expected anything less.

"If you're still looking for a job, I can probably put in a good word for you at *my* job."

Translation: She would recommend me for the janitorial position that just opened up.

"Didn't we have this conversation the last time I saw you?" I said, annoyed.

As usual, Stacey got on my damn nerves. Was there ever a time she didn't though?

Let me put her in her place...again.

"No thanks. I need a job that can afford me the luxury of a *two*-bedroom apartment."

We all, aside from Stacey, started laughing hysterically.

"Besides that, I already have a job, and I start Monday."

"Whaaaaaaat?" Char said. "You didn't tell me that."

"Everything was just finalized yesterday."

"Where you gonna be working?" Jaleesa asked.

"You remember Sam from my apartment complex?"

"The white boy?" Stacey asked.

"Yeah. Well, he started an Internet company about a year ago and wants me to head up the Maryland division. We talked over the money, and it's good. Now he's just getting the offer letter together. I sign it tomorrow and start Monday."

Char and Jaleesa raised their glasses in a mock toast.

"Congratulations," they said simultaneously.

I looked over at Stacey and she was giving the fake smile.

"That's great," Stacey said, lifting her glass behind everyone else. "But you really have to watch out for those Internet companies. They're successful one month and the next month, everyone's out of a job."

"So have you heard from young buck yet?" Jaleesa asked me, ignoring Stacey.

I cut my eyes to Char.

"Dang, Char, you've got a big-ass mouth."

"No, I don't. Ohhhhh, that reminds me," Char began, changing the subject. "You know they left, right? They went back to the Bahamas earlier this week. Cornelius' mom got real sick, so he had to go back early and Broadus went with him. He called me last night from the Bahamas to tell me. He did say Cornelius was sorry for not calling you."

"Oh," I said, not really knowing what else to say.

I didn't know if I was glad or sad to find out this bit of information. I mean, I felt bad for Neal and his mother, but at least he just didn't call me for no reason. I guessed I wouldn't be seeing him again—and that hurt.

Chapter 10

M onday morning I woke up at six-thirty. I thought I could get a run in before I got ready for work, but when I awakened, I got lazy and didn't feel like it. Oh, well, I was up, so I might as well check out the early morning news.

It was the usual. Let's see...there were killings in D.C., fires in Bethesda and what they thought was a kidnapping in P.G. County. I didn't know why I bothered turning on the news in the first place.

I had seen the contract Sam had offered on Saturday evening, and I spent the rest of that evening and all of Sunday reading it. Eventually I signed it and gave it back to him. The deal was just as he had said, but with a few more perks than discussed. He had also given me a company credit card if needed.

What would I need with a company credit card?

I was also guaranteed at least a ten-percent raise for the next three years if I was still at the company. There was a clause in the contract regarding working for another Internet company. I was unable to do so for a total of three years after my departure from his company. Nothing had really alarmed me regarding the contract. It seemed like a fair contract to me so I signed it.

I chose to wear my gray outfit. It was the best one that I had, and I loved it. Wearing it on the first day meant that you couldn't wear the outfit together for the next couple of weeks because everyone at the office would be sizing everyone else up. You could wear the skirt with a different blouse and the jacket with a pair of pants but not the two together for *at least* two weeks. It was forbidden. It's true; check out section forty-two, paragraph six of the women's guide to office apparel.

I had gone out over the weekend and purchased some expensive suits. I had money to do so, so I did. Hooo boy, I had spent some money, too. I loved nice-looking suits. In my opinion, you could pretty much tell when someone had a cheap suit on. Sometimes you were able to get away with it, but trust me, most times you knew. To me, expensive suits just wore better.

Sam had asked if I wanted to ride with him to work, but I decided against it. I made up some excuse about having to run some errands before I stepped into work. I didn't want it to start off like that. This to me would be like any other job—you do not ride up into work with your boss.

I pulled past the building to the parking garage where it was twenty dollars a day to park. (Of course). I really had to check into a monthly plan.

When I got into the building, it was a beautiful high-rise. It had twenty floors and was nestled right in the center of everything. It was as if the building was created first and then the smaller shops were catered around it. Looking at the directory, I could see that there were a lot of businesses in the building. The businesses varied from a catering service to a small financial firm.

There it was, Suite 410, Sam's company, which was titled a very simple SamInc. I couldn't decide if that was keeping it simple or just plain lack of imagination. Regardless, I was proud of Sam for realizing his dream. I had hoped to do that one day in the near future. What could be better than working for yourself? Hey, if I was going to put in long hours, I might as well have been doing it for me, and not some jackass of a boss, Sam excluded, of course. Fortunately, I didn't feel that way about Sam. Not yet anyway. (Only kidding). I just hoped that it would work out. Professionally and financially everything was cool, but how lucrative would this be to our friendship?

We'll find out now, won't we?

Sam was holding the new-hire orientation, which was to begin in another fifteen minutes. There were approximately forty people in the room, most of them being young white males. I noticed that there were only a handful of women, me being the only black one. There was an Asian woman and a few other younger ladies. The young white males had on snazzy suits, so I figured them to be the sales team. Some of the younger ladies had on leggings, short, short skirts or wrinkled cotton pants with loafers, so I figured them to be the customer service representatives.

See, the clothes tell all.

We stood around and introduced ourselves while meeting with each group of people. I was right; most of the white guys were sales representatives and all of the younger females were account managers, which we all knew was just an ostentatious name for a customer service rep. The Asian woman had on a nice suit and introduced herself as Hyung Kim. She did not give me her title, but I later found out that she was in charge of the sales team. The young white males.

You go, girl!

The meeting was about to start when someone walked into the room at the last minute.

Ohmigod! I recognized her right away. I looked at her and she at me. What in the hell was she doing there? She was dressed in a tailored black business suit. She didn't see me at first, but then her eyes met mine, and she looked just as surprised as I knew I did. She took a seat at the table with the rest of us and continued to steal glances in my direction. How did I know she kept looking? Because I was doing the exact same thing.

We went around the room and introduced ourselves, and when Sam came to her, she looked directly at me and stated her name as Tanya Michelle Johnson. This was the girl who was always with Mark, and now she was here with me, in this very same room. I had no idea of her position within the company, but it was killing me to find out. I'm sure she felt the same.

"Well, we can go ahead and take a lunch break," Sam said when it had reached twelve o'clock.

A few people, mostly the sales guys and the customer service reps, already had broken out into their cliques, so they all went out to lunch together. Me, I preferred not to "bond" with anyone and leave business as business, so I was prepared to go to lunch by myself.

I grabbed my planner off the desk and got up from the meeting table. I figured I would just go to the deli on the first floor.

"Hey," Sam said when he approached me. "Want to go out to lunch? We could do Italian and you know that's my favorite," he said with a wink.

I decided to go, but then I found out that Ms. Tanya Michelle Johnson was going, along with someone named Jason who I figured to be one of the sales guys. It was just going to be the four of us. Oh, goody, goody. *Was it too late to back out?*

We all went in Sam's BMW. I found out Sam and Jason went to school together and were best friends. Jason was just as cute as Sam, if not cuter. I don't think he was Italian because I detected a slight accent, which I thought to be Australian. He even kind of reminded me of that actor that was in that movie *The Gladiator*, Russell something or other.

We all went to lunch, and actually, it wasn't *that* bad. When either Tanya or I was asked a question, we answered without looking at each other. To tell you the truth, I couldn't even remember what she had for lunch, nor did I care.

"So what did you think of the orientation?" Sam asked the group.

"I thought you were pretty damn boring, myself," Jason, the Gladiator, said and laughed.

He had this sexy cocky laugh. The kind I knew women swooned over.

"Don't worry, Sam. I thought you were good," I said, looking from the Gladiator to him.

Sam looked in Tanya's direction.

"What about you, Tanya?"

We all leaned toward her (including me). In silence, we waited for her response. It was almost like one of those mystery movies where everyone had their mouths gaped open right before the detective announced whodunit. She barely said two words during this whole lunch and now she was about to speak. *Remind me. Why was she here again?*

"It was okay," was all she said, then took a bite of her food.

We all drew back. She might as well have said that the butler did it.

"I would get a glass of wine, but I wouldn't want the boss to find out I was drinking at lunch," the Gladiator said and we all laughed.

All of us except Tanya.

Eventually the conversation steered toward what our positions were within the company. We knew Sam was the owner, and I had just found out that Jason was the IT guru. He had gone to MIT for four years and then grad school. He was working at Proctor & Gamble, but when he was passed up for a big promotion he decided to leave, and that's when his best bud Sam came along. "Perfect timing," he had called it.

Then it came to Tanya, and I found out that she was going to be the secretary of the company. Sam found her through a temporary agency. He didn't even know her. I didn't know why, but that made me feel better.

Then it was my turn and I let loose. I couldn't talk enough about my actual job title. As I spoke, I glanced over at Tanya every once in a while. She was either fidgeting with her lunch (I still don't know what she had) or was looking through her purse for something, which inevitably she never found. I did catch her giving me a couple of dirty looks and cutting her eyes at me every time I spoke. At one point, I even attempted to include her in the conversation, but she would just look away. When someone else asked her a question, she was more than happy to volunteer information to *them*. I wondered if Sam noticed. She was being very unprofessional, and I decided that if I was going to be in management, I wasn't going out like that. After lunch we went back to the office and continued with our orientation. By the time five o'clock rolled around, I could sum up everyone in that conference room. Keith and Matt were two sales guys who were competing against each other. Throughout the whole orientation, one had a question, then the other. Actually, they weren't even questions. It was mostly them spewing off facts about the company and about other companies. They did their research and wanted everyone to know it. You could see them playing off each other. Both were trying hard as hell to impress Sam with their knowledge of the Internet with megabyte this, gigabyte that. I knew it wasn't just me because after about the hundredth comment, people started giving the gimme-a-break-look to one another. They were slightly behind me because I started the gimme-a-break-look after the twentieth question. Sam, though, never broke his composure, the sign of a true professional.

By the end of the day, we were all exhausted. My mind was overloaded with facts, figures, and projections, mostly from Keith and Matt. I felt good though. It was great to get back to work and use my brain again.

~❤~

"Does that mean she's going to have to get your coffee?" Char asked, laughing.

I had to call Char and tell her about my day and who was in my day.

"Yeah, I'll take that with cream and sugar, please," I said laughing with her.

"If *she* gets you coffee, you'll have more in it than cream and sugar."

We started cracking up.

"It's not that there's anything wrong with being a secretary. I just didn't like her attitude. It's her, not what she does. "

"I know," Char said. "We've all been there, even if our title wasn't exactly secretary. Even when I was a telemarketer, I had a manager who made me pick up his laundry and order his wife flowers once. He used to ask me to get him lunch. He tried to make it sound like, 'If you're headed down to the cafeteria, could you pick something up for me?' He usually gave me money, but this one time he 'conveniently' forgot. You know I tracked his ass down and was like, did you still want lunch because if you do I'll need the money to get it, and then held my hand out."

"You did not, you liar!" I said.

"Aw, right, I lied, but after I got his lunch, I did remind him that he owed me money."

"Did you get it back?" I asked.

"Hell no, cheap bastard!"

After our phone conversation ended, I poured a glass of wine, put in a smooth jazz CD and went back to finishing reading up on SamInc. I wanted to be prepared for everything and anything. Little did I know what I needed to be prepared for had nothing to do with the SamInc. literature I had sprawled out on my table.

Chapter 11

The next morning I walked into the office at seven sharp. Sam had given me a key to open up the office, and when I opened the door I found Tanya sitting at the front desk, which was to eventually be her permanent desk. I looked at her and she at me. I said, "Good morning," and headed straight to my office. There was no answer, but I expected that. Any time I have had to deal with difficult people at work, I would just treat them in a professional manner, like anyone else. No more, no less and this was going to be no different. At least I hoped. If she opted to have this huge attitude with me, then that's fine, but you will not catch *me* being unprofessional. I reached my office and decided that it definitely could do with some more plants. My office wasn't big by any means. It was cozy and had a beautiful picture window behind my desk and a gorgeous view. Since we were on the fourth floor, I could look down and see hoards of people scurrying out of the parking garage to their offices. Sam let me pick my office first. I had taken a liking to this one. I spruced it up a bit with a few plants and some paintings, nothing expensive, just ones on sale at Target. It felt very comfortable. All the managers had an office now and were doing their own decorating. The customer service ladies sat in cubes in the middle of the office and Tanya sat at a desk up front by the door. She was at one end of the office and I was at the other end. This didn't mean much considering the office wasn't that big to begin with, but at least we were at opposite ends. I knew we would have to end up talking some time but didn't want to force it. I was just going to remain my professional self and get on with work. If the situation began to prohibit me from doing my job effectively, then I would address it, but until then I would be fine. Besides, with a temporary agency, she was under contract and might not have been there too long if it didn't work out. Hope sprung eternal.

By the time everyone else had arrived, it was about eight-thirty. Sam wasn't going to be in the office that day, so we had to actually start our jobs without his guidance—not that I needed it anyway.

My day was spent doing Internet research on HMO providers to find the best deal for the employees. I needed one that would be cost-effective yet practical, since Sam was paying for all of his employees' health insurance.

My phone rang at noon. It was Sam asking me to take an interview for him that was coming in at three-thirty. No problem.

"Aren't you coming in at all today?"

"No, I'm at a conference in Virginia, so I'm not gonna make it in today. Then I have to turn around and make it back to D.C. by six-thirty to bartend. It's gonna be hectic today."

"Why don't you just quit bartending?" I asked.

"Are you kidding? I love that job. Besides, how do you think I get all my dates?"

"Goodbye, crazy," I said, "and don't worry. I have your interview at four-thirty."

"Three-thirty," he corrected in a panic.

"I know, I know, I was kidding."

Before I got a chance to hang up, he asked me to meet with him Friday morning at nine sharp to go over some things.

Hmmm, I wondered what about. The rest of my day was spent researching, and I figured if I didn't go through all of the HMOs by the time I left, I would finish at home, and that's exactly what I ended up doing. It was seven-thirty when the phone finally rang. I had no messages all day and no one called me while I was home until now. Not even harassing solicitors asking me to get a credit card with an annual introductory rate of 2.9 percent.

I looked at the caller ID and it was Mark. I had just realized I hadn't talked to him at all since the previous week. I knew he was out of town but I had no idea when he was coming back.

Well, I guessed he was back.

I couldn't decide whether or not to tell him about Tanya. I figured she would tell him if she hadn't already.

"Hey, Mark," I said, picking it up, finally letting him know I had caller ID.

"I hate that damn caller ID," he said.

I brushed aside the work I brought home and tapped my lap for Kitty to come up. She was more than happy to oblige.

"Now you can't call and stalk me. If you do, I suggest you do it from a pay phone. That's what everyone else does," I told him half-kidding, half-serious.

"So what's up?" he asked. "I just got back into town and thought you would like to go out to dinner tonight."

I told him I couldn't because I had too much work to do.

"What work? Now, how is someone with no job gonna have too much work to do?" he said in jest.

Stacey, is that you?!

"I have a job, thank you," I said. "I'm now a human resources manager."

"How did you get that gig?" he asked.

I was hungry. I brushed Kitty off my lap and went to the kitchen where I opened up the refrigerator for my hourly inventory.

"A friend of mine is the owner of an Internet company and wanted to bring me on board. We had dinner last week, and he asked me."

"I hope you signed a contract because working with friends never works. They try to take advantage of you because they know they can get you for cheap."

His last comment pissed me off. Instead of congratulating me, he had to bring up the negative.

He really should've been fixed up with Stacey and not me.

Did he really think I was some sort of idiot that couldn't handle professional business? I decided against discussing it further and quickly got off the phone by giving him the work excuse again. I really wasn't in the mood for his cynicism. Let Tanya tell him. I didn't give a damn.

He must've known he pissed me off because before I hung up, he tried giving me a token "congratulations." I just said, "Gee, thanks" sarcastically and then "goodnight" and hung up mid-sentence of some crap he was saying. Almost immediately my phone rang, and I picked up knowing it was him ready to say something else to piss me off.

"Yesssss?" I asked into the receiver, now completely exasperated.

"Good evening," a deep voice said, a voice with an accent.

Helloooooo?!?!?!? It couldn't be.

"Did I catch you at a bad time?" asked the caller.

"Neal? How are you doing?" I asked in a voice that sounded way too excited.

"Great," he said. "I had to leave earlier than expected."

"I know. Char told me. How's your mom doing?"

I went to the kitchen and fetched a glass of ice water. Was it hot in here, or was it just me?

"She's okay. I just wanted to be back here with her."

"I understand but I am sort of upset that we didn't get a chance to say goodbye," I said wholeheartedly.

"I know. Me, too."

We made some more small talk and then silence.

"I've really been thinking about you a lot since I left," he said. "I had a great time with you that night and I wanted to see you again, but I had to leave."

"I know how you feel," I said. "I had one of the best times I've ever had."

Any other person, I wouldn't sound so out of breath and desperate, but all bets were off when it came to Neal. He made me not care if what I was saying was stupid. I think he felt the same way, too.

"Well, I'm at work, so I can't talk long but I did want to say hi. Oh, yeah, and I got your number and address from Broadus, who got it from your girlfriend. I sent you a letter last Wednesday when I got home. You should be getting it soon."

Last Wednesday? That was the day I had heard they left, so he must've written to me right away.

"I'll be waiting for it," I said again, not caring if I sounded desperate.

"By the way," he began. "I've been looking into coming back to Maryland to visit you. Would it be okay to stay with you?"

Are you kidding? Does he have to ask?

"It would be more than okay. Just let me know."

That hussy Char said she didn't talk to Broadus. She had to, in order to give my address to him. It didn't matter because I had finally talked to Neal. The phone conversation had been short and sweet. It turned everything around. He had missed me as much as I had missed him.

I started to smile at the mere thought of that.

This feeling that I had was weird. It was almost like I drank some magical brew or something. For the rest of the night I couldn't do any more work. I just put on my pure jazz CD, got a glass of wine and—I shouldn't be admitting this but—for the rest of the night, I dreamt of what could've been and quite possibly could still be.

Chapter 12

Friday morning I was in Sam's office. I had come up with an HMO package that was cheap and effective. The only thing was, if women wanted birth control pills, they would have to pay out of pocket. (That wasn't a problem for me since I wasn't getting any anyway, so I didn't need any pills.) We had full medical and dental coverage. This plan would only allow for the employees; dependents would have to pay an out-of-pocket cost. I gathered that was why it was so cheap, but the good news was that there were only two possible participants—Kyung Kim and one of the sales guys, who were married. And they had told me that their spouses had other insurance coverage and they were on their plans.

When I presented it to Sam, his immediate response was no, no, and no.

"Why would we want a healthcare plan that wouldn't allow for dependents?" he asked.

I pulled notes out of my planner and placed them on his desk.

"Personally I think that should be up to the employees. It should be something to present to them. If they're getting free healthcare coverage, they may not mind paying out of pocket for dependents. Just check the rates," I said, pushing the notes across his desk.

"Yeah, if they don't have a bunch of kids," Sam countered while looking over the notes. "Do you have any idea of how much that could cost for *them?*"

"Well, how about if some of the dependents of the employees are covered by another insurance in the household?"

"What other insurance?"

"By a husband, or in some cases the baby's daddy. I think this should be an option. If you want to keep costs down for the company," I continued, "this is definitely an option."

"Okay then, we can present this, but I don't necessarily like the idea."

"Sam, this doesn't have to be permanent. We could try this out while the company is in its beginning stages and see where it goes from there."

He handed my notes back to me. "If we try this, I assume we would have to be locked down in a contract for a certain period of time."

"For one year exactly," I offered. "If it's something that doesn't work out, we'll go on to the next one. This is just an idea so far. I have other plans that we could present to the employees, but I have to tell you that they are far more expensive and the coverage isn't necessarily any better."

He leaned back in his chair and looked up to the ceiling as if he were deep in thought.

I made my final point. "If you want to guarantee employee raises for the next few years, then I don't have to tell you that you have to keep costs low and profits high."

"Okay," he said. "Let's schedule a tentative meeting for next week with other options and you can present all options to the employees," he said, finally satisfied. "But now that you're here, I want to talk to you for a minute."

He got up and walked around me to shut the door.

This didn't look good.

"I know you've only been here a week, but I want you to make some judgment calls for me."

I had no idea what he was referring to.

"You've seen the employees in action." He paused. "What is your 411 on them...and be honest, please. I've already formed my own opinions, and I want to see what you think."

This was an odd question. He must have had some uneasy feelings toward someone in the office to be asking me this. I wondered if it was Tanya. Maybe she wasn't rude to just me. Maybe she was rude to everyone, including outside clients. Maybe he'd noticed the glares I continuously got from her. Maybe he saw her give them to others as well. Then again, maybe it wasn't her; maybe it was someone else he had concerns with. I had everyone pegged that first day in the orientation and wondered if he felt the same.

"To be honest with you, I've made judgments of them as I'm sure they have of me," I said carefully.

Judgment may have been too strong a word. I'd say it was more like observations. Yeah, that's the word I should've used. It sounded less confrontational.

"I consider your management team to be highly competent," I continued.

I sat back in the chair and thought for a moment, choosing my words carefully.

"The customer service reps seem a little cliquish, but they seem okay, and the sales guys are real sharks, and in case you didn't catch that, I just complimented them," I said, joking. "All in all, I think we have a good team in place."

I had validated everyone in the office except one person. I wondered if he had caught that. I wasn't sure how objectionable I could've been at this point.

I decided to let him say something first, if there was truly an issue. He could've just been picking my brain to find out some info. Since he wasn't here a lot, he probably didn't know the real deal.

"Okay," he said. "I just wanted to get your opinion since I wasn't here much."

Okay, now that was just a little weird. I didn't believe he just wanted my opinion.

As I walked out of his office, I looked back at him and he seemed as though there were something bothering him. I'd give him time to come to me with it, but the next time, he would have to be straight and not so evasive. If he wanted to know something, all he had to do was ask straight up.

The rest of the week was cool. I had a few staff meetings and we were beginning to hire. Personally, I would've liked to hire for the secretary position! That girl was really unbearable. I hadn't cracked yet, but there were times when I was ready to take her outside to one of the back alleys and beat her down. I just wanted to stick my foot right up her big ass and bang her head on a brick wall a couple of times, just enough to put her in a coma for a good long while.

Okay, I needed to relax a moment.

I just couldn't believe how unprofessional she was being. Earlier that week when I walked into the bathroom, I caught her with one of the customer service reps gossiping about someone.

Gee, I wonder who?

As soon as I walked in, she ceased the conversation and changed the subject, *quick.* From what I had seen, she sat at her desk and talked on the phone all day. If she wasn't talking on the phone she was taking a smoke break. Mark didn't strike me as the type to like a woman that smoked but, then again, I barely knew him.

Mark called me throughout the week, but I had yet to return his calls. I had just been completely busy. (At least that's the excuse I would give him when I talked to him again.) I still wondered if Tanya had told him that we worked together yet. The way she yapped all day long on the phone, she had to have.

I decided to give Mark a call at his office. Earlier in the week he left his office number on my machine, and I wrote it down intending to call, but just hadn't gotten around to it. I hadn't gotten around to a lot of things. I talked to Char maybe once that week, and get this; I hadn't been out to dinner at all that week. And don't get me started about my workouts. Char and I decided to resume our Saturday brunches over the weekend at Quimby's. I would've preferred just her, but she had already called Jaleesa and Stacey again, so they were on the roster for the weekend, too.

I had heard from Neal a couple of times during the week also. I really missed him. He said he was going to call me with a big surprise. I had no idea what it was. I mean, c'mon, what could it possibly have been? He was way over there and I was in the States. I figured he might have ordered flowers or something like that. Could they even order flowers in the Bahamas to deliver here?

I picked up the phone and dialed Mark's number. His secretary answered and patched me through right away. It was as if he instructed my calls to go right through.

How conceited of me, but that's exactly what it sounded like.

"Good morning. This is Mark," he answered on the other line.

I got up to close my office door. You never knew who was around the corner.

"Hi, Mark, it's Monica. How are you doing?" I asked.

"I'm actually missing you," he said. "I've been trying to get a hold of you all week, and you've been impossible to get to. I've been waiting for you to return my calls. I guess that job keeps you that busy, huh?"

"Actually, it has," I said, setting up the excuse for not calling. "I really like it here so far."

There was silence for a moment and then the million-dollar question came in.

"Why didn't you tell me you and Tanya were working together?" he asked.

I knew it! She probably had told him a while ago, but he wanted me to speak on it first.

"Does it bother you?" I asked, evading the question.

Women could do it, too.

"No, it doesn't. I just figured what a small world this was. So have you guys been out to lunch yet?"

You have got to be kidding? What the hell did she tell him? *Did she happen to mention that she was ready to kick my ass in the mall a few weeks back? I bet she conveniently forgot to mention that.* Aside from the lunch with Sam and the Gladiator refereeing, I didn't plan to share any more dining experiences with her.

"No," I said. "I don't really go to lunch too often. Besides," I continued changing the subject, "I have to cut back on eating since I haven't been working out as much."

"Well, you'll have to make an exception tonight because I want to take you to dinner. It's Friday; I know you can go out tonight. I want to try Bartholomew's. It's the grand opening this weekend, and I just got a two-for-one coupon," he said.

I laughed.

He better have been kidding.

"That sounds good. Seven-thirty okay for you?"

"Sounds okay to me," he said.

I looked down at the phone. It sounded as though there was an echo. As a matter of fact, I noticed my phone had been sounding like that all week. I asked everyone else, but their phones seemed to be working okay. There was also another button lit up. Almost every time I picked up, the button labeled "call" would come on, sometimes as soon as I picked up and sometimes in the middle of a conversation.

I made a mental note to ask Sam about that.

I hung up the phone and saw that the "call" button was still lit up. I'd call the technician later.

I went back to work on my health care proposals. We had decided to present them to the employees on Monday. They were almost ready, so I didn't have too much work to do over the weekend. I decided I was just going to go ahead and enjoy my weekend.

When I got home, I did my immediate check for messages.

None.

Since I got home a little later than expected, I decided to take a shower right away. Mark was going to arrive in an hour or so, so I had to hurry.

As soon as I got out of the shower, the phone rang. I looked at the clock. Right on time. Neal said he would be calling at six-thirty and six-thirty it was, actually it was six twenty-seven. I picked up and immediately drifted into another world.

"Hi, how are you doing?" he asked.

"I'm fine, and yourself?" I sounded like I was on a business call at work.

"I'm great. I wasn't sure, but I just spoke to a travel agent and booked a flight to Maryland next week. I got a good deal, so I booked it for next Wednesday. Is that okay by you?"

I thought for a moment. I wish he'd told me sooner. I didn't know how I was going to swing it. I couldn't take off work because I just started, but he'd already booked the ticket.

"Is it okay?" he asked again, this time sounding a little alarmed that he had to ask twice.

"That's fine," I said, trying not to let him know the situation by my tone, "but I don't think I can take off work."

"That's okay," he said. "I just wanted to see you."

That was what I needed to hear.

"I can't wait for you to come," I said.

He started to laugh and I felt more at ease.

"I can't wait to see you, too. All I've been doing is thinking about you. Your face, your smile, your lips. They're so beautiful."

He knew how to make me feel so good.

"Ohhh," he said, stopping his train of thought.

I loved the way he said "oooh." It was so sexy.

"Did you get my letter?" he asked.

"I haven't checked the mailbox today."

Hopefully it came today because it had been almost two weeks. *Is it that slow to get mail from the Bahamas? Damn!*

After a few more minutes of conversation, time ran out on us again.

"I have to go because I'm at work, but I'll call you this weekend...and Monica?" he added quickly. "Think about me tonight, because I'll definitely be thinking about you. Bye."

I stared at the receiver for a moment before hanging up.

Damn, damn, damn, why did he have to be so far away?

I finished getting dressed to go out with Mark. Why did I almost feel like I was cheating on Neal with Mark? It felt really weird. The more I thought about it, the more ridiculous it sounded. Here I was thinking about a man, younger I might add, and who lived so far away. It didn't make any sense. Was I supposed to not be with another man because I really liked this guy who I would never see except on occasion? I mean, how many times would he come up here to see me and how many times would I go down there to see him? That could get expensive. Every time he called, we could only talk for five minutes because it's like a billion dollars a minute to call from the Bahamas, and I couldn't even call him because he doesn't have a phone. They didn't really need phones down there like we did up here. If he wanted to get in touch with someone, he could just drive over there and do what they call "hail" somebody. I really wished I would just shut up and enjoy the moment, but sometimes my practical side always came out. So far, I had gotten the go-ahead from the girls regarding Mark, but I still wasn't sure. What to do? I knew he was interested but was I? I *felt* like I should be, and apparently so did everyone else. I decided to change the subject in my head. If I really sat down and thought about how I felt about this man, it could get real depressing.

Let's see, what was I going to wear? I decided on the famous little black dress and sandals. It was going to be hot, so I wanted to be ready for the heat. (No pun intended). As a matter of fact the whole week had been hot, and the girls at the office had been showing up with teenie-weenie skirts on and no pantyhose. Now I hated pantyhose as much as the next guy, but if you weren't going to wear any, I didn't suggest wearing short, tight skirts. I don't think you should wear short, tight skirts to the office regardless, but that was another issue. Tanya was actually the leader of the pack on that one. Her skirts started out to her ankles on Monday, but by the time Friday came around, it was a free-for-all. I thought we should've had a dress code. I decided to approach Sam about that one, too. Every company needed a dress code. Sam had given me an agenda for the upcoming months. I was to prepare a new-hire orientation guidebook, and an employee handbook, in which the dress code would have to be included anyway. I also had to come up with personal and vacation time. Since this was a new company, we had no precedent.

I sighed as I thought about how much work that was going to take, but not that night; I was ready to go out and have a good time.

When I finished getting dressed, I had another thirty-minute wait. I decided to fix a martini and just chill for a minute, but I was out of vodka. I looked in the refrigerator and I saw the Bahama Mamas in a pitcher that Neal had made for me a couple of weeks earlier when he was here. Awwwww, I forgot I had those. I decided against drinking all together, and closed the refrigerator door. He was not going to consume my thoughts that night. I was hanging out with Mark, and I'd be damned if I didn't plan on having a good time.

I sat down on the couch and rubbed my foot against Kitty. She loved that. I had to watch getting cat hair on my black dress because she could shed something fierce.

When my phone rang, I checked the caller ID and it came up "ANONY-MOUS."

"Helloooo?"

No answer.

"Helloooooo?" I repeated.

Still no answer.

I hung up. With me, you got two tries and that was it. After that it was usually a solicitor keying up the recording that asked you if you wanted a condo in Bora Bora, or if you wanted to buy twenty pounds of frozen meat. With a real person, you felt guilty for hanging up, but with a recording I had no hesitation.

The phone rang again. I looked at the caller ID and again it said "ANONYMOUS." Since I forgot to turn on my answering machine, I let it ring to see how desperate this person was to talk to me. It started getting creepy on the seventh ring. I picked it up and said hello again. This time there was a pause, and then *they* hung up.

That was it; I turned on my answering machine and decided to wait for Mark downstairs.

Freaks! Mark pulled up on time and saw me, so he didn't pull into a spot. I went over to his truck and he got out to open the door for me.

"Are you okay?" he asked upon seeing my face.

"Yeah. This solicitor just kept calling me and getting on my nerves," I said and hopped in.

He leaned over my lap and pulled something from the glove compartment.

"I've got you something," he said.

He took out this perfectly wrapped gift and handed it to me. I opened it up. It was perfume.

"Thank you." I smiled.

My mood changed immediately.

He stared at me. "You look nice."

"Thanks."

I watched him as he put the key in the ignition and started the truck.

The profile of his face looked funny. Not really funny; it just looked too perfect to have been real. He had high cheekbones and his complexion didn't have one mark on it. I kid you not. There wasn't even a blemish or a mole anywhere in sight on that face. If I didn't know better, I would've guessed he used some sort of bleaching cream because faces like that just didn't happen.

"So are you ready to have fun? I have the whole evening planned, so don't even think you're going to get one of your 'headaches' and roll out on me," he said, looking from me to the road.

I started laughing.

"Let's do it then," I said to him a little more upbeat.

He looked at me and winked.

For some strange reason, I think he took my last sentence literally.

We got to Bartholomew's and it was packed. Since it was grand opening night, there were balloons all over the place. The news was even there and it was total chaos. This was exactly what I needed.

Mark seemed just as excited as me. "Do you know you have to kill someone to get reservations in this place tonight?"

I played along. "So you killed someone, huh?"

"Well, I got juice. I just had to maim somebody."

I busted out laughing.

"See the cops over there?" He nodded toward the sidewalk. "They're waiting for me so, when we leave, you might have to drive yourself home tonight." Mark was certainly in a good mood, and I was thankful for that. When we walked into the place, I saw that it was huge. They were blasting Branford Marsalis throughout the many speakers in each of the corners in the room. I found out that it was actually a restaurant/bar/dance club. They had live bands that played there, and they had everything from theme nights to cigar rooms filled with fine cigars, which I enjoyed on occasion. They must've spent a pretty penny to put the place together. The lighting was astonishing. It was mood lighting in different shades of cool, meaning it was turned down dark and low and gave the room a bluish look. They had small tables that had a tiny spotlight over them to showcase the couples seated.

I gazed around and was thoroughly impressed. "This is nice."

The maitre d' came over and showed us to our table.

Mark held out my chair for me. "So you like this place?"

I nodded. I loved it. The atmosphere was great.

"We can call this our place now. What do you think about that?" He looked at me with serious eye action going on.

I joked off his comment and changed the subject (my specialty).

I really did like Mark, but in no way, shape or form was I going to lead him on. If this was going to happen, this was going to happen at a slow pace.

We ate dinner and had good conversation as usual. He was actually rather interesting. This was a huge change from our first date. I had no idea that he had done charity work with inner-city kids for two years until his job took him away from that. I also had no idea that he had been engaged before. I don't think he meant to let me know about that, but it slipped out in conversation. It seemed as though he didn't want to talk about it anymore, so I dropped it. Besides, it really didn't matter to me anyway.

"So how's the job going?" he asked.

"It's going well. I really like it. I like the hands-on work. Sam's a great boss who actually listens to my suggestions." I laughed. "You know how rare that is in the workplace."

"That's that guy you said was hitting on you in your building, right?"

I didn't like where he was going, but I bit. "Yes, that's him. Why do you ask?"

"I'd try to be a great boss, too, if I wanted to get in your panties!"

He'd just killed it. In one moment, he'd killed it.

After his remark, he took a drink of his wine. When he looked up from his glass, he saw me staring at him with blood pressure rising and all.

"Meaning what?" I asked.

When he saw that the conversation was turning sour, he tried to joke it off. "I was kidding." He laughed. "So anyway, how's Tanya working out?"

I stared for a second before answering his question. This time he didn't look up when I was silent. He was just steady drinking until I said something, and even when I eventually did speak, he started fidgeting in his pocket.

"Why don't you ask her? You still talk to her, don't you?"

He continued fidgeting and didn't look at me.

Woo, hoo, I'm over here!!!!!

"Why would you ask *that?*" he said, finally looking at me.

I sighed. I was finally fed up. "Mark, exactly what is the deal between you two? I mean, we're just hanging out as friends and having a good time, but I'd really like to know."

"I told you, Tanya and I are just friends. We've been friends for a while, and that's it."

"Well, call me crazy, but I get the distinct impression that there's something more than that." I decided not to discuss the mall confrontation. "She's very cold and callous at work, to mainly me, of course, but it isn't limited to just me. She isn't getting high marks with anyone, but I seem to be on the top of her hit list, and I can't figure out why. Think about it; our only connection is you, but she has no idea that we're going out because I haven't said anything." I paused. "Unless you have. She's only seen us together in passing and speaking to each other cordially. I can't imagine her spending all her time confronting women you speak to in a friendly manner."

I sat back in my chair and crossed my arms, waiting for an answer.

He looked at me with a huge question mark over his head. "She confronted you? When? What happened?"

Oops, my mistake.

"Fine!" I threw my hands in the air in defeat and ignored his barrage of questions. "You two are just good friends, so let's leave it at that. It's really none of my business."

He took another sip, grabbed my hand and grinned. "Let's go to the club and get our dance on."He was really going to drop it and not answer me directly. *Ain't that about a bitch!?* I decided to put that conversation behind us because before all this, we were having such a good time and I wanted to resume having a good time.

He pulled me up from my chair and we went to the club section. That side was packed, too. On the "club side" they were blasting Puff Daddy, P. Diddy, whatever, and he immediately pulled me out onto the dance floor. In between drinks, we danced to Shaggy, Blu Cantrell, and Missy Elliot. Then a slow song by Case came on, and he pulled me close to him. *Real* close. So close that I could feel how much of a good time he was having. This was great. I was getting turned on myself, especially when he started kissing my neck. It must've been the combination of liquor and the ambience of the club that made me not mind. Or it could've just been the fact that I was terribly horny. If he'd wanted to take me home that night, I just might've let him. It was the weekend, and besides, it had been a good while since I'd gotten some. I looked around the room and everyone was dancing, drinking and having a good time.

I opened my eyes a little wider when I saw the bar. I couldn't believe it. I squinted and looked again. You've gotta be kidding. Yup, it was Tanya standing there at the bar and staring directly at us. She turned around to the bar, took a shot of something and turned back around to us. She was with that same ghetto-ghetto she was with at the mall. She had on this little tight ass dress with spaghetti straps. Under ordinary circumstances, I would say it was a cute dress, but I couldn't bring myself to do so because it was on her big butt, and it had all her cleavage hanging out. I was talking, about to fall the hell out any second, if she so much as coughed.

I tapped Mark on the shoulder and pointed toward the bar. He nearly fell out his damn self.

"I can't believe this!" He was obviously pissed off. "Hold on a sec, I'll be right back," he said, stomping toward her.

After about two minutes of looking to see what the hell was going on at the bar, I realized I was still standing in the middle of the dance floor, so I walked over toward the bar. Mark didn't see me coming because his back was to me, and she didn't either because she was too busy flailing her arms wildly in anger.

As I walked up on him, I couldn't be sure, but I thought I heard him say something about waiting for him at home.

What home? What the hell was going on?

"Mark?" I called over the loud music.

He didn't hear me over the music, so I yelled louder.

Just then Tanya peeked around him, and I'll be damned if she didn't grab my hair! Mark tried to pull her off me, but she hung on for dear life. I was able to twist around and get my hair loose, and then she lunged at me. It looked like she was going for the eyes but missed and tripped, probably over her big fat hamhock calves. She got up quickly and turned and lunged at me again, this time knocking me down. We were literally on the floor rolling around, pulling each other's hair. By this time the patrons at the bar were looking and cheering (mostly men of course). I couldn't figure out where Mark was, but he needed to get this psycho bitch off me. We began tussling on the floor until two guys—I'm guessing bouncers—grabbed us and separated us. I looked over at her across the room and her boob was hanging out of her dress. Men were still cheering, but now it was even louder. I saw Mark coming toward me. He took my arm and started leading me out the door. As we walked out, I turned around to make sure that crazy bitch wasn't following us, but a bouncer was holding her with her tit still hanging out.

As we walked out, I heard her yelling over the music. "If you leave with that bitch, don't bother coming home, motherfucker! It's over."

She was right about one thing; it was over.

Chapter 13

W hen I got home that night, I hopped into the shower and went straight to bed. I woke up the next morning to my phone ringing off the hook. I think it rang even earlier, but I was in and out of sleep so I wasn't sure. I saw I had four messages and checked the caller ID before listening to any of them. I didn't want any surprises. Mark had called at two-twelve and at four thirty-three in the morning. He also called me at six, and there were two "ANONYMOUS" calls on my ID. I just went ahead and deleted all the messages. There was nothing I wanted to hear. I called Char and told her everything.

"You're kidding," was her response. "Did you kick her ass? That bitch must be crazy. I knew it." When I told her about my previous confrontation at the mall, she was even more astonished.

"Dang, girl! You're gonna hafta get a restraining order. That don't make no sense. Do you still feel like going to Quimby's for brunch, or did you want to go to the gym and get buffed so you can protect yourself from her?" she asked, laughing hysterically.

Leave it up to her to find the humor in this.

"I'll meet you there at one," I said.

No one, and I mean no one was going to keep me away from my chicken fingers with extra honey mustard. I'll diet tomorrow, but today I was too worked up.

I started to get dressed until my phone rang again. *Jeez Louise*. What the hell? Why is everybody so interested in calling me now?

I was in my bedroom and didn't have caller ID in there, so I just took my chances.

"Hello?" I said cautiously.

"Hey, Monica. I hate to call you on Saturday, but I left a message last night and I just wanted to make sure you got it."

It was Sam.

"I'm calling a meeting for all managers first thing Monday morning. Try to be there at eight. Okay?"

"No problem, Sam," I told him and hung up.

I'd decided that I wasn't able to work with that girl, especially now. I was going to suggest her termination. I was going to bring this situation up to Sam on Monday. She had proved her un-professionalism many times at the office and now this. I was sure I could get back-up on this one. I had received numerous complaints regarding her, so I was sure termination wouldn't be a problem. The only predicament I did foresee was the actual discussion regarding her termination. Since I'm considered HR, I'd kept the complaints confidential and in her file. Sam didn't know anything regarding her work ethic, but I guaranteed he'd find out Monday morning.

She was going to prohibit me from doing my job efficiently, and I wouldn't have that, period!

I went downstairs to my mailbox. I hadn't checked it in a while, and I was sure it was overflowing with bills as usual. I opened it up and found one lone envelope. I took it out, looked at it and saw that it was post-marked from the Bahamas. Through all the excitement I had forgotten Neal said that he had sent me a letter.

Good grief; it took almost two weeks to get here.

I opened it up and looked at it. His handwriting was horrendous (what guy's wasn't?), but it was beautiful in the fact that it was *his* handwriting.

I folded up the letter, put it back in the envelope and took it upstairs. I wanted to read this letter in the privacy of my own home.

When I got back to my apartment, I took the letter out of the envelope and looked from front to back. It was two pages and read:

Dear Monica,

How are you doing? I couldn't wait to put my thoughts and feelings of you in this letter, so I started writing it before I left.

Monica, you are by far the sweetest and most charming young woman I've ever met. The quality of your character is beyond measure. I wished my time there had never ended. Your unique personality will be with me always.

I thought about the things you told me concerning your life dreams. You have inspired and motivated me to finish my degree, and for that I thank you. I know it's highly unlikely that we will see each other again, and there is no certainty that this letter will reach its right destination; however, there is one thing I can guarantee. I will always remember you. I will always remember the softness of your lips, your delicate touch, and your wonderful smile. The touch of your hands I shall never forget.

Please write me soon and let me know how you are doing.

Sincerely yours,

Cornelius

I couldn't believe this letter. It was so beautiful, so poetic. The letter was dated the day he left. He was feeling all of these things about me, and I had no idea. What made it even more touching was the fact that he wrote this thinking that we might never see each other again or that I'd never receive his letter. He might've had terrible handwriting, but the words that filled this page were breathtaking. If anyone else would've written this letter it would've been bullshit, but I really believed that he meant every word he put on this piece of paper. His eyes told me so the night we'd spent together.

I started to smile. He actually had written this letter thinking that we might never speak to each other again. It felt good that he felt the same way I did about him but, at the same time, it made me sad. His being so far away was starting to eat at me. I really wanted to hug him for this letter, for making me feel so much better. I hoped he would call that night. I would wait by the phone if I had to.

I was serious, too.

I looked at the time and realized that I was late for brunch with the girls. I ran to my room, knocked Kitty off my bed and opened my closet to see what I should wear.

I felt good. Even after the previous night's ignominy, I still felt good and all because of a letter. I felt better than good. I felt great. So good that I could even go to brunch with Stacey *and* Jaleesa, even though I wished it was just Char. I wanted to tell her what I was feeling for Neal. I wanted her to be happy for me, as I knew she would. I also wanted her to bring me back to earth. She could and would be the one to ground me from this cloud I was floating on. We do things like that for each other.

I started to think back to when she was dating some dude named Christopher. That whole deal was a mess. He bought her flowers and candy every day for like a week. He took her to these nice restaurants and ordered wine and shrimp and the most expensive things on the menu for her. They even had afternoon dates to museums and to the zoo. That's when you know you're a couple. When they don't just want to take you out to dinner and then take you back to their place for "coffee and conversation." Char decided that she was going to hold off on sex with Christopher, which was a good move. She liked him so much that she knew he would wait. Well, he did wait, and wait, and wait. In the meantime, those afternoon dates and expensive dinners just kept coming. He actually *seemed* like one of the nice ones. Just days after their first intimate encounter, he came up with excuses as to why he couldn't see her. The afternoon dates were cancelled altogether and before she'd given him some, he was talking about taking her home to meet his parents. Eventually everything ran out. No dates period—afternoon or otherwise—no candy, no flowers and no phone calls. She'd try to call him and always got the answering machine. She had no idea what had happened. *She* had no idea but I figured it out quick. I warned her, as I know she would've done for me. We ended up going over there to make sure he wasn't dead or *something* because according to her, that wasn't like him not to call. Well, he wasn't dead. It was that *something* that got her.

When he opened the door, we could see that he had some woman sitting on the couch. We didn't see much of her, but I did see that she had short-cropped blond hair and the biggest tits you'd ever seen. He dismissed us quick and practically slammed the door in our faces. I remember that night well. Char and I had gotten drunk big time and passed out at my place.

We'd decided not to trust men ever again, considering a large majority of them were just malicious and cruel. There was probably one percent of the male population that was actually good. If we got lucky, we got lucky and right then I felt as though I got lucky with Neal. Or was this another Christopher? Whatever it was, I was going to trust that Neal was decent. *What else could I do?* If it was a mistake, it would be Char who would ground me as I did for her.

I finished getting dressed in a pair of cropped black pants and a tank top. I looked at myself in the mirror, and it looked as though my stomach was getting a little bigger. Shit! This would be my last time ordering chicken fingers with extra honey mustard and fries, I promised myself.

I finished getting dressed and went downstairs and out into the parking lot. I walked over to my car and saw a black Range Rover double-parked in my parking lot.

Oh, goodness. I *knew* that wasn't Mark stalking me now! Well, evidently I didn't know too much because it was him. I decided to just walk straight to my car and not even look in his direction. I heard him yell my name from his truck but kept walking.

"Monica!" he yelled again, this time getting out of his truck.

There was absolutely no way to avoid him, so I just gave in.

"What do you want?" I asked in disgust. "What could you possible have to say to me after last night? You've got to be the bravest motherfucka in the world for coming down here to see me after that fiasco last night."

I reached in my purse for my keys because I wanted to get the hell out of there as soon as possible.

"Just let me explain," he said, clasping his hands together as if pleading. "First of all, I wanted to give you the perfume I bought for you. You left it in the car."

I snatched it from his hands and threw it down against the asphalt, shattering it into a million pieces.

"There, you gave it to me."

I don't know why I was so angry. I had liked Mark, but it wasn't like he was my man. Hell, it wasn't even like we'd slept together or anything. Wait, I knew exactly why I was so angry. I—like any other woman—just didn't like being played. He must've loved having two women fight for him like that. Men like him are precisely why I didn't have one and I knew I didn't want this one. *Throw him back; this one's no good! Tired ass bitch!*

"Look, I know you're mad and I don't know what to say."

He looked down at the ground for a moment and then back up to me.

"I'd been staying with Tanya for some time. I was getting my place painted and she offered, so I stayed. Nothing happened, which is why she's mad. When she saw us together, she just sort of blew up."

"Sort of?" I asked. "Were you not there last night? That bitch was going for the jugular."

He looked at me with almost pleading eyes.

"Look, I got on her about that and I moved all of my stuff out last night. I didn't realize how crazy she was myself. She always seemed cool."

"Let me ask you a question," I said. "How the hell did she know we were going to be at Bartholomew's anyway? It was like she was waiting for us."

He stammered a moment and scrunched his face up like he was thinking.

"I have no idea; I wouldn't tell her. Maybe you said something to someone at your office and she overheard."

I shook my head.

"She couldn't have overheard because I didn't tell anyone at the office. She knew we were going to be there. Even if I did believe your tired ass excuses, I'm not trying to get involved with someone who has a fatal attraction following them around the whole dang city. I don't have a rabbit, but I do have a cat, and I'm not trying to come home finding her boiling in some pot."

He laughed, but I kept a serious look on my face. I didn't want him to think I was relenting.

He looked at me and told me he totally understood but he was not giving up.

"Monica," he said with his voice softening, "I really enjoyed our time together, and I'm not giving up on you. I find you extremely sexy and smart, and I have a genuine interest in taking this to another level."

He grabbed my hand that was down at my side.

"I think you feel the same."

He smiled, turned and walked away.

How dramatic of him.

I turned to get into my car and heard him yell my name again. He walked up toward me with a single yellow rose in his hand.

"In all this excitement, I almost forgot this," he said and handed it to me. "You can answer your phone tonight or not, but I'll call you later on, and if you choose not to pick up I'll leave you a message. A sweet message," he said. "I want you and I think you know that. I'm going to leave it all up to you. Take all the time you need. I'll be here."

"So what did he say?" Jaleesa asked at brunch.

I stuffed another fry in my mouth.

Char, Jaleesa, Stacey and myself sat in a booth at Quimby's having our usual throwdown. We opted for a booth this time so we could have a private conversation. (Then again, anything that was said at that table that day would end up being repeated the next day by those big mouths.) I had a lot to tell them, actually just Char, but with the tag-a-longs, I had no choice.

"He really didn't have too much to say," I began. "I mean, c'mon, what could he say? I'm just really surprised that he actually had the balls to come over this morning. What the hell was he thinking?"

"I hear ya," Stacey said. "If I were him, I would've just taken the loss and left it alone."

She tilted her head and thought silently for a moment.

"Hmmm, then again, if I *really* liked the person...," she said and trailed off.

"You gotta admit that," Jaleesa interjected. "If nothing was going on and I really liked the person, I think I'd try to explain, too."

Char made a sucking noise with her tongue.

"Aw, c'mon, you guys. What do you think this is? Does she have 'dumb ass' written on her face? Y'all might, but she don't."

She took a sip of her soda to wash down her mouthful of food.

"He could be living with that bitch *and* her momma and still be able to come all the way over to Monica's and lie to her face. They can do that, and if you have any sense," she said, turning to me, "you'll heed my warning."

"Girl, shut up. You're the one who fixed her ass up with him in the first place," Jaleesa said. "Besides, you just jealous cuz you ain't got nobody."

Char looked at me in disbelief. Jaleesa's actually the last person to be talking about taking somebody back.

Char looked as if she was going to read Jaleesa and read her good. When she snuck a glance at me, I shook my head as if to tell her don't do it. I didn't need or want a fight today. I wasn't in the mood. The previous night was enough.

"Let this girl do her own thing," Jaleesa continued. "Personally, I think she should take him for all he's got. I'm just thankful that I didn't let the brotha get any further with me."

Char started laughing out loud.

"You didn't *let* it get any further cuz Mark didn't want your ass."

I'd forgotten that Char admitted to setting Jaleesa and Mark up before.

"He evidently feels guilty, so that should be able to get her something. He'll want to take her out to dinner and buy her things. I'd go for what I know," Jaleesa said. She then turned toward Char. "And just for the record, *I* didn't want *him*."

Silent-for-once Stacey spoke up. "Puh-leese. The way you keep taking broke-down Rakim back? You keep taking his ass back and what has he ever given you? I'll tell you, nothin', cuz he ain't got nothing." She then turned to face me. "Besides, he may feel guilty now, but that'll only last for a week, and I don't give a damn how guilty a brother feels, he ain't buying shit, especially for some woman who didn't give him the skins." She paused. "Or did she?"

They all looked at me, but I kept silent.

"You *didn't* break him off a piece yet?" Jaleesa asked, laughing. "Oh, well, that changes everything. You ain't getting shit!"

"On the contrary," Char said. "Think about it. He didn't hit it yet and is still comin' over beggin' after what happened. I just may change my position on this one. You may have him whupped."

We all laughed. I believe that men don't get whupped anymore. Men may like the sex a woman gives him, and she may be able to get something out of him for a short period of time, but eventually the tables turn. When the woman is playing the dude, he'll eventually turn it around. If he is "whupped," he may be buying you shit, but trust me, he'll be screwing somebody else behind your back, and in the end when you think he's all yours and that you have him "whupped," he may have had about four other women on the side that he's been fucking. The fucked-up thing is that while you were "playin'" him, he'd show up on your doorstep with some STD. So the whole time you thought you had it like that, he played you just as much as you thought you were playing him. I've seen it over and over again. Hell, I've even been through it a few times, minus the STD, of course. I just didn't have that player nature in me and I'm glad I didn't. I valued my relationships—if that's what you wanted to call them—more than that. I looked at it this way; if we broke up, then we broke up. If he burned me, then I felt it wasn't meant to be. I'm not saying it hurt any less; I'm just saying that everything happened for a reason. I just hoped I didn't have to get burned too many more times before shit changed.

"So when is Cornelius coming again?" Char asked, still stuffing her face.

"He'll be here on Wednesday and he's staying until Monday," I said.

"What are you guys gonna do?" asked Stacey.

The waiter came back and refilled our glasses.

"I'm not really sure yet. Unfortunately, I have to work, so I don't know what that is going to leave us to do. I'm going to try to take Friday off though. We'll probably hit D.C. a few times and take it from there."

"I don't even know why you want to bother having him come up here," Jaleesa said. "You guys could never have a relationship. He lives in another country, for goodness sake. Char did say that he was cute as hell though."

"Not just that," Char corrected, "but he's younger, too."

"Go 'head, girl," Stacey said. "Don't sleep on those young bucks. I dated one for a while but he was triflin'. The sex was bangin' in the beginning, but it got so that *I* couldn't keep up. What kind of shit was that? Aren't I supposed to be in my sexual prime? He wanted it all day and all night, but I worked all day and when I came home he was ready to go even before I got my shoes off."

"Was this Eric?" Jaleesa asked. "The one that lived with moms and had no job? I guess he *was* ready to go when you got home, seeing as he had all day to sit around and wait for your butt...and I mean that literally," she said and started laughing.

"Yup, that was him. That's why he was triflin'. He didn't want to get a job and had his mom give him an allowance. He had the nerve to pick me up in her station wagon when we went out one time," she said, trying to stifle her laugh with the rest of us. "To top it off, there was a baby seat in the back for his little brother."

"I thought he *was* the little brother," I said.

That was it. We all started crackin' up.

"How long ago was this and how old was he?" I asked.

"Let's see, I was twenty-seven at the time, so he was like twenty-three."

You know I got silent quick.

"How old is your man?" she asked back.

Damn, I knew it was coming. I made sure to correct her first.

"He's not my man, and he's twenty-four, thank you," I said defensively.

I saw their faces and decided right then that I should've lied and said at least twenty-seven.

"Daaaaaaaang!" Jaleesa said.

She turned to Stacey.

"Can she borrow that baby seat?"

Now I was the center of their laughter. It was funny when we were bustin' on Stacey but now, for some reason, it wasn't funny anymore.

"You can always take him to a movie. Just remember, if it's R-rated, you're going to have to accompany him, or else he won't be able to get in," Stacey said and started laughing again with everyone else.

I didn't think that was funny. Actually, it was kinda funny. I started laughing, too.

"How old is your man, Broadus?" asked Stacey, turning to Char. "Is he twelve, too?"

"Girl, Broadus is thirty, thank you," she shot back. "He's able to get me a drink *without* a fake ID."

More laughter.

Okay, okay, it's not funny anymore.

"Yeah, well, your man wasn't *trying* to get you a drink when he was here. If I remembered correctly, it was Broadus that did all the ordering, mostly for himself, and it was Neal that did all the paying," I shot back.

Laughing, they both looked at Char for her retort.

Oh, now she had nothing to say?

Jaleesa said, "So anyway, what are you gonna do about your girl at work?"

"That's a really good question. I thought about getting her fired. She isn't productive at all. I wanted to say something to Sam sooner, but I felt as though I could've just been being biased considering the circumstances. Now I *know* I'm being biased and I have a right to be. I don't want to work with her, period. She's not professional at all and for lack of a better word, she's pathetic. She really needs to go back to the temp service she came from, and get a lower-profile job. Maybe they could find her a job as a dishwasher or something like that. That's more in line with her qualifications."

When I looked up from my plate after spitting all that out, I realized that I was mostly talking to myself moreso than them. They all just looked at me.

"Damn!" Jaleesa said. "I knew you didn't like her but...damn!"

"Don't *damn* me," I said angrily. *"You* don't have to work with her every day and I'm tired of her attitude and don't let me get started about last night. This isn't just about last night though; she's been working my nerves for a while. She needs to have her ass fired."

"You shouldn't do that." Char took another huge bite of her sandwich. "You should let her hang herself. If she's as bad at her job as you say she is, she'll do just that. Trust me on this one. I've seen cases where someone was fired and then turned around and sued the company, and you being HR and all, that wouldn't be good if she was fired on your recommendation considering the circumstances. Believe me, people like that always hang themselves. Let her do it, and Sam and everyone else will see it, and then *pow!* She's outta there. That's how I'd play it."

"You sure know a lot about this type of situation. Somebody must've done this to you before, only you must've been the 'firee' instead of the 'firer,'" Stacey said, laughing. Char did have a point. Maybe I should wait until she sealed her own coffin. The question was, how long could I stay sane while waiting?

When I got home, it was well past five-thirty. Let's see, I'd been to brunch with the girls, I went and visited my sister and then I actually worked out, only this time I went to the gym and did some weights. That had to be the most powerful feeling in the world. I didn't really care for aerobics too much, but when I lifted weights, I felt powerful, and I liked how it sculpted my body. Just think, if I'd actually stopped eating junk food I would've been lean and mean. I usually just worked out with my male friends at the gym because the one time I went with Jaleesa, she came in full makeup. C'mon now.

We started doing the aerobics and ten minutes into the routine, she had to stop because her makeup started running. It only took one time. I never went with her again.

I couldn't figure out why I didn't work out more often; it really relieved tension, and I felt great after a hard workout. My new resolution was to work out more and eat less junk food. This was something that I promised myself. Hey, if I wanted to stay sane *and* in shape, it would be a requirement. If not that, then it would be a bottle of Jack Daniels, and that could be real punishment on my liver.

I checked my messages and there were three on my answering machine. I pressed the "message" button to listen to the first. It was Neal.

"I just wanted to say hello and that I really miss you. Don't forget me next week. Bye." It was a sweet and simple message. I wished he were actually around so I could've told him exactly what was going on with the Tanya situation. He was definitely the type of person that I could've shared the shit with. Believe me, by the time he came the next week, I would have new shit to tell him.

The second was from Mark. His message was the typical I-told-you-I-was-going-to-leave-a-message-so-here-it-is type. I guess he figured it sounded corny because he attempted to sound sweet with the I-miss-you big finish and something about coming over for a visit tonight, blah, blah, blah. Yeah, whatever. I really wasn't in the mood. It just wasn't working with him. Contrary to popular belief, it had nothing to do with Tanya. She didn't even factor into the equation. It was something else. He seemed really cool on paper, but why wasn't I head over heels for him like I was for the guy that was across the Atlantic Ocean or whichever ocean. Could it be the fact that he was so far away that made it so tempting? Maybe subconsciously Neal was the perfect guy. He was far, far, away, but you could easily brush off scrubs by saying that you already had a man but didn't have to actually live with him. I could deal with that. (How about that for reasoning?) The trade-off would be that you wouldn't get sex when you wanted/needed it, but if that meant that I didn't have to deal with a man's bullshit, then I was all for it. Hook it up!

I listened to the third message and it was just a female voice on the machine. She called me a bitch and something, something. I couldn't make it out. It sounded like whoever it was (like I didn't know) was slightly drunk and wasn't enunciating properly. It didn't sound like her, but it could've been one of her friends like ghetto, ghetto from the mall. She's pulled that one before. I couldn't believe she didn't feel ashamed about what happened the previous night. I thought maybe she would've felt an iota of remorse, but evidently she didn't, and that was the worst part of the entire thing. What would it take for her to feel some remorse and how long would and could she keep this up? *More importantly, how did she get my damn number?* I just thought about that. My number wasn't even listed yet since I'd just moved, and I knew *I* didn't give it to her. I guess two and two equaled Mark again. Why did everything negative lead back to him?

I made myself a drink and sat back and put in my Jill Scott CD. I didn't know if it was her or the martini, but I was feeling a little more relaxed. Thank you, Char, for getting me that martini kit for my birthday. Fuck Tanya, fuck Mark and fuck missing Neal. I was chillin'.

When I woke up, it was completely dark. I looked at the clock. It was nine-thirty. I figured I had been asleep for about two hours. I think I was drunk, or should I say slightly tipsy? (It sounded better.) I had made two more martinis (damn you, Char, for getting me that martini set), and then Char called me telling me she'd be over at ten to hang out. I didn't have anything better to do, so I was down for it. We'd probably end up playing Scattegories or my personal favorite, UNO.

I quickly jumped in the shower and put on my cotton pajamas. Since it was just her coming over, I figured I'd be as comfortable as possible.

I heard the phone ring and, in the dark, I looked at the fluorescent number lit up on my caller ID. It was Char on her cell. Maybe I wouldn't have company that night after all. Either way it didn't matter to me. I picked up and she was laughing.

"Hello?" I said.

"Giiiiirl, are you still up because I'm on my way over."

She sounded drunk and not slightly either.

"I *know* you're not driving over here with your drunk ass self. (I know I had nerve but at least I wasn't driving.) I told you to watch that."

She'd done that before and had gotten into an accident and landed her butt in the hospital and almost in jail.

"Girl, knock off the preachin' shit. For your information, I'm *not* driving. I'm calling you to tell you that I'll be over in ten minutes, so just make sure you have your butt up."

She's not driving? Then how the hell was she getting here?

Before I could ask, she told me that she was hungry and had ordered a pizza to be delivered. Oh, no she didn't! Now I would have to pay.

"Whatever," I said. "Just hurry up before I fall asleep again." I walked over to the Venetian blinds and closed them. I didn't want anyone looking in when I turned on the lights. Nosy ass neighbors.

"Girl, wake your lazy ass up. I'm ready to get my party on," she said and then hung up.

I walked to the other side of the room in complete darkness and flicked on the light.

I was so glad to be tipsy because drunk Char could really get on your nerves at times. It *had* been a while since just the two of us hung out, so I was welcoming her visit.

The doorbell rang and I ran to my room to grab my wallet. That had to be the pizza guy. I opened the door, forgetting that I only had my cotton tank and shorts on. The delivery guy, whose name was Jamie according to his bright orange nametag, had to be no more than eighteen. He didn't even see my face. He just stared at my body, grinning from ear to ear, telling me that the pizza was thirty dollars.

"Thirty dollars?! What all was ordered?" I asked him.

"Uh, I think, I'm not sure." Jamie took off his cap and fumbled around for the receipt.

Oh, gimme that.

I grabbed the receipt that was taped right on the front of the box and saw that she'd ordered one large pepperoni, one large cheese and one large with everything.

Oh, see, now she was pushing it.

I reached into my wallet and gave him a fifty-dollar bill. He looked at me like, "What? You want change?" I gave a look back like, "You'd better gimme my change!" He handed me my change in practically all ones, claiming that this was the only thing he had even though I saw in between that wad of ones there were plenty of tens and twenties. (Slick move, Jamie my boy). He then gave my body one last up and down as I slammed the door in his face.

Was this girl smoking crack, too? Why the hell was she so damn hungry? I put the pizza on the coffee table and immediately grabbed a slice of cheese. Since I planned on chillin' with my girl tonight, my diet would start tomorrow. I poured myself another martini and turned the radio on. Pizza and martinis—what a nice combination, I thought, as I turned the radio up. The radio stations were at the clubs, so I picked the station that was jammin' the most and sat back, put my feet up on the coffee table and ate my pizza and drank my drink. Now this was how I like to spend my weekends. No fussing over what to wear, how to wear my hair, how much makeup to slap on my face. None of that. I could just sit back with my feet up and relax.

I started thinking about Neal again. I wondered what he was doing right then. Knowing him, he was at work slaving away. It seemed as though he always had to work. Whenever he called me, he was on his way to work, on break at work or had just left work. I really couldn't wait to see him again. I closed my eyes and pictured his smile. I then pictured his body. He had a cute tight body. It was perfect. I did peek at his butt when he was there and it was just as tight as the rest of his body. I thought about his torso, his eyes, his lips and especially his hands. They were strong like a man's but not dirty like one. I knew this because when he spent the night he gave me a massage and it felt so good. I thought about how those lips kissed mine and how I immediately drifted into heaven. It was wonderful.

When I opened my eyes again, I looked up at the clock and it was ten-thirty. *Where the hell was she?* This is why I was always late when I went to meet her someplace. It didn't matter where she was going; she was *always* late, forever on CPT.

The doorbell rang and I walked to the door with drink in hand. I opened up the door ready to cuss her out, and lo and behold there was Char, but she wasn't alone. She was with two guys! One of them being...Mark.

I am going to hurt this girl one day; I swear to it.

They must've seen the shock in my eyes because they all yelled, "Surprise!" like it was some damn birthday party.

Mark gave me the same once-over that Jamie, the pizza guy gave me. Char walked past me and into my apartment with the guys following. I didn't even know who the other guy was.

Char laughed. "I told you I wasn't driving!" *Ha! Ha! The comedian was at it again.*

I grabbed her arm and led her to the kitchen. Once we were in the kitchen, I peeked out into the living room to make sure they weren't able to hear what I was going to tell her.

"What the hell's going on? Gee, thanks for telling me that Mark was coming with you along with some guy I don't even know."

I peeked out again to make sure I wasn't too loud.

"I was gonna tell you when I called," she said, obviously drunk, "but they told me not to."

They or Mark?

Ten to one, Mark was behind all of this.

"Girl, who cares? Let's just hang out and have a good time. They brought some Bailey's, so let's just party," she said, grabbing my elbow.

"You sometimes remind me of a drunk." I snatched my elbow from her grasp.

"Only sometimes?" she said and we started laughing.

Again, she had gotten away with being her usual slick self. I guess it couldn't hurt. What else was I doing anyway?

We walked back into my living room with glasses for the Bailey's and found them sitting on my couch chillin', feet up and all. I looked over at Mark, and he was still staring at me, only this time he was looking in my face trying to read whether or not I was going to kick him out.

"I really missed you," he said, back to looking me up and down, and I could've sworn he just licked his lips.

"I just saw you," I said, trying to make light of the situation.

"I know, but last night in bed, I thought about you, thinking you would never talk to me again, so I dreamt about what I thought I would never have."

Damn, this guy has got confidence, but I made sure not to show any weakness. Think boiling rabbit.

"And now?" I asked.

"And now I realize that all good things come to those who wait. And I'm one that's willing to wait."

Actually, if done properly, rabbit stew wasn't that bad.

His dark eyes said so much more than his words. I couldn't call it at this point, but I felt something genuine in his words. Either that or the liquor was finally getting to me.

Char grabbed my arm and directed me toward her nameless guy friend.

"Monica, I want you to meet my new friend, Jackson," she said.

He looked at me and grabbed my hand and shook it hard.

"Nice to meet you," he said, withdrawing his hand to reach past me to one of the pizza boxes on the table. He smelled like rum.

We spent a good portion of the night dancing, eating and drinking. Char decided she wanted to play *Cooley High* and turn off the lights, and the next thing I knew, we were all in the dark. Char and dude (I forgot his name) were on the couch doing whatever, which I didn't want to know. The only thing I knew was that I was going to be shampooing that couch first thing the next morning.

I had gone outside to the balcony because it was hot inside my apartment. When Mark came out to join me, I was neither surprised nor disappointed. We had danced closely, and to tell you the truth, he had really turned me on. I felt like he really was interested in me and not just on the sexual level. I never told anyone this, including Char, but I actually believed him when it came to Tanya. He told me that he had stayed with her because of whatever reason, but that was it. I could tell that he really liked me. He liked me a lot. I actually liked him, too, but I hadn't admitted it to anyone. I barely admitted it to myself. I mean, there were no fireworks or anything like that at this point, but he definitely turned me on.

At least he was from the States.

As we stood out there on the balcony, I looked at Mark and tried to make light of the situation yet again. It was what I did best.

"So it's too hot in there for you, too, huh?" I asked.

"Actually, it's hotter out here," he said, doing what *he* did best.

Instead of wasting time staring at me as he usually did, he went straight for the gold by grabbing my waist and pulling me to him. He kissed me with his full, luscious lips. He pulled back and then kissed me again, this time parting my more than willing lips with his sensuous tongue. Even if I were hesitating, the lower portion of my body wasn't, and I could feel the deep, intense tickle of her wanting more.

He reached his hand under my tank top and felt my stomach.

Damn, did I do sit-ups today? I knew I shouldn't have had that second slice of pizza.

His hands moved upwards from my stomach to my now heaving breasts where they stayed. His kisses moved delicately from my lips to my neck, and then his eager lips replaced his hand that was on my breasts, kissing them softly. This felt so damn good. It had been a while since I had this feeling all over my body, and I was enjoying it to the fullest. He took my hand and guided me back into the apartment.

"Where's Char?" I noticed that the still darkened apartment was now empty.

"I saw them take off a few minutes ago. Do you mind?" He let go of my hand and let it drop to my side.

The ball's in my court. *What to do?* I thought for a moment. Was I going to let this happen tonight? I thought again...*Hell yeah*, it had been a while, and it was right about time.

He took my hand again, led me to my bedroom and shut the door. And that night, I felt a sensation that I had not felt in a long time, and it was amazing.

Chapter 14

I woke up Sunday morning with a huge headache. I hadn't drunk like that since college. What the hell happened? I had no idea. Well, I had some idea. I got up and looked into the mirror. I looked a mess. My hair was tousled all over the place, and I had dark circles under my eyes. The last time I had looked like this I had that blind date with...Mark.

I couldn't believe we did it! I stared at my reflection in disbelief.

We...had...done...it, I thought to myself, enunciating every syllable. We had finally had sex.

I quickly rinsed my face off and walked out to my living room to find a piece of paper and a yellow rose on my kitchen table.

Good morning/afternoon,

I just wanted to let you know that I had a great time last night. I really want to see you again, so I'll call you today to find out your plans later on in the week.

Sincerely,

Mark

Sincerely? And where the hell did he find a yellow rose? Well, it had finally happened, so I supposed I wouldn't be hearing from him anymore. I couldn't say that I was really sorry about that. I had an urge and he was there to satisfy that urge.

I checked my caller ID and saw that four people had called. I pressed the "message" button on my answering machine and there was Neal telling me that he was sorry that I had missed his call and that he would try later on.

And that he did. He left me two more messages with the second sounding a bit more peeved. I can't believe I didn't hear the phone ring. I walked out to the living room and saw the jack taken out of the wall.

That's why I didn't hear it. Somebody unplugged the phone. It could've been done by accident, but I really didn't think so.

I guess I should've been mad because Mark left so early without saying goodbye, but I wasn't. I was actually glad that I didn't have to make breakfast for him. I just wasn't really in the mood for that. Not the breakfast but the I-just-had-sex-with-you-last-night conversation. I could at least say that the sex *was* all that. It was all that and then some. I didn't expect any less from him. I had come twice, and it was explosive, a feeling I'd seldom known before. It was wonderful. I actually felt good in a relaxed sort of way, kinda like I ran a marathon. Maybe he'd be calling, maybe he wouldn't, but again I say, I didn't really care. At least, not right then. I just wanted to relax and enjoy that beautiful Sunday morning. I had come to one conclusion though; I had decided that I wasn't going to say anything to Sam regarding Tanya and Friday night. I had decided on Char's suggestion to let her hang herself. That would be the best bet.

I made myself a cup of coffee along with a cold slice of cheese pizza. Diet was going to start tomorrow, when I got rid of this pizza. I didn't want to waste any; I paid for it, *remember?* I fed Kitty and she thanked me by rubbing up and down my leg, sort of like a man. Just kidding.

I pulled out a *Vogue* magazine and started flipping through it. Back in the day I was always told that I should become a model. I would take that as a compliment, but I think the people that said that just said it because I was tall. Models had this certain look, which I knew I didn't have. Besides that, they have to weigh all of ninety pounds. Although I wasn't fat, I knew I was *well over* that. I could've become a writer though. I had good writing skills in junior high and high school that could've turned into something more if I'd pursued it. My favorite classes were always

English. I enjoyed reading Thoreau, Poe and Chaucer, and poetry came so easy for me. I'd write things off the top of my head and my classmates thought it was the cleverest thing that they'd ever heard.

As I got up to get another slice of pizza, my phone rang. Caller ID said "out of area," so it must've been Neal. I quickly picked up the phone and I was right. I started to smile when I heard his voice.

"Hey, baby? How's it going?" he asked.

Did he say "baby?" How cute.

"It's going great now, that I heard from you," I said, taking a huge gulp of my coffee.

"I tried calling you last night, but no one answered."

I took another mouthful of my coffee, not sure of what to say.

"I know. I got the messages this morning. I had some friends over and didn't hear the phone," I told him. That was the truth, sort of.

"Oh," was his reply. "I just wanted to call you and give you my flight and what time I'll be at BWI."

I grabbed a pen and pad and took down the information.

"So everything's okay with me coming?"

Why would he ask that?

"Everything's more than okay," I told him.

"I'm looking forward to seeing you, but I have to go because I'm on my way to work."

"I know, you're always on your way to work." I laughed.

"It seems like that, doesn't it? I'll call you when I get the chance, either later tonight or tomorrow. I miss you."

I missed him, too. I missed him so much I couldn't even explain it. I'll never be able to explain how deeply I cared for him, how much I think about him and how much I would love to hold him right now. I just didn't understand it. Would I feel this same way if he were here with me now? I even felt a little guilty about the previous night with Mark. I knew there was nothing I should feel guilty about but I did.

I spent the rest of the day with the obligatory "me time." I shampooed the couch, polished the table, my bookcase, and a few other wooden things, and then I polished off the pizza. Since my dieting started tomorrow, I'd better get rid of it today. What's the sense in starting a diet on Sunday anyway? To me, Sunday was considered part of the weekend.

By the time I finished my housework, it was late afternoon. I couldn't decide what I wanted for dinner, so I ended up not eating anything. I couldn't believe it was already late afternoon and no one had called. Not even Char. I picked up the phone and dialed her number, but then thought about it. I really didn't feel like talking to her, especially about Mark, and I knew she would ask, being the nosy bitch that she was. I don't know why I even slept with him. Oh, who was I kidding? I slept with him because I wanted some and I was *extremely* attracted to him. However crass it may sound, it was the truth and he lived up to *all* expectations. I still felt guilty though. Neal was hardly my man, especially living in another country. If I looked on a subconscious level, some part of me could've slept with Mark just to get back at Ms. Thang. I know, I know, real mature, but oh well, it was done and there was nothing I could do about it. More importantly, what would she do if *she* found out? I made my bed and I had to lie in it.

That reminded me; Sam wanted to have a meeting with me first thing the next day. Something told me that I wasn't going to like it. I'd already decided that I wasn't going to say anything to Sam about Tanya and let her go ahead and do her hanging, but if she got in my way at work, there would be a problem.

As I got up to feed Kitty, my phone rang. I checked the caller ID (why is it you *always* look at the ID when you're avoiding talking to someone) and it was Char. Nope, I didn't feel like to talking her. Maybe the next day, but not then. I listened to her leave her frantic message on my machine.

"Giiiiiirl, call me when you get the chance. I've got some news for you!"

Uh-huh. She could either: A–have nothing to tell me and just want me to pick up if she thinks I'm here or B–actually have something relevant to tell me, relevant meaning good gossip. In any case, my curiosity got the best of me and I picked up and started breathing hard like I just ran to the phone. (Everyone has done that before.)

"You chickenhead, you know your ass was there the whole time!" she said.

"No, I wasn't, I just got in, and anyway, what's so important that you have to tell me? Probably nothing but I'll bite anyway," I said, sitting down on the couch preparing myself for one long conversation.

"Well, check this little bit of nothin' out. Do you remember Stevie? Oh, wait, I don't think you ever met him. He was at that party you decided not to go to because you were dating asshole John…"

Don't talk him up, please, or next week *he'll* be calling me.

"What's your point, please?" I interrupted.

What did I want to eat? I was hungry.

"Oh, yeah," she said, getting back into her train of thought. "I talked to him this morning and he told me…"

"Hold up, since when do you talk to a Stevie? You've never mentioned him before," I said, interrupting her again.

"Yes, I did. You just weren't listening, as usual."

She got me there. Char talked so much I just learned to pick and choose what I listened to. That sometimes meant that she would call me out later for something she told me, but I didn't see the relevance in it at the time, so I chose not to listen to it at that point. That's how I was able to tolerate her never-ending babble.

"He told me that your girl is el prego, and I'll give you one guess by whom?"

I sat up on the edge of the couch. My heart began to speed up with anticipation. I knew exactly who she was referring to.

"Wait a minute. How does this Stevie know those two in the first place?"

"Oh, puh-leese. They go waaaaaay back. Stevie used to mess with Tanya before Mark got a crack at her. That's how nasty she is, but he says they're 'just friends' now. Kind of like Mark says he and Tanya are 'just friends.'"

Smart ass.

"He said she told him last week that she was pregnant with Mark's baby, but didn't tell Mark yet. I still don't think he knows. That's why Stevie told me not to tell anybody," she said, satisfied.

"Then, why are you telling *me?*" I asked, already knowing the answer to that one. She had a big mouth, that's why.

"Who are you going to tell that runs in that circle? The big question is, did Mark know when he slept with you last night?" she asked and then got dead silent.

"He might not even know about the baby. You said so yourself."

"*Slut!*" she yelled through the phone. "I *knew* you two did it and your triflin' ass wasn't gonna tell me. How was it? I heard it was big as shit."

"I didn't say we slept together," I said, trying to clean it up, but I knew the cat was already out the bag.

"Girl, shut up! It's too late now and I now know the truth. So how was it, really?" she asked again in a more serious tone.

"It was okay," I said, giving in. After I said it, I thought about it; nobody wanted to hear that sex was just okay. They wanted to hear about the fireworks, the swinging from the chandeliers and the whips and chains, but I wasn't going to get into all that. Besides, it was none of her business. I shouldn't have even been telling her that much.

She kept trying to get more information out of me, but I wasn't tellin'. I wanted to know what was up with this baby thing.

"Brunch next weekend? By then, I should have more to tell you," she said.

Not good enough.

"Girl, you'd better tell me something sooner. I have a meeting with Sam tomorrow and am back and forth about whether or not I'm going to say something about this ongoing soap that has seemed to engulf my life."

"You'd better take my advice and just let her do her thing."

"I know, that's what I'm thinking about doing," I said, sitting back on the couch again.

"I'll call you as soon as I hear something."

What was I going to do? Especially with this new information looming in the wings. Couldn't Char have talked to this Stevie *before* last night? One thing I knew for sure, I was going to cut Mark off for good; at least until I found out something. The sex had been great, but as for any type of relationship, I didn't need this drama in my life. Now that this situation could step up a notch with the whole baby-momma-drama thing, I was definitely getting the hell out while the getting was good. Dick was not worth all that.

Chapter 15

I had gone out to the park for a jog at seven, and when I returned it was eight-thirty. When I was out there, I ran into Janice Beauvoir walking her dog. I hadn't seen her since Quimby's a few weeks back. She had a lot to tell, but as usual had nothing to say.

It was all the same shit. She was still dating the same guy, had the same job and was thinking about getting a Mercedes since her man was going to finance it for her.

"My man tells me all the time that he would just love to buy the finer things in life for me because I'm worth it and there isn't a damn thing on this earth that I don't deserve and you know what, he's absolutely right," she had told me in the park while her dog relieved himself. "I don't really want to jump the gun but he's thinking about marrying me. He told me so. We even looked at rings," she continued to tell me.

She said all of this as if it was all his decision. The sad part was that it probably was all his decision. Women can be so eager to get a man, that even if it was the wrong man, they would take it (him) anyway. I never understood that. Several of my female acquaintances back in Philly got married to the wrong man and are now divorced. Some were married for as long as eight years and some divorced after only a year. They waited all their lives for *that?* They could at least say they had the perfect little wedding. Gee, that's real important. That's a lesson that I've definitely learned. A wedding a marriage does not make. If you have to live with somebody for the next fifty years, wouldn't you want him to be as compatible as possible? The thought of living day in and day out with somebody that gets on your nerves is just ugggggh! It makes me sick to even think about it. If I'd ever married, say Frick or Frack, Kenny or even video porn boy, I *guarantee* I would've been divorced by now. I'd be willing to bet money on that one.

Then my thoughts drifted to Mark. Could I actually be involved with *him?* The answer came as quickly as I'd asked the question. Fuck no! I could imagine Tanya calling my house every day looking for him. She probably knew my car from work and would end up showing up and slashing my tires. I still don't rule out coming home one day and finding Kitty in a pot with some onions and carrots. That girl was really unstable. I find it hard to believe that one of her friends didn't tell her about herself yet. If Char or I had ever acted like that, we would've been slapped into reality by each other a long time ago. I could count on her for a good slap across the face, and she could do the same with me. That's how good of friends we were. We had each other's backs like that. She was my girl.

After taking a bath and relaxing, the clock read nine-thirty. I was beat down. I just wanted to chill and go to bed. I didn't do a single lick of work over the weekend and it felt good. I had a great time, even Friday before what I now refer to as, "The Incident." I just wondered what it would be like on Monday when I had to see *her.* I came to the conclusion that she was going to just be non-existent to me. There really was no other alternative. She had pushed me into a corner with her actions. Now I felt as though I couldn't even be professional with her. She left me no choice. I figured, with her track record, she would eventually hang herself-as planned-and be out the door sometime the next month.

My thoughts were interrupted by the phone. I looked at the caller ID and it read "ANONYMOUS." It couldn't be a telemarketer Sunday night, so I picked up.

"Hello?"

"Hey," was all the male voice said.

Gotcha!

It was Mark. Aw man, what did *he* want?

"I just wanted to call and say what's up?" he said.

I was still silent. He waited for a response and when he didn't get one, he proceeded to talk.

"Do you want me to come over later?" he asked. *Now* I was definitely ready to say something.

"No," I said.

After a pause, I gave him an excuse, which he probably didn't deserve, but I gave it anyway.

"It's too late and I'm getting ready to go to bed."

Damn! After I said it, I realized my mistake. This was just what he wanted to hear.

"Perfect timing then," he said right on cue.

Let me nip it in the bud.

"Mark," I began, "I'm really tired and I have a meeting I need to get ready for in the morning."

Then I felt a little bad, so I again relented a bit. I imagined how I would feel if I'd just slept with someone and the next day they were cold to me. Oh, wait, I didn't have to imagine; that's happened numerous times before. Besides that, I wasn't sure of what the real deal was. For all I knew, this could've been some big misunderstanding.

"If you want to, you can call me at work Monday or Tuesday this week and maybe we can hang out," I said, making sure he knew it had to be early in the week because Neal was coming on Wednesday.

I was waiting for him to question why those specific days but he seemed satisfied with this and said okay. Great. That was easy enough.

I lit some candles, got a glass of wine and pulled out the latest James Patterson book I'd been meaning to read for the past six months. That night, I just wanted to chill.

Chapter 16

I got to work earlier than usual on Monday. No one was there, so I had to open up. Tanya wasn't there either. I really didn't expect her to be because she'd been showing up late the past few weeks. I wondered if she'd told anyone she was pregnant—if she actually was pregnant. I also wondered who would be first to find out if it was true or not, Char or me. My money was on Char. I wasn't all that eager, considering I'd already decided to cut it off with Mark. I just needed to tell *him* someday.

I opened up my office and turned on the lights and the computer. I looked at the clock on the wall and it was only seven-thirty. I was up that morning at five because I couldn't sleep. I'd been so restless lately, and I hadn't the foggiest idea why.

I saw my voicemail light and realized I had two messages. The first was Neal leaving a message at eleven thirty last night. It said that he wanted to call me at home but didn't want to wake me up so therefore settled for calling my voicemail to say goodnight.

I thought that was really nice of him—corny but sweet.

The second was from Sam reminding me about the meeting that we were having that morning.

How could I forget?

I reached into my locked files and pulled out the health care proposal

I'd been working on and started on it. I still had to make a decision on whether or not to have dependents included on the plan.

At least Tanya had coverage for her and her kid, I thought.Why was I jumping the gun? This could all have been a huge lie originating from her big mouth. Regardless, it was still a possibility. I was upset with Mark for the alleged baby, but I was more upset with myself. If I'd fallen for that load of crap and found out it wasn't true, I was turning into a lesbian. You heard it, right here, right now.

Well, I wasn't going that far, but you get it.

I did take consolation in the fact that I hadn't admitted to anyone, besides Kitty, how I was starting to feel about him. I may have acted tough on the outside, but the truth was, he could've been a possibility, a definite possibility.

Slowly but surely people had started coming into the office, one by one. I still hadn't heard anything regarding Tanya. It was nine-thirty and she wasn't in yet; even though we were to arrive by eight-thirty.

What a surprise that was.

Sam came in about nine forty-five, apologizing because he was stuck on the phone at home. He started telling me about some client who wanted facts and figures from him and blah, blah, blah, but I wasn't really listening to him. My thoughts were elsewhere.

What if Tanya *was* pregnant and Mark was the father? How long had he known, if he did know?

How *did* she get my number?

I still couldn't get past that.

How did I even get tangled in all this in the first place? It seemed no matter how much I tried to mind my business, I always got served up a dish of drama with a side of crazy. Sam asking me to come to his office interrupted my thoughts again. I followed him and stood behind him as he unlocked his door, turned on the lights and went through the exact same routine I'd gone through just hours before. We walked into the office and I shut the door behind me at his request.

His office was a pigsty. He had magazines and books all over the place, and it smelled like someone had left an old pair of socks stuck in one of the corners.

I began to sniff around the room to indicate I smelled something not very favorable.

"I know. When I'm not here, the office gets kind of dank," he said, pushing papers off the chair he now wanted me to sit in.

"You should have Tanya open it up when she comes in the mornings." I was hoping to draw up some info on her. She could've called him that morning and left him a message as to why she wasn't in yet.

It didn't work. He just nodded. "Good idea."

We started out the meeting discussing the health care proposals. I gave him updates on them. We'd decided to present a rough draft to the employees before taking any further action.

That ended that topic, on to the next.

"Monica, how's everything going? Do you like it here?" he asked.

Of course, I did and told him that, too.

I thought back to what I could've possibly said to someone.

"I think you're doing an excellent job and I really enjoy working with you," he said. "I just want to make sure you are happy here."

Again, I reassured him that I was, but now I was really interested as to why he kept pushing the issue.

"It's been brought to my attention that *in error*, someone overheard you talking about your position and how dissatisfied you were."

What?!?!?!? What the hell was he talking about?

"I said no such thing. I don't even know who I would've told, if I did say something remotely like that. I don't know anyone like that," I said, sounding somewhat defensive, which wasn't helping my case any.

From the outside looking in, it sounded like a classic case of *Thou doth protest too much.*

Sam sat back in his chair and cocked his head to the side.

"That's the thing; you don't seem to talk to anyone about anything other than work-related issues. I just wished you'd come to me and told me that you were having problems. I thought we were tighter than that. I don't want you to just up and find another job and leave me high and dry," he said, getting up and walking toward the water cooler that sat catty-corner from his desk.

"Do you want a glass of water?"

No, I didn't want a glass of water. I want you to tell me who "accidentally" told you this bullshit.

I shook my head no and waited for him to continue.

He leaned over to get some water from the cooler. "I told you this job was probably going to bore you."

I couldn't stand it any longer. "You've got to be kidding. I like my job, I like working with you, I like everything. Sam, you know me; if I had a problem, I'd come to you first. I thought you knew I was more professional than that," I said a little disappointed. "I have to ask, where did you hear this from? You have to understand my position. I'm sitting here defending myself against false accusations about something someone, who I have no idea, said regarding *my* career."

He looked down. He was just as uncomfortable as I was, and I could tell he understood my position and really wanted to tell me, so I pressed on.

"Sam, this will go no further than this office, I swear it, but if I know who said it, maybe I can understand why they got this impression."

He was still silent, but only for a moment. "This can't leave this office." He looked at me, waiting for my reaction.

"I promise it won't," I assured him.

"Tanya Johnson, our receptionist, accidentally hit the button to your office when you were on the phone and overheard you speaking to another company."

Say no more. That explained it all. You just don't know how my blood was boiling. It took all of my energy to look Sam in the eyes and say nothing as he continued.

"It was a complete mistake, but she stated that she was concerned for the company."

Yeah, I'm sure she was. My thoughts were all over the place at this point. That bitch must've been listening to my phone calls. It all made sense now. That must've been why that damn "call" button was always lit up next to my extension every time I was on the goddamn phone. Not only that, she outright lied. I wasn't on the phone with some company or anyone else for that matter regarding my position there.

Where to start? I wanted to go to my office so badly and pull her file. Her file with all the unprofessional shit in it that she'd done since day one. I wanted to show Sam the customer complaints we had regarding her. I also wanted to show the internal complaints we had on her, and most importantly I wanted her ass fired! This had nothing to do with work, but I wanted to break it down about Friday night but didn't want to go out like that because if I were to speak on it right then, Sam would've damn sure seen my unprofessional side. Ghetto bitch would've been up in there that day.

Bring it down Monica; bring it down.

When Sam finished, I calmly (or as calm as I could be, considering) told him that I was never on the phone with another company regarding my position there and that I had no clue what she was talking about. I tried to reassure him that if I did have a problem, I would come to him first.

By the time I left the office, I felt like I'd been kicked in the stomach. Sam was listening to me, but I'm not sure if he *believed* me. Even if he had, I'm sure there would always be something in the back of his mind wondering. Look at it from his point of view. He had no idea of our issues, so why would she just lie on me like that? Obviously he didn't understand the animosity we felt for each other. How could he?

As I got up to leave his office, I felt the anger burning up inside of me. I wondered how many other calls she'd heard and what was to stop her from listening again. I'll tell you what was to stop her. *Me!* I knew I should've calmed down first, but I couldn't help myself. I wanted, no I had, to say something then.

I started walking toward the front of the office when I remembered that I promised Sam that our conversation wouldn't leave his office. Damn! Maybe I was better off not knowing.

I started walking to the front of the office to where her desk was anyway. I wouldn't say anything; I would just...I didn't know what I would do. When I reached her desk, I saw that she wasn't even there. Pamela, one of the sales girls, saw me at her desk and told me that she had called in that day because she had a doctor's appointment. *Just as well*, I thought. At least now I was forced to calm down before dealing with her, and deal with her I would.

I walked back to my office and shut the door for the remainder of the day. I couldn't deal. This girl was seriously trying to make my life a living nightmare.

It was seven-thirty when I got home. I'd stayed late because I couldn't get anything done after my meeting with Sam, and that was at ten that morning. I tried, but my mind just wasn't in it. Every time I thought about that girl, I just got madder and madder. Char hadn't called me at work all day. I was kind of glad because I would've spewed off at the mouth and I wanted to be home to talk to her. That way I could get as loud as I wanted, and I wanted to get loud.

I turned some music on and plopped down on the couch next to Kitty. I just wanted to sit there for a minute to get my thoughts together. I picked up the phone and dialed Char's number. Her answering machine came on. I left a brief message and told her to call when she got in.

Bitch, Bitch, Bitch, Bitch. I couldn't get that bitch out of my head. I was angry with myself for letting her get to me but, under the circumstances, who wouldn't be pissed off? Man, I would've liked to have just pulled out every bit of her peasy, jacked-up, nappy hair one by one right about then. Evidently this girl wanted to scrap. I don't know if she thought that it wouldn't get back to me, or *did* she want it to get back to me? I didn't know. The point was that she'd said it, and now it was on.

"Riiiiiiiiing."

I picked up the phone on the first ring, thinking it was Char. It wasn't; it was Neal. He was on his way to work and just wanted to say hello. He helped me forget about her for a hot minute. He always made me feel good, no matter what.

"Is everything okay?"

I thought about telling him everything, but I didn't want to burden him with my squalid tales of calamity so I just lied.

"Everything's great," I said, forcing a smile so it would sound more genuine. I learned that from my telemarketing days.

I was glad he even cared enough to ask.

We talked for a few more minutes and then he was off to work. He was coming that week and it would be a nice change. Sam had given me Friday off, so that would be cool. I wasn't sure that I wanted *her* there without *me* being there. Who knew what other lies she'd come up with? I'll tell you what I did know, I knew that she was out for blood, and she was doing anything to get it. I was going to play it by ear and see how it went, but if I went on instincts, I knew it wasn't going to be a pleasant next few days.

Two minutes after I hung up with Neal, my phone rang again. This time it was Mark. He wanted to come over and hang out.

I did tell him to call me either Monday or Tuesday, but that was *before* and I really wasn't in the mood. Besides, he had ties to *her*, and his being there would probably just piss me off more. But more importantly, it just might be detrimental to my health to hang out with him. That psycho bitch had proven that she took no prisoners. Plus, I still wasn't sure of the baby situation and didn't want to do anything until I found out for sure.

I told him no, but he kept begging and pleading.

"Monica, I really do want to see you."

"It's not a good time right now," I said, fixing a martini.

What was wrong with this guy? After about the twelfth time of him asking, I gave in and signed my own death certificate by telling him yes. Partly because he was bringing food from Giovanni's, which was my favorite Italian restaurant. (My diet would start the next week because Neal was coming and we were more than likely going to go out to eat, so what would be the point?) I also had a hidden agenda for him coming over. I wanted to find out what the hell he was telling her or even what she told him.

I jumped in the shower and tried to decide what to wear. Fuck it. I was just going to throw back on my shorts and tank top. How presentable did I have to be to kick someone's ass? Okay, I was kidding, but if I found out something that even smelled sour, his ass was gonna be splattered up against my living room wall.

He said he'd arrive at eight-thirty; he showed up at nine-fifteen.

I never understood why he and Char didn't get together.

As promised, he showed up with a full spread of Italian food. He said he wasn't sure what I liked so he brought over lasagna, fettuccini with clam sauce, and veal parmigiana. Along with this spread, he had a bottle of cabernet sauvignon.

"What's all this?" I asked when he broke out the picnic basket and a little red and white-checkered tablecloth for us to sit on.

He started moving my coffee table to the side so that he could put down the tablecloth.

Sitting down on the now checker-covered carpet, he said, "I just wanted to make this special."

He tapped the tablecloth next to him, indicating for me to sit down and then reached into the basket and pulled out the bottle of wine.

He reached back inside the picnic basket and brought out a beautiful bouquet of flowers.

"I thought you might like these, too," he said, handing them up to me because I was still standing above him, amused at his meager attempt to woo me.

I thanked him and walked to my kitchen to put them in a vase. This would've been nice if it were another person, (not naming names) and under other circumstances.

While eating and drinking, we had a decent conversation, but he didn't mention anything about Tanya. I would say he didn't know anything because he was the type that would've definitely said something about it eventually.

"I'm supposed to be going on a retreat with the kids from my youth group in two weeks," he said as he took a bite of the lasagna. "They've been looking forward to this all week."

"That's great. How many kids do you have in your group?"

"Twelve, but all of them are not going with me."

"Thank goodness for that." I laughed. "I couldn't see you with twelve kids by yourself."

We spent the next couple of hours eating and drinking—as much as I hate to admit it—having a good time, but I did have to get up for work the next day. I think he sensed that I was just about to give him the blow-off when he kissed me. His tongue slipped in between my lips and gently tickled my tongue. I felt my lower body respond, but I couldn't do it again. I just didn't feel like it. Too much had happened that day, and none of my questions were answered. I apologized and told him that I had a good time but I was tired. He looked disappointed but took it surprisingly well. We got up from the floor, and I escorted him to the door.

"Goodnight," he said and kissed me again, this time putting his arms around my waist like we were a couple. I discreetly pulled away and went back inside and shut the door. I looked at the picnic scene on the floor and had to give him props on that one.

You know, I realized I hadn't thought about *her* for the remainder of the evening. Damn! Messed it up. Now I was angry all over again. *Bitch!*

Chapter 17

I woke up Tuesday morning feeling a little calmer. (Yes, I was still thinking about it.) I still didn't have a chance to talk to Char about it yet. She didn't call me back the previous night. I wondered where that tramp was.

I'd decided to be calm about the entire situation. There was going to be no scene or no scratching her eyes out. I was just gonna chill. Just stick to the plan and let her hang herself. Don't get me wrong, she was definitely going to know that I wasn't the one to mess with, but I was going to give her fair warning and that was it. If I ever caught her so much as glancing in my direction incorrectly, then I'd take other measures.

I got up, took a shower, fed Kitty, got dressed and fixed a breakfast of eggs, with cheese, of course, toast and coffee.

I grabbed one of the fashion magazines and sat at the kitchen table and relaxed. I had on a nice forest green suit and I didn't want to mess it up, so I tucked a napkin in my blouse. Somehow I spilled coffee on my blouse and had to change anyway.

I left thirty minutes earlier than usual because I was ready. When I got to the office, once again I was the first one there. Or so I thought. I unlocked the door to see Ms. Thang sitting at her desk. She glanced up at me, and then right back down to what she was doing.

Perfect! This was prime time to get my message to her without the others being here, so there couldn't be a scene.

I just stood at the door and glared at her. She was fidgeting with papers on her desk and didn't look up; although I knew she realized I was staring hard. I shut the door and just lingered there for a second. Then I walked straight for her raggedy desk and stood right before her. Even more perfect, she was sitting, and I was hovering above her. The exact position I wanted to be in.

Realizing she had no choice at this point, she looked up and this time met my gaze.

Take it home, girl, but remember, be professional.

"Stop listening to my calls," I said in a deep stern voice. "I know you've been pulling that shit for a while now and it's gonna stop."

I started walking off slowly before turning back around. (Dramatic, huh?)

"Oh, and don't even think about telling any more lies regarding anything having to do with me, period. If you have a problem with me, you need to address me and me only. It's called being pro-fession-al."

I enunciated the word professional nice and slow just for added insult. I didn't even wait for her reaction. I just turned and walked toward my office. I thought that was fair warning without getting ghetto, but with just enough of an insulting tone to piss her off.

I walked into my office, turned on the light and sat down behind my desk. I wondered what her reaction was.

Was she pissed? Was she shocked? Either or was good.

I didn't have to wonder too long because when I looked up, she was standing at my door, staring at me. I gazed at her casually and asked her if I could help her.

"Bitch, who do you think you are?" she started.

Uh-oh, pull out the Vaseline.

I just looked at her with no reaction whatsoever.

"I know you spent Monday night with him, and I know you've been spending the weekends with him because he never comes home on the weekend."

I continued to let her talk.

"And as for that so-called business trip he has in two weeks, I know he's going to the shore with you! Why don't you just go and find your own damn man? I don't want to have to drive by your house again to make sure he's not there. I'm serious; stop seeing him," she said and stared at me again; this time with eyes of fury.

Just then, I realized I was dealing with a nut. Tanya looked crazier than Carrie on prom night, but I still looked at her with no reaction.

Keep your game face on.

"First of all," I began calmly, "evidently there's a problem if you have to keep your man on a short leash, and that problem has nothing to do with me. Mark and I are friends and nothing else. I don't know anything about his weekends, and I sure enough don't know anything about a trip to the shore. You're barking up the wrong tree."

I looked at her and saw she had tears in her eyes.

Awwww, poor baby.

If she wasn't such a pain in the ass I would've almost felt sorry for her. *Almost.*

"Look, I don't have to justify any of my business to you," I continued. "Your so-called man isn't doing anything he doesn't want to do. Instead of trying to make life miserable for any woman he comes in contact with, you need to go straight to the source. I'm gonna let you know now, you're wasting your time with me. Maybe he doesn't want to be with you. Did you ever think of that?" I said, adding the nail to my coffin.

I knew she was pissed already but oh, well, evidently no one told her about herself yet, so I took the opportunity to do so.

The look of hurt turned into a look of contempt as she began to smile maliciously.

"Well, he wasn't saying that when he knocked my ass up, now was he?" she said, self-satisfied.

I tried to show no reaction but how could I not? There it was, straight from the horse's mouth (literally), no more speculation, no more rumors. That answered the question, and just for the record, I found out before Char.

"Well," I said, maintaining composure again, "that's something you're going to have to deal with." And I finished with "good luck" but in that sarcastic I-feel-sorry-for-you way. It came out like that because truthfully, at that point, I did feel sorry for her. I knew for a fact that Mark wasn't the settling down type. I knew that because he was with me two nights earlier. I wondered if he knew about the baby. I wasn't going to be the one to tell him. F-that. I was so out of it you just don't even know.

~❤~

Later that afternoon, I kept running into Tanya, and each time she had that smug look on her face like she was the lucky one with the man and the baby.

I thought of Patti LaBelle's song "If You Only Knew."

The day was rather uneventful after that. Sam was out of the office all day and Mark had called me three times already but had to leave messages because I wasn't at my desk. Thank goodness because I definitely didn't want to talk to him. What was I gonna say? I had to find a way to cut it off. It's a real shame though, because before all of this, I did like him. He *seemed* like a decent guy, but he had too much baggage, and he just wasn't worth all that. Even if it weren't for Evil-een out there, I didn't think I could see myself in a one-on-one relationship with him. In order to cut it off, I could make up an excuse but I'd tried that before and he just came on stronger. I could tell him that I wasn't ready for a relationship, but he wouldn't care because he'd just say that he wasn't either. What if he really didn't know what was going on and he was totally innocent? Like I said before, maybe she was pregnant and maybe she wasn't.

I wouldn't put it past her to lie to keep a man. I thought he was cool and all and the sex was great, but in no way, shape or form did he have it like that with me. I wasn't the one doing drive-bys (don't think I didn't catch her saying she didn't want to have to drive by my house *again* and check up on me, so obviously this was a routine thing for her) and threatening other women he came across. The more I thought about it, the more I realized how pathetic it all was. Maybe down the road, *way down the road*, I could've seen us together, but something just kept holding me back. Now I realized it was the strong chokehold of Tanya.

I began to think about Neal again. He was coming the next day. I'd been excited about it and still was, but now it was different. The day's events had killed the excitement a bit. He was coming in at eleven forty-five p.m., and I was going to pick him up at BWI Airport.

Come to think of it, I guess I was still excited about it. I'd just been preoccupied by the unforeseen events of the day.

When I got home at seven I was tired, mentally more than physically. Mark had left two more messages for me, and the last one almost sounded like he was begging. "Give me a call as soon as you get this message," it said. If I didn't call him that night, he'd probably end up calling me for the rest of the week while Neal was in town, and Neal would think I was some sort of bimbo that had men calling me all throughout the night.

I put on some sweats and decided to take a quick run. It was the beginning of August and the sun was still blazing at that time of day, but it wasn't too bad. It wasn't like I was going to pass out from heat exhaustion or anything. Besides, I really wanted to get out, and that's exactly what I did. It felt great. I ran two miles and then stretched in the park. When I got home, I was sweaty and my ponytail was matted down to my head and drenched with sweat.

I went to the refrigerator to see what I had to eat—nothing as usual. I shut the refrigerator door and grabbed a towel from my linen closet to wipe my sweat-soaked face. I sat down on the couch and finally checked my messages. One from Neal telling me he would call me that night and couldn't wait to see me; one from Mark (surprise); and one from Janice Beauvoir. *What the hell was she doing calling me?*

"Monica, hon," her message said. "I got your number from Char. I was trying to get together with you maybe like this weekend and hang out. I finally convinced my man to hook you up with a lawyer buddy of his. Did you catch that? I said 'lawyer.' If not this weekend, then maybe next weekend. It has to be soon because I'm about to go on vacation and won't be back for a week, so let me know soon. Bye, sweetie."

I really hated the way she talked with all the sweeties and hons. It was worse than those crazy white women on *Sex and the City*.

I was going to kill Char for giving out my number. Where was she anyway? I hadn't heard from her in a few days.

I took a shower and washed my hair. When I finished, I wrapped my hair up in a towel and went into my room to get dressed. I was looking for my sweat shorts to put on when my doorbell rang. (Would it be any other way?)

I yelled "just a minute" as I scrambled around to find something to wear besides a towel.

The doorbell rang again. I reached to the bottom of one of the drawers and found a T-shirt and a pair of shorts to put on while I was still soaking wet. I ran to the door and opened it up without even looking through the peephole. Big mistake because standing there was Mark with more food and a bottle of wine in his hands.

(Okay, now it's played out.)

"What are you doing here?" I asked. "I came to see you," he said, smiling. "Aren't you gonna let me in?" he asked.

Was I gonna let him in? That was a good question.

"Mark, I just got back from running and just got out of the shower. It's not a good time right now," I said, not moving.

Now he was staring hard at my nipples that were protruding through my wet T-shirt.

"I'll call you later," I lied as I started to shut the door.

He looked up from my chest and pushed his way in.

"Uh-oh, I've been calling all day and I'm still waiting for a call back. I'll just wait for you in person, thanks," he said, shoving past me and parking it on the couch.

"Mark..." I sighed.

"Look, I really want to see you," he interrupted. "I don't know why you haven't returned my calls and it doesn't matter. I'm here now and I'm not leaving until you let me know what's up."

I looked at him and like a man on a Sunday afternoon, watching the football game with a bucket of chicken and a six-pack of beer, there was no way he was moving off of that couch.

"Let me get dressed. I'll be right back." I said and hurried to my room.

I took off the T-shirt and shorts and started searching for something dry. As I resumed looking through my drawers, there was a knock at my bedroom door and then *boom!* Mark was in my room staring at me in all my glory.

"Get out, please!"

He stood there with this roguish look in his eyes. I tried to cover myself up with my hands, but that was doing no good.

"Damn, you're fine," he said, still staring.

"Get out!" I repeated, this time only louder. He must've thought that I'd said come in and ravage my body because he was walked toward me taking off his jacket and loosening his tie.

"Did I stutter?" I grabbed the first thing in my dresser to cover myself up. It was a pair of red lace panties, which I'm sure turned him on more.

He grabbed me with physical strength and pulled me toward him. Not the I'm-gonna-rape you-physical-strength, but the passionate I-want-you-and-want you-now physical strength.

I was standing there against him totally naked. He put his left hand on my right breast and began to suckle my nipple. Then he kissed my neck and worked his way up to my chin and then to my lips where his tongue parted them and met mine. I got that sensual sensation down below.

Damn, the man knew how to kiss, but I couldn't do it. I wasn't getting involved with him again; especially after that day's events.

Fatal Attraction. I remembered the movie well.

He continued to gently kiss me while tenderly massaging my breast. I pulled away, and he started walking toward me again with sheer determination in his eyes. I wanted some so bad, but it wasn't worth all the drama.

Or was it, maybe just this one last time. You know, like a goodbye fuck.

I knew that if I let him have me again, it would be all over. I thought about earlier in the day when Tanya enlightened me with her information, and I pulled away again. This time he stopped.

"What's wrong? Monica, I really like you, and from last night I thought you liked me, too."

I decided it was time to talk.

"Mark, let me get dressed because I have some things to say to you."

He looked confused, but still didn't move.

"Let me get dressed and we'll talk."

He turned and walked out like a sad puppy that was just scolded. I shut the door behind him and hurriedly put on some clothes. When I walked out to the living room, he was sitting there drinking a glass of wine with the food untouched.

"What's wrong?" he said, looking up at me.

"Mark, right here, right now, tell me the deal between you and Tanya. I know I said it wasn't my business before, but now I feel it is. I want to know."

He looked perplexed but not surprised. "Where's all this coming from?"

I hated it when men responded to a question with a question to keep from answering one they didn't want to. Hate it, hate it, hate it.

"Just answer the question, please." I was getting irritated, and in case he didn't hear it the first time, I rephrased it for him. "Are you and Tanya in a relationship?"

He took another sip of wine. If he didn't quit stalling and answer me soon, I was gonna stick that glass of wine right up his ass!

"Okay," he said, throwing his hands up in the air as if it were an inconvenience for him to answer my question.

"Tanya and I dated a while back. I told you that. We've been friends for a long time, and I'm always there for her and she's always there for me."

He got silent. I knew he wasn't going to leave it at that because I had some more I wanted to know.

"It just didn't work out between us and now she's like my sister."

"Ohhhhh, I see," I said, cocking my head to one side. "So are you still fucking your sister?" I asked, getting straight to the point.

He looked at me.

"No, I'm not. I know she's trying to get back with me, so I'm sure she told you that we're still sleeping together, but I'm telling you *we are not,*" he said with strong conviction.

I stared at him for a moment letting him know I was sizing up that last statement he made.

"How about this then, do you still live with her?"

"I stayed with her in the past because I was getting a new room added on to my apartment. She said I could stay there for as long as I needed, so I did. Any more questions, warden?" he joked nervously.

I thought for another moment. He wasn't going to get off that easily.

"That night at the club you told me you were getting your apartment painted and that's why you stayed with her."

He sighed heavily.

Gee, I'm sorry; was this an inconvenience for him?

"They're painting the apartment along with adding a new room. Of course the room they add needs to be painted."

He took another sip of wine.

"Where is your apartment, anyway? The only numbers I have for you are your cell phone and your work number. Why can't I have your home number?"

He stood up. "Monica, what's with all the questions? I can't believe I'm falling in love with someone who doesn't believe a word I say."

Did he say falling in love? That caught me off guard, *but only for a second!* I asked the question again, ignoring his last statement. (Nice try, buddy).

"I live at 1422 Castle Boulevard in Silver Spring in apartment 304, and the reason I don't give out my home number is because when I met you, I was already having the room added—along with being painted," he said sarcastically. "And my phone's disconnected until they're done."

"When's your apartment going to be completed?" I asked. "I met you a couple of months ago, and they're still adding on the room?"

"They had to stop because I didn't have all of the funds right away for them to finish. They're starting back up next week and should be done in September."

This was turning into the Spanish Inquisition. "So, you've been living with Tanya since then?"

He sat back down on the couch. I guess he gathered this might take a while. "I've been staying with friends here and there, but, yes, you could say I've been staying with her most of the time."

Damn, he had an answer for everything. They always did.

He grabbed my hand and pulled me on his lap and kissed my shoulder.

"I'm going to have to have a talk with Tanya," he said with a softened tone. "If she's been harassing you, I'm gonna say something. You should've told me. I would've fixed it for you. I want to do things for you."

Do things for me? He's the reason why I'm being stalked; he and his crazy "sister" roommate.

I jumped up from his lap. No big deal. The fact of the matter was even if all of his explanations were true, I still didn't want him like that. He may have been good for sex, but now even that had been tainted by the simple fact that I wasn't trying to have all the drama that was just clinging to his ankle for dear life, like a pitbull to an attacker. I didn't know if he was telling the truth or not, but I could tell you this, somebody was lying. He claimed that he didn't have sex with her anymore, and she was claiming she was pregnant by him. Now, unless she was the Virgin Mary the math didn't add up. The truth had to come out sometime and when it did, I was gonna be as far away as possible from that fan when you know what hits it.

"I can't believe that," Char said in between bites of something she was chewing in my ear over the phone. "So he denied everything, huh? Do you believe him or her?"

I really didn't know, and I wished I didn't care, but as much as I hated to admit it, I still did.

"After I asked him all those questions, you know he rolled up outta here quick," I said.

That had been a good thing because I wasn't in the mood to have to deal with him all night.

"That's really bad," she said. "We're supposed to believe that he's been staying with ghetto girl for months and hasn't gotten any? Yeah, okay and I'm a virgin."

"Now we *know* he's lying," I said, laughing. "So you really don't believe any of his explanations?"

"Are you kidding? You can't possibly think that he's being truthful."

I walked into the kitchen and opened up the refrigerator.

"But what if it was true?" I asked, shutting the refrigerator.

"Girl, wake up and smell the cheap cologne that he sports. I can remember the days when you could spot a liar a mile away, and now your gift is gone. It must be the age thing creeping up on you."

"You're the one that fixed me up with him," I reminded her.

There was nothing like pointing the accusing finger when you were ass out in a situation. If you were going down, take someone down with you.

"I know, and that was a mistake of mine," she admitted. "I really thought he was okay, but after all this you just told me, I would head in the other direction ASAP. Besides, if you don't, Tanya's gonna git you," she said, laughing.

"Oh, please, that girl doesn't dictate what I do in my life."

"That's okay. I got your back," she said, still laughing.

Even just thinking about her pissed me off. I hoped Char didn't really think I was afraid of her. She knew me much better than that.

"So when's Neal coming again?" Char changed the subject.

I told her.

"Make sure you get some from him, with that tight little ass he's got."

"You're so stank," I said, cracking up at her nasty self.

"Uh-huh, that's why you laughing, you ho."

My other line clicked. It was ten o'clock and I knew it was Neal because he said he would call that night. I said goodbye to Char and clicked over.

Nothing like dumping your girls for a man.

"Good evening," Neal said on the other line.

"Hi, Neal. What's up?"

"Nothing much. I can't wait to see you tomorrow. I've really been thinking about you a lot for some reason," he said.

The truth of the matter was I had been thinking about him less lately only because of this never-ending saga that was going on. But I lied anyway and told him the same.

"Me, too."

You know, I just realized that I almost forgot what he looked like. I just remembered that he was extremely attractive...at least to me anyway.

I *was* a little liquored up that night.

We talked forever about everything—the flight; what we'd do when he got here (and no, not that); how we were going to go visit my sister; just everything. Neal was the type of guy who was extremely optimistic about everything. He told me that his mother had taken a turn for the worse with her illness but he had hope. He was praying for her. I told him about my aunt who had had cancer and about how she lived for years in remission before she passed away the previous year. We talked about writing. I didn't realize that he wrote poetry sometimes. That would explain that poetic letter he wrote. He told me if he remembered, he'd bring his scrapbook of poetry he'd been keeping since he was fourteen. We even laughed about our first sexual experiences—don't ask me how we got on that subject— and how he was still recovering from his broken heart from his first girl- friend at the tender age of twelve. (He could've left that part out.)

By the time we got off the phone, it was one in the morning. I hoped he was on a phone card or something because his bill was gonna be sky- high. I went to bed feeling much better knowing Neal was coming the very next day.

The next morning I was up early again. This time I took a run and had a breakfast of eggs, turkey bacon and a croissant smothered in butter and strawberry jelly. (Remember, my diet now starts next week because Neal's coming tomorrow.) After I threw down, I was still early, so I did the norm and left for the office. I would've been there nice and early, but of course, there was an overturned tractor-trailer on I-95, so I ended up getting to the office fifteen minutes late.

I walked in and sure enough Tanya's desk was empty and hadn't been touched so I knew she wasn't there. Good, I'd get some time without any of her smirks or her smart-ass comments.

I walked past Sam's office and said, "Good morning." He was in there drinking coffee and working on the computer.

"Hey, girl," he said, waving from his desk.

"How professional," I joked and walked to my office and did my customary routine. First lights, then computer.

I had one phone message. *Did I wanna know?* I listened to it anyway. It was from Mark. He apologized for the night before and told me that he had had a talk with Tanya. (Great—that day shoulda been a good day.) Then how about he ended the message with "I miss you" and "I love you?"

Whaaaaaaaaaat? Hold the phone. He loved *who*, cuz it sho' nuff wasn't me.

I was erasing that message when my phone rang. I picked up and it was Janice.

"Did you get my message? Didn't I ask you to call me back?"

Actually, she didn't and I told her so.

"Oh. Well, can you make it out this weekend?" she asked, getting straight to the point.

I told her that I had out-of-town company coming and I couldn't make it.

"It's gotta be next week then," she said this time not even asking. I'll tell him everything is copasetic for next week." She hung up. Why the hell was everyone trying to fix me up? Did I look *that* desperate?

"Knock, knock," said someone at my door.

It was Sam.

"Lunch today at one okay for you?" he asked.

I agreed. He said it would just be us at Luigi's.

Oh, no, what was in store for me now?

"Everything cool so far?" Sam asked at lunch.

"Everything's great," I said, taking a bite of my chicken Caesar salad.

"You're doing a great job and everyone really likes you," he said.

I looked at him in astonishment.

"Really?"

"Yup," he assured me.

He reached toward the center of the table for the salt and began to sprinkle generously.

"I wanted you to be the first to know," he said, still sprinkling. "I got another account in Virginia, and I want you to open up the office and get it in order. Don't worry. I know it's a farther commute and I would pay you for it," he said with an ecstatic expression on his face.

I was really happy for him. He worked really hard.

"That's wonderful," I said, leaning over the table to give him a hug.

It really seemed as though our differences from before had been cleared.

"I just wanted to apologize for the other day, too," he said out of the blue. "I value our relationship more than that—business and professional—and I know you wouldn't do anything like that. It's just that it's a new company and I don't want..."

"Say no more," I interrupted. "I completely understand," I said, grabbing his hand.

I think he blushed a bit.

"Now that that's over, there is something I need to talk to you about." He was getting serious. "I'm thinking about letting the secretary go."

Happy New Year!!!!!!

"Why?" I asked.

Oh, God. I hoped I wasn't smiling.

"I don't know if you noticed, but she's not very competent and that's only when she's there," he said, shaking his head back and forth.

Did I notice?!?!?

"As a matter of fact, she's out sick again today. I can't afford to have no one there when we have client calls coming in," he continued.

I took a sip of water before speaking.

Remember to show no elation.

"So is this definite?"

I cocked my head and raised my eyebrows in mock concern while waiting for his response.

Okay, take the animation down a few notches.

"Pretty much."

Yessssss!!!!

"I got a message from her brother right before we left for lunch telling me that she is pregnant and in the hospital. I don't know why he even told me all that. Besides, I don't know if I even believe her at this point because she has lied about so many other things."

Just then the waiter came up and asked how our meal was. *Great timing.*

"Everything's great," Sam said smilingly to the waiter.

Now get lost; I wanted to hear the rest of the story.

Sam took another bite of his linguini.

"This is really good; you should try some," he said, putting some on a fork and pushing it into my face.

"No, thank you. You were saying?"

"Oh, anyway, I told her to bring a note in from her doctor," he said. "Do you think that's being insensitive?" he asked.

Remember, be fair and professional.

"Not really," I told him. "She does have a track record of calling in and now you're just asking for some proof," I said, completely agreeing with him.

She had finally hung herself, and it took her less time than I originally anticipated.

After lunch I went back to my office and shut the door. I immediately called Char at her job and told her the whole pregnant story.

"So you think that could've been Mark calling in for her?" she asked.

"I dunno. Does she even have a brother? I never knew anything about a brother," I said, grabbing a pencil from my top right-hand drawer.

"I couldn't tell you, but I bet you I could find out from somebody. I'll call you back," she said and hung up and off Sherlock Homey went.

That son-of-a-bitch. I bet you that was him calling, and if she comes in with a note from her doctor, that's the exclamation point on this whole story. Now that Sam had confided in me regarding her, I felt it was okay to go into his office the next day and ask him about the doctor's note, and I sure enough was going to.

Later that afternoon, Char called me back with the 411.

"Okay, here's the deal. She doesn't have a brother—I know that for sure—but she has been seen with some dude. So what if this other dude's the father and he was the one that called in for her?" she said.

I pondered that for a moment. I wished I knew for sure.

So for now Mark got off again. There was no way I could know for sure. Damn, damn, damn! Back to square one, not knowing if he's a big fat liar or not. I still didn't know why I cared so much. It just bugged me because I wanted to know if this guy had been trying, and I do mean trying to play me and I had no idea how I was going to find out. How?

Think, think, think.

Just then my phone rang. I picked it up on the first ring. Well, well, well, it was Mark himself.

"Hi, honey?" he said. "What's up?"

I got it! I figured out how I could get it out of him.

I looked at my phone to make sure the "call" button wasn't lit. She could've come in within the last few minutes.

"Mark, do you know that Tanya has called out sick again today?" I said, setting it up. "Sam's thinking about letting her go."

"What? I called him this morning and told him that she's in the hospital. She's sick," he said.

BINGO, BINGO, BINGO! That was it. So it *was* him that called pretending to be her brother and telling Sam she was pregnant. I should've been a detective. So now he definitely knew that she was pregnant, but was it his? That was now the million-dollar question.

"What's wrong with her?" I asked.

I chewed on the eraser end of my pencil in anticipation.

"She has some sort of stomach flu," he said without skipping a beat.

Why was he lying? Maybe he thought it was none of my business, I'd give him that, but this was just too weird.

Before I could say anything my second line rang. I put Mark on hold and picked up. It was Char. I told her my latest information, but it seemed she had some late information herself.

You'd think we'd actually *work* at work.

"It's his," she said. "I just spoke to his best friend Jerry and he told me that, yes, Tanya's definitely pregnant and that Mark's the father because he has been telling everybody so. That is, everybody except you," she added.

You know, I wish I could've been surprised, but, alas, I wasn't.

"But wait, get this," she continued. "He also said that they are planning a wedding for sometime next year."

Now, *that* I did not know.

I asked if I could call her back that night. I didn't want Mark to hang up. I clicked back over to him and he was still there.

"What took you so long? I missed you," he said, trying to sound cute.

Asshole!

"Mark, Tanya told Sam that she was pregnant and that's why she's in the hospital," I said lied. "Her brother called and confirmed it." I emphasized *brother*.

I wish we had been face-to-face so I could've seen his expression that I was sure was an amalgamation of "caught" and "oh, shit."

He didn't say anything.

"By the way," I continued, "will I be invited to the wedding next year?"

No response again.

"Then again, that would really be considered poor form—the woman you're marrying and the woman you love together in the same room. Tacky, tacky," I said.

He finally spoke up. I was beginning to think we'd gotten cut off.

"Monica, let me call you back. Someone's trying to call me on my other line," he said and hung up.

I guess he couldn't get a lie together fast enough so he took the easy way out. I guarantee if he *ever* had the gall to call me back, he would get his feelings hurt.

I felt good. Not that I needed it, but I finally had an excuse to get rid of that dead weight.

He was history. The only thing I could think of was that I was so happy that we had used condoms because I have no idea where she had been. Come to think of it, I didn't know where his triflin' ass had been either. Yuck.

Chapter 18

Finally the day was over, and I was going to pick up Neal at the airport. I was so happy. I hoped I remembered what he looked like. I'd just look for the cutest guy on the plane.

I got home at five—I left a little early—and cleaned my apartment from top to bottom and gave Kitty a bath. I got a quick workout in and had time for some dinner. I only had a salad because I was so nervous. Why in the hell I was so nervous I didn't know. I was anxious to see him in person again. I thought about how much fun we had when he came for vacation. I just hoped that he had that much fun *this* time.

What if I bored him to death? I had to keep him occupied, and I wasn't sure what to do. I was hardly a Maryland/D.C. tour guide considering I had just moved in the area myself.

Char called me around nine that night, and I told her about my conversation with Mark. She immediately started laughing.

"I guess we won't be hearing from him anymore," she said.

By the time I got off the phone with her, it was ten-thirty. Since I lived about forty minutes from BWI airport, I decided to leave and just go to an airport bar and have a drink. I hated going to airports, but if I had to, going at night was the best, especially a weeknight.

You never had the crowds and you never had problems parking.

When I first arrived at the airport, I was calm but by the time I walked in the sliding-glass front doors I was nervous as hell, and when I found Gate 4C, his gate, I was a total wreck.

I looked around for the nearest bar. I just needed one drink to calm my nerves down.

What if he didn't remember what I looked like? We might even pass each other, not remembering what each other looked like.

I found the only bar open at that time of night and sat down. I asked the bartender for a glass of wine. I didn't want anything too heavy because I didn't really eat and I didn't want to be falling all over myself when I met up with him again. That would make a real nice impression.

When the bartender came back with my glass of wine and told me that it would be $7.50 I nearly fell over. I forgot they overcharged at the airport.

"Waiting for your boyfriend or husband?" the bartender asked, smiling at me.

He was a cute guy. He had dark hair and green eyes.

"Neither," I told him.

I didn't feel like explaining, so I picked up my drink and walked to one of the tables. I couldn't believe it. I was at the airport picking up a guy from another country. It just seemed so uncanny but exciting. I couldn't wait to see him. I had no reason to be nervous. It wasn't like it was a blind date. I had been out with him before. I talked to him almost every other night on the phone, and we shared so many things about each other. This was a relationship that wasn't based on sex, as me and Mark's had been. I actually respected this guy. (No offense to Mark—okay, some offense to Mark). I felt as though I knew so much about him, and I didn't have sex to cloud my judgment. We hadn't even been intimate yet, but I bet we would within that week. I mean, c'mon, he was staying a week with me. More than likely it was going to happen. What if *that* changed everything? What if after sex he didn't want to come visit anymore? What would I do then? I'd just go with the flow. There was nothing else I could do. For right now I just planned on showing my out of town, or should I say, out of country guest a good time, and then we'd take it from there.

I looked down at my watch and it was eleven-thirty. The time had passed rather quickly. I left the bar and went to wait at the gate in case his flight was early. When I found his gate, I immediately checked the schedule and flight 783 was on time. I looked around and most of the people at the gate were young women. They must've been waiting for their husbands to come back from the Bahamas. Maybe they were there on business, or maybe that's just what they told their young girlfriends-slash-wives when they were actually there meeting up with some young island pineapple. A possibility.

I sat down in the vacant seats and looked at some woman who was at the gate across from me who brought her cat. Now why the hell did she have to bring her damn cat? I'm sure the cat's pissed at her stupid ass for dragging him out late at night. I know Kitty would be.

I caught some flight attendants and pilots walking through the airport with their luggage.

They all looked the same, especially the attendants. Most of them were tall, but not too tall, and they were thin. All the women had their hair pulled back in buns or tight ponytails and the male pilots were the exotic-looking types with deep tans and dark hair and dark eyes. They all walked through the airport like they owned it. They just talked amongst themselves and didn't notice any of us commoners sitting on the sidelines waiting for their brethren to land the planes that our loved ones were on.

Okay, that was enough killing time.

I looked up at the clock and it was now eleven-fifty. One of the children of the women shouted excitedly, "Look, here comes Daddy!" I looked out the huge picturesque window and saw a plane crawling toward us. That was his flight. He was getting closer and closer. I was *real* nervous.

When the plane pulled up to the gate and the passengers started getting off, I almost peed on myself. I watched as each person got off. First there was an elderly white man, then an older black man, then a few more women, then a black male.

That wasn't him, was it? He wasn't as cute as I remembered. I *was* drinking an awful lot that night, but damn, this guy was nowhere near cute. Then he did the best thing he could've done. He walked straight to his wife and kid and gave them a big hug. After breathing a sigh of relief, I turned back to the gate and as soon as I turned back, I saw him. I felt a smile form on my face.

Be cool.

He was just as gorgeous as I remembered. Just in case, I waited in the wings and just watched. He saw me almost immediately and walked right to me. I stood there just smiling.

~❤~

What do I do now? I started walking toward him, and it was like I was walking down a large corridor to my death, not knowing what was on the other side.

Not the right analogy.

Finally we met face-to-face. We just looked at each other for a moment, and then he dropped his carry-on and gave me a big hug. I hugged him back just as hard and then we pulled apart. Then right there in the middle of the floor he kissed me on my lips. He didn't slob me down; it was just a quick peck, but it was perfect. I almost melted. If this were a movie, this would've been a pretty damn good one, a five-star classic even.

His kiss was warm and soft. I didn't have to tell you what the bottom portion of my body was doing.

Down, girl, down.

We started walking toward the baggage area while talking about his flight. He told me that he almost missed it because Broadus forgot he had promised to take him to the airport. When we finally got to my car and I paid the five gazillion dollars to get out of the parking lot, we were still talking. Anything I said, he was listening to me intently and offering his opinion. It was like we didn't miss a beat from his last trip. He was refreshing. He had a mind of his own that it wasn't just focused on sex, as mine was, but we wouldn't get into that right then. I'm sorry but that kiss at the airport said it all.

We were silent for a little bit in the car, but it was okay. I think we were both just happy to see each other again. In the darkness, I could feel him looking at me.

"Do you know I was actually nervous to meet up with you again?" he finally said.

"Really? Why?" I asked.

I knew the answer but I wanted to hear it from his beautiful lips that were perfect for sucking.

Calm it down.

"I don't know. I thought there could've been a chance that what we felt for each other the first time wouldn't be the same this time."

"Oh," I said, pausing. "So what do you think now?"

"Think about what?"

"Think about your feelings regarding this trip now?"

"I think I was crazy for even being nervous," he said, smiling.

Those lips...

"I was afraid I wouldn't remember what you looked like," I admitted.

"I know. I kind of forgot what you looked like, too."

"Am I what you remembered?" I was taking a real chance on that question.

"No, you're much more beautiful than I recall."

Five extra points for him. That would bring his total now to seven thousand, five hundred and thirty-three.

There was just this comfortable feeling I had with him. I was able to relax and not have to be a certain way, and it felt good. With Mark it had been different. I felt like he expected me to be something I wasn't.

How dare I even mention the two in the same sentence?

When we got home I introduced him to Kitty again, who after a few sniffs of his shoe couldn't have cared less. It was now one-ten in morning and I knew I should've been getting to sleep, but I was just so excited. What the hell; a few more minutes wouldn't hurt.

He looked around the apartment.

"The place is just as I remembered it."

"Oh, you remember the place, but you don't remember *me?*" I said, taking his bag from his hands and placing it on the living room floor.

He laughed.

"The detail of your exquisite beauty is much too intricate to contain to memory, but now that I see it a second time, I will never forget."

We both laughed. I told you he was good.

"Oh, you're good," I said, going to the kitchen.

I poured us a glass of wine and we sat on the floor talking some more.

"How's your mom?" I asked.

"She's doing a little better. She's really sick though. I just hope she makes it until Christmas."

Wow, I had no idea her illness was that far along. I felt bad for him. I could tell from our conversations that he was really close to his mom.

"My mom raised all of us kids on her own. My father left for the States when I was two and didn't look back. I don't even really remember him," he said, bringing the glass of wine to his lips.

"She must be a remarkable woman."

"She is. I admire her so much." He took another sip. "I just hate it that she has to go through this."

He looked down at the carpet, obviously uncomfortable.

He had this deep, strong passion about him. I could tell he wasn't afraid to show emotion unlike so many other men. He had this quiet strength about him.

I looked at him and leaned over and kissed him on the mouth. I didn't really care if it was too forward or not. It just felt right, so I did it.

A few more minutes turned into a few more hours and after talking to him for so long I told him that I had to get up in the morning for work and that I really should be getting to bed. He agreed.

I wasn't sure if he was going to stay on the couch or in my bed because we hadn't discussed sleeping arrangements, so I left it up to him. I wasn't sure of a lot of things. I wasn't sure if I should wait until he made the first move regarding the sleeping situation but I didn't have to. He came out and asked me what I would be more comfortable with. Now that was a funny question. Of course I turned it around on him and told him it didn't matter to me and that wherever he felt comfortable, I felt comfortable. So off to the bedroom we went. (Good move, huh?) He wanted to take a shower first, so I showed him where the towels were and told him to help himself.

As I climbed into bed, I heard the shower turn on. I could picture what his body looked like underneath all those clothes. I could picture the water streaming off his back and into the crevice of his well-defined posterior.

I changed into my cotton shorts and tank top and got into bed and pulled the covers right under my nose. I felt like a kid in anticipation of the big bad monster that was going to be coming out of the bathroom in the next few minutes. (If I were lucky, the monster would be bigger and badder than I expected.) Next thing I knew, Kitty jumped up on the bed next to me and made herself comfortable on the other side.

"Oh, no you don't; you're gonna have to find another place to lay your hairy cat butt this week," I said in a whisper and scooched her off.

I lay back down and just waited. About ten minutes later the water stopped and he came out of the shower. He walked out of the bathroom with just a towel on, but I only got a glimpse because he walked out to the living room to retrieve some clothes out of his suitcase.

He came back into the bedroom with a pair of boxers on and nothing else. Nice chest, and as I remembered, he had those nice broad shoulders. He jumped into bed and leaned over to kiss me.

"Goodnight," he said, now lying on his back.

"Goodnight, John Boy," I said back.

"Huh?"

"Nothing."

Chapter 19

The next morning I woke up to the smell of coffee, turkey bacon and eggs. I got up and walked out to the kitchen to find Neal standing over the stove making breakfast. "Good morning," he said, winking at me. "I bet you didn't know I could cook."

Actually, he did tell me, but I didn't have the heart to wipe that grin off his face, so I just looked surprised.

"No, I didn't know."

It really did smell good.

He grabbed my shoulders and steered me toward the table and sat me down. He poured some coffee and served me breakfast.

"You didn't have to do this," I told him as I took a bite of my bacon. *Mmmm, real good.*

"I know, but I wanted to. I felt bad for keeping you up last night, so therefore I wanted to give you a nice meal before starting your day."

I could've fallen in love with his accent alone. I told him that we could go out to dinner that night if he wanted to.

He said that was fine and offered to take the Metro to my job so that we could meet and go to that Italian restaurant I was always talking about. How practical can a man be? I agreed to have him meet me at my job and then got up and went to the shower.

~❤~

I got to work feeling as light as a feather. It was actually a good feeling knowing I had someone at home waiting for me. What really would be nice is if he were waiting for me butt-naked with a leather thong on.

"Monica, come to my office, please?"

It was Sam, and he had that "I mean business" look.

When did he get here? I was hoping to have some time to myself to just sit and think about Neal, but no such luck. I was being summoned.

I got up and walked to his office. When I arrived, he was sitting at his desk working on the computer.

"Good morning, Sam," I began.

I was about to tell him that Neal was meeting me at the office to take me to dinner, but when I saw his face, I realized that he was visibly upset about something.

"What's up?" I asked curiously.

He asked me to come in and shut the door behind me.

"Tanya had her brother call in again this morning," he said, sighing in aggravation. Who could blame him?

I wanted to tell him that it wasn't her brother that was calling, but why bother?

"I need your opinion. Do you think I should fire her now or wait until she comes in? I've already called the temp agency and they are sending another secretary over, but I told them this would only be temporary."

He sat back in his seat and tapped a few keys on his computer.

"If this new temp is any good, I want to keep her, but I need to know if I can fire Ms. Johnson."

Hell yeah, I'll do it.

Remember, be professional.

"Well," I began. "You haven't seen her confidential file, but she has already had numerous complaints, internal as well as external, regarding her competency in this position. You can fire her, but truthfully I wouldn't risk it. She'd have a lawsuit for the simple fact that she hasn't gotten any written or verbal warnings put into her file. *But* in our favor, if you do decide to fire her, we did hire her under a ninety-day probationary period, and she hasn't yet met that requirement as per the contract, so therefore you could fire her under that clause."

He just looked at me.

What?

"When did you become such an HR specialist?" he asked, laughing.

"That's what you hired me for. What did you think I was doing in that office all day, picking my nose?"

"What's *your* opinion then, Miss HR superwoman?" he asked.

Be professional.

"If anything, it's a moral issue. You're able to fire her, but she may really be sick. In my personal opinion, I'd use the temp until she comes back. I'd definitely have her bring a note in from her doctor, and if she doesn't produce a note, I'd use that as write-up number one. Three strikes and you're out."

I thought again.

"Actually, I would write her up now regarding her business ethics."

"What about them?" he asked.

"Let's see, how do I put this? *She has none!*" I said half kidding-half serious. "Seriously, I have a file on her a mile long with complaints. That's worth about two write-ups right there," I added.

He started laughing.

"Personally, I would give her another chance."

As I said the words, I couldn't believe it myself. I was actually defending her, considering she had been nothing but a straight-up bitch to me, but I really felt that it was the right thing to do at that point in time. I didn't hate her; if anything, I felt sorry for her. She was one of those weak-minded girls that didn't have any sense. She was and probably would always be running up behind some man.

I just hoped I wouldn't regret opening my big mouth in her defense.

~❤~

After lunch I went back to work on the proposals. They seemed to never get done. I needed to call a meeting with all the employees to decide which health care plan we were going to choose for the company but really didn't feel like it. To make matters worse, I knocked off early and ended up leaving at two-thirty to meet Neal at home.

When I got home I walked through the front door and didn't see him anywhere in sight, but I did hear the shower. I could smell fresh flowers. The apartment looked spotless. When I saw Kitty, she was sitting on the couch just looking up at me. It seemed as though she were impressed, too.

I put my briefcase down and walked to the kitchen. I opened up the refrigerator and saw a pitcher of Bahama Mamas. I grabbed two glasses and poured us drinks. I let them sit on the counter top while he was in the shower and I changed out of my work clothes.

When I finished, I just lay on my bed thinking. I was really nervous at first, but this was really cool so far. I enjoyed his company and he seemed to be enjoying mine. Even after the trip, I would've loved for him to come back again, or I could even go down there for a visit. No matter what, I definitely wanted us to remain as friends, at least.

I heard the water stop, so I sat up on the bed. No sooner than I sat up, Neal came out of the bathroom. He didn't see me right away, but I sure saw him. I saw every bit of him. He was butt-naked. The monster looked even better than I had imagined. He walked into the room and saw me.

"Shit!" he said before he hustled back into the bathroom. "I'm sorry," he apologized. "I didn't know you were home."

He was apologizing to *me?* Believe me, he had nothing to be sorry about.

I was still in shock, so it took me a second to say something.

"No, it's my fault. I just assumed you heard me fiddling around in the kitchen."

The next time he came out he had on a pair of shorts and nothing else. He still looked good, but I liked him just a little better minus the shorts.

"The place looks great," I said, looking around and changing the subject.

"Thanks, I saw some guy in the parking lot selling flowers, so I bought some for us," he said as he walked into the kitchen. When he came back into the bedroom he had the two fruity island drinks with him and handed one to me.

"I didn't know you were coming home early."

"I didn't know I was either, but I decided to head out early. I thought we could eat at home tonight."

(Didja hear that? I said "at home.")

"I went out to lunch and I didn't really feel like going out to dinner, too."

"That sounds good to me," he said. "What do you want me to make you?" he asked.

"You don't have to. I thought we could order out," I said.

"Let's save the money; I really don't mind cooking."

Was this guy serious or what? Flowers, drinks, cooking. This was perfect.

He checked my refrigerator and decided on pork chops, vegetables and baked potatoes. All through his preparation time, he asked me questions about what I did exactly at work. After explaining it to him, I realized just how boring it sounded.

When he was done, we sat down at the table, had dinner and a few more Mamas. He had a great sense of humor and more importantly, he actually thought *my* jokes were funny. No one got my sense of humor but I could tell that he really thought I was funny, or he did a good job faking it.

After dinner, we both did the dishes; he washed and I dried. Boy, I really got over. I didn't have to do a thing.

Can I keep him mom, please?

Since it was only five o'clock, we decided to go for a walk. The weather was beautiful, and I wanted to give him a tour of my neighborhood. The leaves on the trees were the ideal shade of green. The flowers were in full bloom and we could smell every ounce of their exquisite fragrance. This day epitomized summer with the sun beating down hard in forceful rays that felt warm on my skin, while the gentle breeze caressed our bodies with just a small hint of relief from the blazing summer sun.

Since I had left early I didn't want to run into Sam in the parking lot, but there was no way, considering he'd most likely be at work for another hour or so. He was busy in meetings all day, so I didn't even think he noticed me taking off early. Even if he did, I deserved it because I had been working weekends for the past few weeks. (So why am I trying to talk myself into not feeling guilty for leaving early?) When I looked at Neal under the late sweltering summer sun, it made me forget my guilty feelings with a quickness.

When we got back to the apartment it was nearing seven o'clock. I checked my phone and saw that I had four new messages. Sheesh, we weren't even gone that long. I hoped it wasn't Sam trying to call me telling me that he had some emergency at work and was looking for me. That was always the way; as soon as you left early just one time, then that was when all hell at the office broke loose and everybody and their grandmother was looking for you. Never failed. Neal went to go sit on the couch next to Kitty, and I checked my messages. I checked the first one, a hang-up. I checked the second one, a hang-up. I checked the third one, and guess what? Hang-up. When I got to the fourth one it was Char telling me that she tried calling me at work and got my voicemail and to call her that day. It was important. (Uh-huh). I asked Neal if he minded if I called her for a sec, and he said he didn't. The phone rang four times before she picked it up.

"If whatever you have to tell me was so important, why did you let the phone ring four times?" was the first thing I said when she picked up.

"Sorry, girl, I couldn't find the caller ID, and I thought you were Visa stalking me," she said.

I turned around to see Neal playing with Kitty on the couch. *I got a kitty he could play with*, I thought.

I realized what I had been thinking (shame on me) and quickly turned my thoughts back to my friend on the other line.

"I just found out your girl Tanya was in the hospital and is pregnant," she said.

"I know. You already told me," I reminded her.

If she was going to gossip, she needed to keep it straight.

"Yeah, but did I tell you that Mark is definitely the father?" she said.

She was definitely losing her Midas touch.

"Yeah, you told me that, too, and mind you, I already told him about himself, remember?" I said, getting irritated.

Was this girl on drugs? She runs her mouth off to so many people that she forgets whom she told what to.

"Well, I just found out that she got out of the hospital yesterday, and your boy has been missing in action. He was supposed to pick her up from the hospital, and he didn't and she hasn't heard from him since; I bet I didn't tell you that, did I?" she said with a smart ass notation to it.

"Who cares? That's not my problem."

"I'm just telling you because she may do some more drive-bys or phone calls if she thinks he's there," she warned.

Too late.

"My bet is she already has. I've already had a few anonymous calls here." I lowered my voice.

"Poor Neal probably thought that I had some stalker harassing me or something."

Come to think of it, I did.

"Now if you don't mind, I gotta go."

"Wait!" Char yelled over the phone. "Did you get some yet?"

I hung up on her without even justifying that question. If I had gotten "some" as she so put it, I probably wouldn't have even told her because the same way she was telling me about homegirl's business is the same way she would be telling my business to everyone else. That's my girl and all but, she had a huge mouth.

My phone immediately rang again. I thought about not picking it up but did when I saw the caller ID.

Shit!

"Hey, Sam," I said, trying to sound casual.

He was home.

"Hey, I know your man is here, so I thought you two would like to come up for dinner," he said. "I had to find out through Kimmi at the office. What's up with that?" he said jokingly.

"Why Sam, I didn't think you cared."

I looked over in Neal's direction. He was still sitting on the couch.

"Sure we can come up. We already ate dinner, but you can meet him. Say around eight?" I said.

"Eight's good. I knew that's why you asked for tomorrow off. There had to have been some sort of agenda," he said.

He didn't even say anything about leaving early. Maybe he didn't notice, but then again, if I knew Sam, he didn't really care. I was a good worker, and if I wanted some time off, I was sure he knew I was good for it.

I asked Neal if it was okay even though I had already agreed, and he said it was fine. I had told Neal about Sam once or twice, but I never told him that he had been trying to get with me back in the day. That wasn't of any importance anyway.

"I'm really having a good time," he said, sprawled on the couch petting Kitty.

"Don't get too comfortable; you may not wanna leave. Besides, we haven't really done anything yet."

I walked over to the couch and plopped down next to him and Kitty.

"Wait until we really start going out, which unfortunately won't be until tomorrow."

"That's cool. But I just really enjoy it here with you," he said, smiling sheepishly. "I can't wait until you can come down to my country, I want you to see how I live."

The truth was I really couldn't wait either. I could actually say I knew someone in the Bahamas to hang out with. Someone to take me away from all those tourist traps and show me the real country, and show me how Bahamians really lived.

"I don't think the Bahamas is ready for this," I told him and gave him a wink while running my hands up and down my body.

The next thing I knew, he put his left arm around me. I thought that was nice. He took his arm from around me to reach for something on the coffee table and accidentally brushed my right breast. I think I jumped a bit because he just looked at me but didn't say anything. We stayed that way for a few seconds until he spoke again.

"Are you ticklish?"

This was the kiss of death question. If you said no, they wanted to test you to see if you were lying, and if you said yes, then that was the go-ahead to start in on you. I chose the safe route.

"Are you?" I asked back.

Didn't matter because his hands were all over me. He found out the answer to his question quick. I kicked, I screamed, I wriggled to get away, but he was just too strong for me. He tickled me until I had tears coming out of my eyes. I hated that. No one had done that since I was five years old when my oldest sister tickled me until I cried. I begged and pleaded but he just kept right on a ticklin'. I twisted and turned until he stopped. When he did stop, he was lying on top of me on the couch. (I'm telling you, this is better than *any* movie. It was perfect.) When I opened my eyes he was looking at me. He wanted to kiss me. I know he did. I wanted to kiss him just as much, probably more. He slowly started leaning in to me when the phone rang.

Damn!

He quickly let me up off the couch to get the phone. I wasn't going to answer it, but since I wasn't getting any lip action I might as well have.

I picked it up and immediately the person on the other end hung up.

I'm gonna kill that bitch.

I decided next time I picked up the phone and it was "ANONYMOUS," I was gonna tell her that he was not here and then I was gonna hang up.

This was the thanks I got for saving her fucking job!

At eight o'clock we went up to Sam's and had a good time. Since we had already eaten dinner, Sam was nice enough to offer us dessert and coffee. He said it was a crème something or other. Whatever it was, it was good.

It was also very rich. I could just taste the calories going from my mouth to my hips and settling there for all eternity. I really would have to start my diet soon but I'd wait until Neal left.

Sam and I did very little shop talk as not to bore Neal. He and Neal actually got along very well. Sam has always been the type to be interested in other cultures and found it very fascinating when Neal told us about his.

"Maybe I can go with you when you go down to the Bahamas sometime," Sam said, turning to me dead serious.

"Yeah, that would be fun," I said just as serious.

Not! The point of a vacation from work was to get away from your boss, too, *hellooooo?!?!?!*

We stayed there for two hours before we decided we had enough. I mean, damn, I had to see this guy all day at the office; I didn't want to spend my nights with him, too.

We said our goodbyes and while Neal started down the steps, I told Sam that I would be in for a few minutes the next day and to call me at home after that. I might not be home but I *would* be checking my messages. I didn't want to miss *anything*.

When we got back downstairs to my apartment, I started to open the door when I felt his hands on my shoulders. He started massaging my neck; his warm, strong fingers digging gently into my back felt soothing. I bowed my head and let him continue.

"Your boss is actually cool," he said while still massaging.

Don't stop.

"I know. He's a good guy. He was the first one to introduce himself when I moved here," I said, now forming circles with my head as he continued. I could feel his breath on the back of my neck. Then I felt his soft lips kiss that little spot on that lower section of my neck. I turned around to face him. He was looking past my physical being and was now searching into my soul with his deep eyes. He didn't lean in to kiss me, he didn't say anything; he just stared. It was almost as if he were making love with my inner being.

"I just want to remember this moment forever," he said while his face slowly approached mine to make this surreal encounter physical.

I could feel his hands run down my spine. God, this felt magnificent. His arms were now around my waist and holding me tightly as he continued kissing me. First it was just his tender lips kissing mine, but that turned into his sensuous tongue teasing my willing tongue. It was sensuous *and* passionate. I couldn't describe it even if I tried.

After about a few seconds or so (I wasn't sure), he pushed away and left me standing there with my eyes closed and wanting more. When I opened them, he was still just staring at me.

"You're beautiful, Monica," he said.

"You're just as beautiful," I said back to him.

Was that stupid? Telling a man that he was beautiful too? But he really was, and I wanted him to know it. Well, *he* didn't think it was too stupid because he leaned in once more and we resumed our kiss. My heart was racing and I was ashamed at myself for feeling like a schoolgirl. But it felt so good that the feeling of shame didn't last very long. I hadn't realized that I had already unlocked the door, so when we leaned on it, we stumbled into the apartment to a startled Kitty. We looked at each other just as startled and then busted out laughing. I reached behind us and turned on the lights. He reached around me and turned them off.

"Let's leave them off," he said, grabbing my hand.

I didn't know what to say, but I didn't have time to say anything anyway. He scooped me up in his arms and carried me to the room like Richard Gere did with Debra Winger in *An Officer and a Gentleman*. He was taking control, and I had no misgivings about it whatsoever. He laid me down on the bed and stood over me. He took off his shirt and revealed his strong, well-defined chest.

Am I breathing? Did I forget to breathe? I don't want to die now, here on this bed. Breathe, dammit, breathe!

He slowly started to unzip his jeans. *Should I be making a move now? Could he see how nervous I was? Get a hold of yourself girl. He must think I'm fifteen. Lord knows this wasn't my first time, so be cool.*

He unzipped his jeans to reveal his Calvin Klein boxers. I loved those. I wasn't really a brief girl, and I couldn't stand bikinis on men. Why do they feel it necessary to wear those damn things? You think it would be painful to have something on that tight.

He took off his boxers and was now standing over me like some naked Greek god. I couldn't see everything (and by everything, you know what I meant) because the only light in the room was the glimmer of the moonlight from outside. He lay on top of me and took off my shirt, my bra, my shorts and then slid me out of my panties.

Thank goodness I wore the cute matching ones. I was going to wear them all week. He wasn't gonna catch me looking a mess.

He gently rested his naked body on mine and started kissing me again. This time it was all over my body. He started with the forehead and worked his way down to my toes where he, without hesitation, began to encircle each one with his tongue.

Yup, toenails manicured and painted. I don't play.

For the rest of the night he kept me in ecstasy. Before he pleasured me with penetration, he pleasured me orally. His tongue took my body to places that I had only dreamt about until that moment. His tongue moved with such quick repetition I felt as though he were licking a succulent cherry lollipop, trying to get to the surprise, gooey center. No one, and I mean *no one*, had ever done that before. As he gently placed himself inside of me, I felt the force of his passion rain all through my body. That night he was my man and I was his faithful concubine.

Chapter 20

D ammit! I was late. I looked at the clock and it was already eight-thirty. I told Sam I would come in this morning for a couple of hours. I looked over at Neal and remembered the night before. It had been just what the doctor ordered. I couldn't have asked for any better medicinal remedy. I had multiple orgasms with this man and I never had the pleasure of that experience before. *Never!* This man knew what he was doing and the wait was well worth it. He knew every place to touch me to make me feel good.

As I looked at him and lay thoughtfully, I wished I could've stayed home and just made love to him all day, but I couldn't and I was already late. Then again, since I was already late, maybe I could just stay home.

No, no, no. I gotta get to work.

I got up and called Sam. He must not have been in because Tanya answered the phone. I didn't even bother to leave a message with her. Chances were that he wouldn't get it anyway. I just hung up before saying anything.

Paybacks, bitch. Now you knew how it felt.

I quickly showered and got dressed. I went to leave and saw that Neal was still asleep. I leaned down to kiss him. He deserved to sleep in. He worked hard. (Wink, wink).

By the time I got to work I was later than I expected. Whenever you were late, there had to be an accident on the road. I'm sure that's a written rule somewhere.

Luckily, when I walked in Tanya was not at her desk. I didn't really expect her to be either. When she *was* there, she was always in the coffee room gossiping or in the bathroom putting on more tacky-ass pink lipstick.

I walked past Sam's office and through the glass window I saw he had Tanya in there. She was sitting with her back toward me, so she couldn't see me.

Great, I suppose she's telling on me now. I can hear it now.

"Sam, I want to do what's beneficial to the company so therefore I need to tell you that Monica is late. I suggest her termination."

I laughed to myself at the prospect of that. At this point, I believed that wasn't as farfetched as it would seem.

I got to my office and turned everything on with my daily routine. Then my internal line rang. *Damn, can a sista take her coat off?*

It was Sam.

See, I told you.

"Yes," I said, trying to sound as pleasant as possible.

"Monica, could you come in here, please?"

"I'll be right in."

Damn, damn, damn!

I walked toward his office and saw she was still there. I took a deep breath and knocked on the door. Through the glass window, he waved his hand in the air to invite me in. It seemed funny as I thought about it. Invited me in? Do you invite someone to their execution?

"Monica, have a seat, please," he said in his business voice.

I looked over at Tanya who was staring down at the ground looking her usual pissed-off self.

"I've been speaking with Ms. Johnson regarding her performance. I thought it would be beneficial for both of us if we had our HR rep in here," Sam began.

I nodded in agreement.

I looked on his desk and saw that he had a full glass of water placed directly in the center. He always got some water and didn't drink it when he was uncomfortable.

"Monica, Ms. Johnson's on probation. This is a formal warning, and if she has one more unexcused absence, I'd like to recommend her termination. Please issue Ms. Johnson the verbal warning paperwork and have her sign. If you have any questions, let me know. Thank you, ladies," he said, pretty much dismissing us.

We both walked out of his office in a single file with her following me. I'd asked her to come into my office for her signature, but she started walking directly toward the front of the office to her desk. I repeated the request to see her in my office, but this time a little louder in case she didn't hear me the first time. She turned on her heel and followed me into my office mumbling under her breath. I just hoped she didn't decide to make a scene, but just in case, as soon as we got to my office, I shut the door and took a seat behind the desk. I motioned to the chair on the other side of my desk and invited her to have a seat, but she just stood there. This time I insisted she have a seat.

She still said nothing but sat down.

Oh, Lawd, why must I be tested?!?!?

I pulled out the paperwork and fully explained it to her, making sure to dot every "I" and cross every "T." I knew she wasn't listening because as I was explaining she was biting her nails.

And this woman was going to be a mother? Hooo, boy, she was a mother, all right!

After the full explanation, I handed her the paperwork, and I'll be damned if she didn't grab it out of my hands and sign it.

"This will go into your permanent file."

She said nothing.

"You do understand that if there are any more warnings, you will be terminated."

"I'm sure you would like that, wouldn't you?" she said, finally breaking her silence.

I looked her up and down trying to figure out if I was going to give a response to a question that was obviously meant to stir up an argument.

"Now, why would I like something like that, Ms. Johnson?"

"Since you and Mr. Boss man are all tight, you probably got it like that," she said, glaring at me.

"Does Mark know you're fucking the boss?"

She crossed her arms over her huge chest and tilted her head staring at me from across the desk. "If he did know, I bet he wouldn't be with you now, would he?"

What the hell was this girl talking about?

I didn't say anything. I was really curious as to what she was talking about, and I just wanted her dumb ass to keep going.

"I don't need this job anyway. Mark and I are getting married, and he's going to take care of me. So now what?"

"You do what you gotta do," I said. "Just make sure you quit before you try coming in here with another unexcused absence because then we'll quit for you."

She sat up on the edge of her chair. It totally pissed her off that I wasn't showing the reaction she wanted, plus I wasn't done; it was time for the dismissal.

"So if you don't have any further questions, please leave my office and resume your work," I said looking down at my paperwork to let her know that *now* I was done.

Unfortunately, she wasn't.

As she got up from the chair, she gave me a warning to leave Mark alone. I wanted so bad to tell her that I was not seeing him. Nor did I ever want to see him again. She could have that triflin' poor excuse of a man, but even if I did, she would think I was just lying to protect "my man," so I didn't even bother; besides, it was none of her business.

"Goodbye," I said. I didn't even look up from the same paperwork on my desk.

With that she walked out and slammed the door loud enough for people to look toward the direction of my office.

I really had no idea how stable this girl was—or wasn't for that matter. For the rest of the morning I got dirty looks and sneers from her. Maybe I had made a mistake in defending her job. It was clear that she shouldn't be in a professional environment, and I didn't see that changing any time soon.

I went to make copies of another proposal. Sam told me that the secretary should handle things like that. Be real. I wasn't going to give her any of *my* work. The truth was, she was unreliable and lazy. I bought her more time on this job, but I guaranteed she would fuck it up soon. At least the company's ass was covered, and that was all I cared about.

When I arrived at the copier, she was already there making a copy of something, *hopefully her resume.* When she saw me, she immediately took her time and started to dawdle at the machine. I just stood there patiently and waited. She'd make a copy and then decide that it was too light, then too dark and then not centered enough and make more copies. Never mind. I'd just come back later because if I had to stand behind her looking at the back of her raggedy head making those copies, I just might've taken a two-by-four to it, so let me go.

As I was walking out of the room I heard her snicker and mumble something under her breath. I just sighed.

Crazy, crazy, crazy.

When I got back to my office I heard my phone ring. It was an outside line. I ran around to the other side of my desk and picked it up.

"Well, there you are," said some white girl; I had no idea who.

"I had been trying to reach you all day yesterday and I got nothing but your voicemail," the voice said.

Ohhhhh, it wasn't a white girl; it was just Janice Beauvoir again.

"Oh, sorry, I had to leave early yesterday. What's up?"

"I just wanted to confirm our little outing for next week. I talked to my man and he said it's a go. His boy wants to meet you."

"Janice," I started. She seemed to have been looking so forward to this that I didn't know how to tell her that I really didn't want to go.

"Oh, yeah, I spoke to Charlize and she told me that you have a guest from out of town," she said. "I wish I could've met him, but I have so much to do this weekend."

Who wanted her to meet him?

"Janice," I tried again. "I don't know about this whole going-out thing next weekend."

"Oh, c'mon, you can't back down on me now. I already told him we were good."

I looked down at my phone and the "call" button was lit up again.

Ah, hell nah. I know this bitch wasn't still listening in on my conversations.

"Janice, I gotta go, I'll call you early next week and let you know. Bye."

Before she could utter another word, I quickly hung up and went to the front of the office to her desk. She wasn't there. I went back to my office and the line was still lit up. What the hell? Oh, well, in any case, I was going to get the phone people and fix that thing. I wasn't trying to have her hear *any* of my conversations.

When I got home it was almost three in the afternoon. (What happened to just working the morning?) When I opened the door, Neal immediately stepped out from behind it and grabbed me, throwing me down on the couch and smothering me in kisses. Then he lifted me up and carried me to the bedroom where he gently laid me down on the bed. He practically ripped off my clothes and we did it for the rest of the night only to stop for some food and water. Now this was the best "welcome home" present I could've asked for. When we finally took a break, it was dark outside. I looked at the clock and it read nine thirty-three.

"Are you hungry?" I asked.

"Yup."

"Do you want me to fix you something?"

"Nope."

"Then what do you want?" I asked, smiling slyly.

Oh, c'mon, like I didn't know the answer to that one.

He got on top of me and we went at it again, and again, and again. After what seemed like an eternity, he climbed off of me with both of us sweating profusely.

"I had no idea," I said.

"No idea what?" he asked, turning to me.

"That you could do it like that."

"Like what?" he said, grinning from ear to ear.

"Like a wild tomcat in heat." I was laughing.

He started laughing, too.

My smile faded and I looked at him with tender eyes.

"What's your family like?" I asked.

"Like any other family, I suppose."

"What do your sisters do?"

He thought for a moment. He looked so handsome just staring at the ceiling with his arms behind his head. I kept forgetting that this guy was only twenty-four. He just seemed older.

"My sisters and brothers are all in the hospitality business. That's a lucrative field over there."

"You have how many sisters and brothers exactly?" I asked.

"Two sisters and five brothers," he said, still looking up at the ceiling.

From the way he had always talked about them, I got the feeling that they were very close. Especially since his mom got sick.

"It's good that you guys are so close." I placed my head on his bare stomach.

"Isn't your family?" he asked astonished.

"We're a solid family. By that I mean that we all know we love each other, but we don't go around saying it. I can't remember the last time I told my mom that I loved her, but I know she knows it."

"That's a shame. I can't tell them enough how much I love them."

"Every family is different. Like I said, I don't say it all the time, but they know. I don't feel I have to say it, and they don't have to say it to me. It's just something we know about each other."

"So what about career goals?" I asked, changing the subject.

"I don't know. I want to finish school and then maybe get a job in the computer field."

"Doing what?"

"I don't know yet," he said, sounding a bit irate so I dropped it.

I started reaching for my robe that I thought was on the bedpost, which it wasn't.

"I'm going to get a sandwich. Do you want one?" I offered.

"I'll go with you."

We went to the kitchen naked and opened up the fridge. There were some leftover pork chops from the previous night, so we ate those. He then opened the freezer and pulled out some chocolate ice cream. He put his index finger in the carton and took a taste.

"Mmmmmmmm, good." Then he put his finger in it again, but this time he started walking toward me. He gently pulled me toward him and put the ice cream on my right nipple. He looked at me, smiled and proceeded to suck off every little chocolate drop. When all of the ice cream disappeared, he continued to suck my now chocolate-less nipple. I was getting excited all over again and when I looked down, I saw he was excited, too, and off we went for round four, or was it five?

Who cared?

The next morning we woke up at seven-thirty. I jumped up thinking I was going to be late for work, but then I realized that it was Saturday. Yippeeee. All day with Neal. We had decided on a few things. I talked my sister and her husband into going to Six Flags with us. Neal had never been to an amusement park, and I figured he'd like it, so we decided to go. The day was perfect. It was beautiful and sunny with minimal clouds. It was going to be a clear eighty-four degrees.

We had met Sharon and Tim at their house in Bowie, and they drove all of us to Six Flags. Once we got there we immediately got on the biggest roller coaster we saw, and then we ate like pigs, which continued throughout the day. I think I had a hotdog, hamburger, funnel cake and Italian ice. Neal had double what I had. He thought the best ride was the water-log ride. I myself thought it was the haunted ride. We really had a ball there. Now I really did feel fifteen all over again.

When we came home it was nearing midnight. Since we had met Sharon and Tim at their house that morning, we still had to drive home, which was a good thirty minutes away. I was way too tired, so I let Neal drive. I'll admit, I was a little skeptical knowing that they drove on the other side of the road in the Bahamas, but I took my chances. I trusted him.

When we got home we both jumped in the shower (together, of course) and then into bed. We were tired but not *too* tired, if you know what I mean.

We finished the marathon that we had begun the night before and that *really* put us to sleep. It was the icing that topped that double chocolate fudge walnut cake.

The rest of the weekend couldn't have been better. On Sunday we drove to Philadelphia so he could meet my parents, my brother, my oldest sister and her family. We spent the night at my oldest sister's house because I would've felt weird staying with my mom and dad. They probably would've had us stay in separate bedrooms, and we weren't having that. Not that we did anything at my sister's house. I thought that was nasty, so we would just have to wait. We even went to a club on Sunday night. It was my favorite club by far—Warmdaddys on Front Street. On Sundays, they had jazz night. They also had a reggae room, which I thought he might enjoy. Then we went to an after hours club and didn't get back to my sister's house until five the next morning. A few hours later on Monday morning we had breakfast with my parents. We finally left Monday afternoon.

I did have to admit that we had the best time, and although he was slightly nervous at first, I knew he ended up having a great time. My entire family liked him. My dad was totally taken by him, which was rare. It must've been the island thing.

It just seemed like time was moving too quickly. He was going to be leaving the next evening, and I didn't want him to. He actually should've been leaving that night, but we ended up calling the airlines and getting him a flight for the next day.

I never even got a chance to show him D.C. I wanted him to see the Lincoln Memorial, the Washington Monument and the White House, but because we had spent most of the time with my family in Pennsylvania, we never got the chance. We could save that for next time.

When we got back to Silver Spring, we were yet again beat-down, but in a good way. I could take Tuesday off, but I didn't want to. I really needed to get on the ball at work. Lately I had been slacking, and I had a lot of ground to make up. Before his visit, I was excited about him coming; when he arrived, I was excited about him being around, and when he left I knew I was going to be upset. I'd use that to my advantage. Maybe I'd be so upset that when he left I'd submerge myself into my work. (Yeah, right). He said we could wait until next time to do all of the sightseeing we missed this trip. (Exactly what I was thinking because there was definitely going to be a next time). We fell asleep in each other's arms, totally exhausted. I remembered thinking before I fell asleep that these were the best few days I had had in a long time. I just hoped there were more to come.

Chapter**21**

As expected, the next morning I didn't want to get up but did anyway.
I told Sam that I would come in but I was only staying for half the
day. I had to take Neal back to the airport that night, and I wanted to
spend some time with him before he left.

I jumped in the shower and got dressed. I didn't wake Neal up because
if he was as tired as I looked, then I knew better.

As usual, I was the first one at the office. I even beat Tanya, who since
her "medical emergency" had been coming in earlier than me.

When I checked my voicemail there was one from seven-ten this morning.
I checked that one first. "Hi, sweetheart. Since you didn't wake me up and
I didn't get a chance to thank you for the best time ever, I thought I'd call
and leave a message for you. I love you."

I couldn't believe it. I knew I had been feeling it, but I wasn't sure if I
was going to say it out loud. Saying it out loud made it official. Was this
sudden? I don't think so because we had had an instant connection the
first time we met, and we had been talking via telephone almost every day,
and then there were the letters. To be quite honest, I think I was feeling
something before he came for this visit, but I never admitted it. Now it
was in my face just staring me in the eyes.

Now what? What were we supposed to do about it? He lived in another friggin' country, for goodness sakes, and I lived here. We would what...see each other every three months or so? What?

My bliss had turned into sadness so quickly. Before I could even think about it any further, my phone rang.

Outside line.

It was Sam telling me that he needed to call an emergency meeting with me as soon as he got in, which wouldn't be until nine o'clock. I asked him what it was in reference to and he said he would tell me when he got there. Now I had to sit and wait for another hour and a half.

Meanwhile, co-workers started filing in. When I looked up I saw Sonja, one of the customer service reps, standing at my door.

"Good morning. How are you?" she asked.

"Good morning, Sonja."

"Did Sam tell you what happened Friday afternoon after you left?"

"No. What happened on Friday?" I asked alarmed.

"Michele and Tanya were fired on the spot," she said.

I looked at her in astonishment. *Damn, I was only gone for half a day.*

"What happened?" I asked, knowing I should wait for Sam, but I wanted to know then.

"Tanya was caught stealing money out of the petty cash fund and has been for some time now. She told us about it a few weeks back, but we didn't believe her. Someone caught her red-handed yesterday and turned her in. Then we found out she has been listening in on phone calls via the switchboard."

Shocker.

"What about Michele?" I asked.

"Same thing. Stealing," Sonja said. "And then yesterday we caught her in your office."

"My office?" I said. "What in the hell was she doing in here?"

"Don't know. Sam caught her in here looking through your files and trying to get in your drawers."

I turned around in my chair and looked at the files. Everything was as usual. Thank goodness I locked my files and drawers every night.

"Well, did she say what she was looking for?" I asked.

"Don't know. Sam had her in the office for like two hours Friday, and when they came out she grabbed some stuff off her desk and left. He got all of us together at the end of the day and told us that he had fired those two."

Sonja then excused herself to go back to her desk.

One-half day. Not even that. I was gone a couple of hours and all this happened? I pretty much knew about the phones, but I couldn't prove it, but stealing money, too? We kept at least five hundred dollars in that petty cash fund. I wondered how much she stole and why didn't Sam call me at home? Then again, I was out most of the weekend, and come to think of it, I didn't check my messages when we got back the previous night. Anyhow, there was nothing left to do but wait for Sam to come in and fill me in on the rest. I had no idea what to make of this.

It seemed as though that was the big thing on Friday. Everyone was sitting around talking about it, and when I would walk by they would just look at me as if waiting for me to say something. I wished Sam would hurry the hell up. No sooner than I had said that, he walked in. I followed him to his office, not even giving him the chance to open the door or take off his jacket.

"I suppose you heard?" he said.

"You supposed right. What the hell happened here on Friday, and why didn't you call me?"

"I did try to call you, but I got no answer and didn't want to leave this on your answering machine. Besides that, it wasn't that big a thing; I didn't want to mess up your day off, especially with your man here. Did you two have a good time?" he asked.

"He's not my man, thank you, and yes we did. Now tell me the deal. What happened?" I asked again.

He asked me to shut the door and then proceeded with the conversation I wanted to hear.

"Jason caught Tanya stealing from us, and several other employees backed him up. Evidently she had been bragging about it," he said disgustedly.

"What about Michele?" I asked.

"Same deal. Both talking too much. I guess they told the wrong person. Michele did admit it eventually."

"And the listening to phone calls?" I asked.

He shook his head.

"She decided she wanted to listen to one of the sales reps' phone calls and was doing it on the speaker phone, and somebody overheard it. Not too bright, huh?"

"I thought she had been doing that to me before, but I had no proof, so I didn't say anything," I said.

"I brought her in the office to talk to her, and I have to tell you, Monica, she launched a full hate campaign against you."

"Now why am I not surprised?" I asked sarcastically.

"She was going on and on about how *you* did this to her. *You* wanted her fired because you didn't like her because she was having a baby by the man *you* wanted and that *you* were a boyfriend stealer and would fuck anything you could get your hands on. She was brutal," he said.

"Sam, I didn't tell you, but that girl hates me."

"Ya think?" he said, chuckling.

"Everything she said was a lie. I made the mistake of dating an acquaintance of hers, and boy, have I been paying for that decision ever since. We've had a few confrontations in *and* out of the office."

I told him about the mall and about the club.

He looked shocked.

"But you were the one who wanted to give her another chance when I was ready to fire her," he said, confused.

"I know, I know. That may have been my fault, but I was also thinking in terms of a lawsuit. You have to be careful when letting somebody go."

"So is SamInc okay in this case?" he asked.

I smiled at him. "I think so, especially with her admission." We talked a few more minutes and then I went back to my office to work. Sam said that since I was HR I should hold a meeting regarding what happened on Friday. I didn't have a problem with that. As a matter of fact, I thought that would be a good thing, so I agreed, but it would have to wait until the next day because I had a man to get home to.

Of course I didn't tell *him* that.

When I opened the front door, it was quiet. Even Kitty wasn't sitting on the couch looking up at me. I walked in, put my briefcase down and headed straight for the bedroom where I found Neal and Kitty sitting on the bed together. Neal had on a set of headphones and was listening to something with his eyes closed. Kitty looked up at me and jumped off the bed, which must've startled Neal because he opened his eyes.

When he saw me, he smiled.

"Hey," he said.

"Hey, yourself. What's up?"

He immediately got off the bed, and came toward me and threw his arms around me and kissed me.

"I was just chillin' listening to some Beres Hammond."

Now how did I know it was reggae? I looked at him and realized that he would be gone. I was taking him back to the airport that night, and I wasn't sure when I was going to see him again. I couldn't even think about it without getting a lump in my throat. This past week had been amazing. I had the best time, and I can confidently say that he did, too. He told me almost every day he was here. We had learned so much about each other's cultures and even more about our personalities. I knew he liked chocolate, chocolate chip ice cream, and he knew I didn't. He even brought some reggae tapes for me to listen to; and I introduced him to one of my favorites, Barry Manilow and the Copacabana. (Seriously, I'm not kidding.) I also introduced him to jazz. He seemed to really like Boney James (one of my favorites, too) and Alex Bugnon. Then there was Chet Baker and of course, Charlie Parker. He wasn't really feeling them yet, but give it time.

"I thought we'd have dinner in since this is my last night and all," he said with a hint of sadness in his voice.

So that's what we did. We had dinner and made love for the rest of our time. The first time we made love it had been hungrier, but this time it was softer and gentler. We wanted to savor each and every one of our last moments together.

~❤~

I took him to the airport at ten o'clock that night. When we got there I walked him to his gate. I couldn't believe it. I was actually fighting back tears. That really hurt.

"Well," he said, "I don't wanna keep you up tonight like I have been all week."

I nodded. He really wasn't keeping me up, but I didn't want to stay any longer for fear of letting loose tears. I mean the air in this building was filled with pollen and my allergies might've started up and I wouldn't want him to think I was crying for him or anything.

"Maybe you can visit me toward the end of the year," he said.

"Yeah, maybe," was all I could muster.

He held out his arms and gave me a strong hug and didn't let go for what felt like an eternity. He then looked at me with his pretty brown eyes and kissed me square on the lips with a desperate passion, a kiss that wanted to linger just a little longer but couldn't. I wanted the same.

I pulled back, ran the back of my fingers against his cheek and immediately turned around and walked toward the exit.

That damn pollen.

~❤~

"You really sound pathetic." Char sure knew how to make me feel better.

"Gee, thanks."

I had called Char as soon as I got home for comfort. My mistake, but I knew she would be up.

"I can't believe you are actually upset over young boy. He must've been good in the sack."

If she only knew.

The truth of the matter was that it was more than just sex, but I didn't feel like explaining this to her. I didn't want to tell her that I had—no, we had—a magnificent time together. Words could barely describe the feeling I had that whole week. It felt weird knowing that he wasn't going to be there when I got home from work anymore.

~❤~

The next morning was work as usual. I thought with Neal gone, I would be able to dive right into work, but it was a lot harder than I expected.

"Wanna go to happy hour tonight?" Char asked with her early-morning phone call to me at work.

I didn't feel like happy hour, but it beat going home to an empty apartment—no offense, Kitty—so I decided to go.

By the time five rolled around, I realized I had actually gotten a lot of work done. I expected the opposite. I held the health care meetings I had been putting off for the last three days, and I even did some more research and came up with a new plan. I was also able to hold a training class for the new employees that started on Monday. As long as I kept busy, maybe I wouldn't miss him so much. I had all these feelings, but I couldn't have told anyone, at least not in the detail that I wanted to—especially not Char. She may have been my best friend, but she wouldn't have understood, seeing as she had a new date pretty much every day of the past week. Wasn't she ever going to get tired of that? I knew I was. That reminded me. I hadn't heard anything about Mark or his crazy girlfriend. Janice called and left a few more messages reminding me about that weekend's blind date. That girl wasn't going to give up, and quite frankly she was working that last itty, bitty nerve that was just hanging on for dear life. I had decided to go on the date, but that was it. After that, no more blind dates, no more fix-ups and no more nothing. I was done. I knew I said that before, but this time I *really* meant it.

She was supposed to call me later on in the week to remind me. Or should I say she was going to call my answering machine and remind *it* because I wasn't answering. I planned to talk to her as little as possible and that especially included anything regarding the blind date.

Thank goodness for caller ID. Hee-hee.

I was meeting Char at Quimby's. As I walked in and looked around I was surprised to see her there already. I thought I had at least a good fifteen minutes before she showed up. She was sitting with two guys when I walked over to them.

"Here she is now," I heard her say to one of the guys.

They both looked in my direction and smiled.

Oh, Lawd! Let the games begin.

I wondered which one she was trying to set me up with. One guy was about six feet two inches tall, had a nice body and a chiseled face. Looking good. His buddy, on the other hand, was about five feet eight inches tall, had a spare tire and reminded me of a weeble wobble.

That wasn't the best part. He also had a gold tooth right in the front where everybody and their grandmother, aunt, uncle and cousin Pookie could see. That would most likely be my guy. As soon as I reached them "Goldie" immediately extended his hand.

"Well, hello. My name's Bruce," he said.

I turned up my nose. It just wouldn't have been complete if his breath weren't kickin' like Billy Blanks.

"Hi," I said, not offering my name.

"Your friend here tells me that you are in Human Resources," Bruce said. He said, "Huuuuuuman Resources," while breathing directly into my face.

"Yeah, I am."

I turned to Char, hoping she would get the message.

"I'm going to find a table," I said.

She got it.

We excused ourselves and went in search of a table.

"You're so lucky I already got Max's number," she said.

"No, *you're* lucky I didn't just turn around and walk the fuck outta here. Don't be tryin' to set me up with no gargoyle. Did you *not* smell his breath?" I asked.

She started laughing.

"Girl, that didn't make no sense!" she said.

We found a table and sat down.

"Did I tell you that I have a hot date this weekend?" I said to her.

"No, with who?" she asked, clapping her hands.

"I have no idea," I said.

I saw the puzzled look on her face, so I explained further.

"Janice has been hounding me to go out with her and her man. Her man has this uppity friend that she set me up with."

"And you're going? Are you crazy? You'll probably be bored all night long."

"I already told her yes but this is it. I told *her* and I'm now telling *you*, don't be settin' me up with anyone else because I'm not going," I said, taking a sip of the drink I just ordered.

"Yeah, yeah, yeah, you said that before."

I took another sip while looking around for a waiter. I was hungry.

"What if he's like your boy Mark? Wouldn't that be funny?"

"Hilarious," I said sarcastically.

"Speaking of Mark, have you heard from him? Or from *her* for that matter?" she asked.

"Not at all, and don't talk them up either," I warned.

"I guess you won't be hearing from *her* anyway, considering she's probably spending all of her time looking for a job. We might even find her on the corner of U Street holding up a sign saying 'will work for food,'" she said, laughing.

"I don't find that funny since she is with child," I said, taking a sip.

"I know. Not only that but word on the street is that she and Mark are having problems," she said.

"Surprise me, that does not. What type of problems?"

"They were supposed to get married, and now they're not; he's supposedly seeing someone else and has moved out of their apartment."

"That's a shame," I said, shaking my head back and forth. "I couldn't even imagine being in that type of position. I understand mistakes happen, but women need to plan things out better for themselves and stop relying on a man to take care of everything because they are not always going to be around. Case in point."

"Amen to that," she said. "I guess you got the last laugh," she said while guzzling down her vodka tonic.

Yeah, last laugh. Real funny.

I got home from the uneventful happy hour about nine o'clock. Neal had already called me and left a message. I was sort of glad I missed it. At this point, I would've preferred to have just let this past weekend dissipate from my mind. I also had three more messages, according to my answering machine. I listened to the first one, and it was from some woman selling something. Now, how are you gonna leave a message for me regarding some shit you are selling? Like I'm gonna call back. The second one was from Mark.

Damn, we sho' nuff talked him up.

"I just wanted to call you and say hi. I haven't talked to you in a while and there are some things I feel I need to explain to you. I really do miss you and would appreciate you calling me back. I'll be home waiting for your call." There were some things he feels he needs to explain to me? Did he actually feel? Well, that was a new one.

The third message was from him again.

"I have been sitting here thinking about you, and I haven't been totally honest about some things. I really would like to talk to you and explain. I want to be with you. I can't do anything but think about you. Please call me back."

Oh, just stop it. He had just done too much shit to me and we weren't even all like that. Did you think I was going to open that can of worms back up again? That was the good thing about Neal; he wasn't about games. Maybe that was just an American thing. Didn't they ever grow up? This fool is thirty-something years old and still trying to play children's games. He should've known that I was not the one to play. In the words of the Notorious B.I.G., "If you don't know, now ya know." I wondered what Neal was doing. Why couldn't I get him out of mind? No matter how hard I tried, I couldn't do it. He meant so much to me. *Did I just say that?*

Was I in love with him like that? I couldn't have been. I'd only known him for a month. Nah, I just really missed him. That was it.

~❤~

My phone rang at ten-thirty. I had a pretty good idea who it was but checked the caller ID just to be sure, and I was right. I picked up anyway because if I didn't he would probably show up like he did last time.

"What do you want, Mark?" I said, getting right to the point.

"I forgot you had caller ID," he said, laughing nervously.

"What do you want?" I said again.

"Monica, don't do this to me. I really missed you, and I need to see you again. Do you even realize how much I have been thinking about you?"

"Can't imagine," I said, not budging.

"Well, I'll tell you. I've missed you so much. I want, no wait, *need* to see you again. I want to take this to the next level. I'm ready."

"What about Tanya? You remember her; she's your pregnant girlfriend."

Let's see his comeback for that one.

"I know. I haven't been totally honest with you."

I thought we had already established that.

"Tanya and I were together, but that's over. I haven't been involved with her in a few years. I was staying there, and yes, we did sleep together a couple of times, but that's it."

"You don't say?" I said, cutting him off.

"But we're definitely not in a relationship. I even moved out and back into my own place, so we can be together," he said proudly.

Whoa, Nelly.

"I didn't ask you to do that," I said.

"I know, but I wanted to. I wanted you to see that I'm serious. I'll still be in the baby's life if it is proven that it's mine, but I want nothing to do with her."

Proven that it's his? So it's one of those cases.

"If I could just see you this week," he said.

"I'm really busy this week; maybe next week sometime," I said, putting him off.

"That's fine. When?" he asked.

Now he was pushing it.

"Call me next week and I'll let you know. Now goodnight," I said and hung up the phone.

I really had no intentions of seeing him the week. I just wanted to get him off my phone. I didn't care if he moved out or not. That had nothing to do with me. As I've stated before, I didn't want nor did I need the drama. I figured if I blew him off enough, then he would get the hint.

Who was I kidding?

Mark called me every day for the rest of the week. If he didn't reach me at work, then he called me at home. I usually let him reach me at least once because if I didn't I knew his ass would show up at my door, and I was not having that. He sent flowers to the office, offered to take me to lunch and dinner, and then offered to come to my apartment and give me a massage after, and I quote, "my long and exhausting day at work."

Get real. I knew I was being cynical, but could you blame me? I had been put through the ringer with this guy. I wasn't about to play the fool again. At least not with him. I'd save that special honor for the next boob I went out with.

By the time Friday came I was really dreading the double date with Janice, her man and the next boob. I was doing more research for Sam when Janice called and told me that she was going to have to reschedule for the next night because her man had to work late. That was fine with me. I just really wanted to go home and relax anyway.

Char called me and wanted to go to happy hour, but I was beat. I didn't want to do anything. Maybe rent a movie and order pizza. *That was it.* I had a taste for pizza. Don't nobody call me; don't nobody come a knockin' on my do' wanting to go out. I was in for the night.

I left work at five and went straight to the video store and rented the 1967 version of *Romeo and Juliet* with Olivia Hussey. I usually only watched that on Valentine's Day, but I was in the mood for it that night. I could go for a scary movie, so I rented one of those Chuckie doll films. I think it was the latest one. All I had to do was order my pizza when I got home and then I was set. My diet would start tomorrow, so I ordered a large pepperoni with mushrooms. Wait, diet can't start tomorrow, I would have some pizza left over and would eat it tomorrow, so therefore we'll start the diet on Monday, since I was going out tomorrow night anyway.

Man, I hadn't done that in a long time. I used to do it all the time in Philadelphia, but since I had moved out here, I had been doing nothing but going out to happy hours and clubs. It was always the same thing. The shortest guy in the club would end up hitting on me and wouldn't take no for an answer. I was never rude, so they would follow me around like a sad puppy dog for the rest of the night. Man, oh, man, watch out when they bought you a drink. That meant you were fair game all night. I don't know about some women, but I refused to meet my husband in any damn club. The sad thing is that I would see the same guys week after week. Of course they could say the same thing about me since my ass was there just as much as theirs. I decided *that* was going to stop. If anything, I would maybe meet the girls to go to happy hour every so often, but that was it. Brunch was okay, too. I needed to cut down on my spending because I had plans to buy a house. I wasn't sure where, maybe in Bowie near my sister, but wherever, it was time. Maybe even Chevy Chase, but that would be some money. I tried to wait until I got married and then we would buy our house together, but by the time that happened we would be living on Mars in space shuttles. Oh, well. I also had my eye on the new BMW. Sam had just gotten a new one, and it looked all that. I don't splurge on too many things, but when I do they are big things.

It was about eight o'clock when I put the first movie in and my phone rang. It was Neal. I was so happy to hear from him. I hadn't talked to him since he left because we always seemed to miss each other.

"Hi, Neal," I said

"Hi, gorgeous."

That made me smile.

I loved when he called me "gorgeous." That wouldn't work for anyone else, but for him it did. He told me he put in vacation time around Christmas and would love for me to spend Christmas in the islands. That was a good idea. I could see myself going to the beach on Christmas Day. I told him I'd see what I could do but chances were good that I would be making my Christmas an Island Christmas. We planned our vacations like any normal couple would plan their dates. It was only September and I wouldn't get to see him until the end of the year. Could I even wait that long? We decided that we would schedule time to talk on the phone so we weren't missing each other as much as we had been. We decided on Mondays, Wednesdays and Fridays. This way we wouldn't miss each other's calls (seemed kind of bizarre). By the time we hung up, I felt a little better knowing that we had made a tentative date for December, but I felt a little bad that we might not make it until then.

Me being the positive person that I was, I figured that the Monday, Wednesday, and Friday calls would probably turn into Monday, Wednesday calls and then just Monday calls and then call-you-when-I-call-you calls.

Stop it! No more thinking about Neal. Just put the movie in and enjoy it, *dammit.*

I got through the first hour of the movie when there was a knock at my door.

Now what?

The thought of whom was on the other side of that door made me cringe. If it wasn't good ol' Jamie, the pizza guy, I didn't want to see ya.

I knew Char was out on a date, so it couldn't be her, unless the date ended early. I bet you it was her coming over here because the date ended early, and she didn't want to go home. I opened the door and guess what? It wasn't her. It wasn't even my highly anticipated pizza man. It was Tanya.

I just stood there with the door open, waiting for her to say something. When she didn't, it was me who spoke first.

"Yes?" I said with more attitude than curiosity as to why she was standing at my front door. I had no idea.

"Where is he?" she said, trying to peek around me and into my apartment.

"Who?" I asked, knowing exactly whom she was referring to but wanting her to hear for herself how damn ignorant she sounded by coming over to look for her man.

"Don't play with me," she said, still looking past me and into my apartment. Oh, uh-uh. This girl was buggin' now, and I'd had it.

She was a true nut.

"Go home," I said. "Your so-called man is not here."

I shut the door in her face but she continued to bang on it screaming, "I know he's in there! Mark, you'd better come out! Maaaaaaaaark!!!"

This scenario played out better than any movie I had ever seen. I laughed to myself each time she screamed his name on the other side of my door. *Why me?* How did I ever meet that asshole? Oh, yea, thanks, Char.

"Maaaaaaark, come out! We can work this out," she said while screaming at the top of her lungs.

The neighbors must be loving this.

I picked up the phone and called Char. She was on her date and wouldn't be home. I decided to leave her a message anyway.

Beeeeeeeep.

"Char, it's me. Listen to this."

I held the phone up toward the door.

"Maaaaaark, please, I didn't mean it!" she screamed from behind the door.

"Now you know that is the crazy bitch who showed up here looking for her man. This is serious payback for you," I said and hung up.

"Don't think this is over." Tanya was obviously talking to me.

Somehow I knew it wasn't. I went to the TV and ejected the *Romeo and Juliet* tape I was watching and put in *Chuckie.* That seemed to be the better choice.

"You need to say something to her. That girl is beyond crazy," Char said.

We decided to go shopping for my date, and Macy's was having the first of its many "last and final sales" of the year.

"You don't think I tried?" I said.

"I can get some of my friends to hook you up and beat the shit outta her," she said with a laugh.

"Nice thought, but no thanks. Speaking of thugs, how was your date last night?" I asked.

"You must've been there because this guy was actually straight-up thug. He thought he was Tupac or something. He picked me up in one of those gangsta-lean cars. You know, like the ones that jump up and down in those Snoop videos."

"I thought they just had those on the West Coast."

"Well, I'm here to tell you they don't just have them on the West siiiii-iiiide," she said, making what I guess was a gang symbol.

"Oh, guess who called me yesterday?" she asked.

"How the hell am I supposed to know who called you?"

"Your girl Janice," she said, laughing.

"Now why she gotta be *my* girl?" I asked.

"Cuz she is. Anyway, she was telling me about your man for tonight."

"What did she say?" "He's tall, has a nice butt and a great job. She told me his name but I forgot," she said, looking up into space as if trying to remember, when in actuality she was probably thinking about her own date.

"Well, remember. She didn't tell me anything valid about this dude and I'm the one going out with him. She's supposed to call me this afternoon. My guess was she didn't even know who he was. She was just playing it by ear and was gonna take the first taker that decided to go tonight," I said. We both started laughing.

"Did she ever tell you about her man?" asked Char.

"She doesn't say too much about him. The only thing I know is that they've been dating for a while and have now been talking about marriage. What do you know?"

"Pretty much the same thing, but they are supposed to be putting a rush on that marriage thing," she said, glancing at me as if she knew something I didn't.

"What?" I asked.

"What, what?" Char was still glancing at me as if she was dying to tell me something.

I knew how to get it out of her. All I had to do was change the subject. She was anxious to tell me anyway, and if she saw that I didn't care about her bit of gossip, it would kill her, and she'd spit it out.

"I'm still not sure what I am going to wear tonight," I said, looking at this ugly ass purple skirt on the fifty percent rack.

"What do you think?" I asked, holding it up for her to see.

It worked—hook, line and sinker.

"Giiiirl, if I tell you something, you have to promise not to tell anyone," she said.

If I had a dollar for every time she said that...

"I won't. Now spill it!"

"Your girl is expecting," she said.

"Uh—dummy? You already told me that."

"No, not *that* girl, you idiot; your other girl."

"What other girl?" I asked. Maybe if she'd stop referring to everyone as "my girl" I'd know who the hell she was talking about.

"Janice, dummy!" she blurted out.

"Damn, not her, too. Who told you?"

"I told you that she told me. She and her man are planning a wedding in December. She'll probably tell you tonight, so act surprised."

Char must've had the biggest mouth in all of Maryland.

I wonder how much of my business was out there?

After our shopping excursion, Char and I went out to lunch and of course I got my chicken fingers with extra honey mustard and fries. I was going to have something lighter since I was going out to dinner, but those chicken fingers were just calling me. I couldn't say no. Besides, I had to have them one last time before I went on my diet Monday.

After stuffing my face, I went to visit my sister and her husband in Bowie; it was four-thirty by the time I realized how late it was. At least I did find something to purchase at Macy's when I went shopping. Since we were just going to Dave and Busters and then probably drinks afterwards,

I got a cute jean skirt with a tank top that had sparkles on it. I also got a matching chain-link belt. The look was very in style, and I felt I only had a few more years to pull off such a hip look, so I got it. Char ended up buying a leopard print skirt and this tiny tight black shirt. It was cute too but it stank of hooch all over it, especially if I knew how she was going to wear it. She would put her false boobs in, then she would put the long weave in her hair and slob on the makeup and be off to the races. She would end up looking like those same girls in rap videos, but hey, if that's the look she was going for, then so be it. Personally, it wasn't my taste.

Char and I were such opposites I sometimes wondered how we became such good friends. Did I mention that she had a big ass mouth, too? I still couldn't believe that about Janice. I knew it. I bet that's why she wanted to go out with me so bad. She wanted to rub in my face that she had a man, who more than likely was a male model look-a-like. She would show me the huge diamond ring he bought her for their engagement, and then she would tell me about the little bun that she had in the oven.

I guess she graduated from talking about *The Firm*.

Everyone always warned me she was in competition with me, only I wasn't with her. It was everyone else who told her what I was doing with my life. I just couldn't figure out why she kept nagging me to go out with her. She never wanted to go out before with her other broke-down male friends, and now she couldn't set up the date fast enough.

I bet my guy was ugly. I bet he had the gold teeth, stank breath and the whole nine. That seemed to be my specialty nowadays. What if he were that guy that Char and I met at the bar the other night? I knew I had bad luck, but damn. That would just take the cake. Well, we were going to a public place, and if that was him, I'd just take off on my own, especially if his breath was smelling like a dirty old shoe. I'd be outta there so quick.

When I got home, I checked my messages. Janice left one telling me that she gave the guy my address and he would be picking me up first and then we'd all meet at Dave and Busters.

Awwwww! Dave and Busters. That's where Neal and I went and had an awesome time. It was almost like our place, and I didn't want to taint it by going with some goldie.

I thought it was a little presumptuous for her to give dude my address like that. *I* would never do that. I was sure she didn't know him like that and it *was* a blind date to me, so I *knew* I didn't know him like that. The only person that really knew him was her man, and I didn't know her man, so that led me back to I didn't know this man coming to pick me up at my apartment. I already had enough crazy people knowing my address, like Tanya *and* Mark.

I started getting ready because according to Janice's message, he was going to be here at seven-thirty. That gave me two hours to primp. Then again, primp for what? I turned on the TV and got in another hour of TV watching. I started getting ready at six forty-five. Forty-five minutes was long enough for this fool.

When I jumped out of the shower it was seven-ten and when I finished my hair it was seven-twenty. I threw on my clothes and was back sitting in front of the TV at exactly seven-thirty. Damn, I'm good!

Before I could pour myself a much-needed glass of wine, my doorbell rang. As I walked to the door, I prepared myself for anything and everything. Here comes shorty; here comes baldy; here comes creature from the black lagoon. I was ready for whatever. When I opened the door I saw that I wasn't ready.

Whoa, momma, before me stood this honey. I mean, if Greek gods were tall, black men with broad shoulders and chests of steel, this would be him. I swear I almost passed out.

"Hi, I'm David. It's finally nice to meet you," Greek god said, extending his hand.

"Hi, David. I'm Monica."

Silence.

"Shall we go?" I said.

More silence but uncomfortable this time.

"Uh-sure," he said, and off we went.

When we got to his car I saw that he had a Hyundai Sonata. So what? I used to have a Hyundai, too.

"I have a BMW, but it's in the shop so I have to drive my brother's car tonight," he said.

"I used to have a Hyundai myself and they're very...reliable," I said, lying about the reliable part.

Cheap ass Hyundais.

"Uh-huh," he said as he got in the car and left me standing by the passenger side. Let me just say something right quick: I'm not one of those girls who expects men to open doors for them all the time, but damn, on a first date when you're trying to make a good impression? C'mon.

He was already in the cheap ass Hyundai starting the car when I went to open up the passenger side.

Surprise; door was locked.

I knocked on the window to indicate, duh, I can't get in and he leaned over and opened the door.

"Ooooops, I thought I unlocked that already."

That's what happens when you don't have power locks in a cheap ass car.

I got in the car, and he immediately turned on the radio to blasting rap.

"It's dance party night at the Ritz, and they're jammin'," he said, bopping his head back and forth to the music.

I just nodded.

"So how do you know Janice?" I asked over the loud music.

"What?" he said.

"How do you know Janice?" I asked again but this time louder. You think he'd turn it down just a tad.

"Met her through my boy. I wanted to get with her, but she was already dating my boy, so I was like, nah, I'm gonna leave that hunney alone."

That was real nice.

"So how do *you* know her?" He turned down the music so *he* could speak.

"Longtime acquaintances."

"Oh."

Greek man had a very nice profile. It was well chiseled and defined and his hair was cut nice and short. I looked down at his suit and realized something I didn't notice at the door. He had on a red suit with what looked like a black muscle shirt under it. How did I *not* notice that at the door? Maybe if I'd jumped out of that cheap ass car then while it was only doing thirty-five, I would've been okay, maybe just a few scrapes and a broken bone or two.

We pretty much stayed silent for the rest of the trip. I did try to make small talk that seemed to fall on deaf ears. All of his answers were one word like "yup," "nope," and "maybe." If this fool didn't want to go out, then why did he come? I didn't ask to be fixed up. Damn, not only did I owe Char for my first date with Mark, I was gonna hafta get even with Janice, too. I had a lot of paying back to do, and believe you me, I was gonna collect with interest.

When we arrived at Dave and Busters it was crowded as usual. That could've been a good thing. Maybe I could've found someone else to hang out with because this guy was not the one. I wondered what Janice's guy must be like to have a friend like this. Like they say, birds of a feather...

To my surprise when we walked in, I immediately saw Janice ordering a drink at the bar. I walked up to her and left my date behind. I wanted to tell her that he was a dud, but I didn't have time because he was right behind me, checking out my ass, I'm sure.

"Hey, hon," Janice said when she saw me.

Since dude was behind me, I thought I could give her the you've-got-to-be-kidding eyes, but she looked right past me to him.

"So how's it going?" she asked.

"Fine," he answered.

He must've been referring to himself because I *know* he wasn't referring to me.

"Come on, my sweetie and I found a table and we are ready to get our drink on and have some fun," she said.

"You guys order some drinks and come over to our table," she said, motioning toward the back of the room, but I couldn't see where with all the people scattered.

I ordered a beer for myself and turned around to see what what's-his-name wanted. When I spotted him, he was checking out some girl that had walked past in a tight, little black skirt.

F-that, let him buy his own drink.

"I'll have a shot of tequila," he said. "Make that two, so I don't have to come back."

Great. Now I was out with an alcoholic.

I cut my eyes and turned back around to the bartender and ordered his shots. When the drinks came, of course, he was nowhere in sight. I reached into my purse and pulled out a twenty and handed it to the bartender. I scooped up the drinks and walked in the direction that Janice motioned toward a few minutes earlier. I couldn't see her. I just kept walking to the back of the room until I saw her sitting in a booth with two guys. One guy was my lovely date and the other guy I couldn't make out because he had his back turned toward me. But I figured that must've been her man. As I got closer she saw me and waved me over. When I got to the table, I almost fell over. There was Janice, there was my date and there was none other than...Mark.

What the...?!?!?!?

He almost fell over when he saw me, too.

"What took you so long?" Janice asked.

"Uh, sorry," was all I could manage.

"Did you bring my shots?" asked the town idiot.

How this guy went from a Greek god to the town idiot in less than an hour was beyond me, but somehow he did it and with much success.

I handed him the one and gulped down the other. I needed this more than he did.

"Well, I want you to finally meet my man Mark," Janice said proudly.

I had no idea what to say. I waited for him to say something first but, when he didn't, I put my drink in the one hand and hesitantly extended my other hand out to him.

"Nice to meet you."

"You, too," he said while shaking my hand.

"Mark's in computers," Janice said, boasting.

This I knew.

I sat down in the booth next to Mark since Janice and the idiot were taking up the other side.

"Now that you are here, there is something I want to tell you," Janice sang.

Mark must've known what she wanted to tell me because he immediately interrupted.

"She doesn't want to hear it now. Tell her later," he said with a sense of urgency in his voice.

Now I *really* wanted to know.

This *was* a movie, wasn't it? A bad one. It had to be. This guy just appeared wherever I went. If I went to hell, he'd be the one fanning the fire. If it wasn't him, it was his crazy girlfriend, or rather, other girlfriend. *Again I ask, why me?* I just couldn't figure out how he could've *not* known that it was me who was coming on this friggin' date. I couldn't believe I didn't see this coming. If she would've referred to Mark as Mark instead of her man all the time, *I* would've known. I couldn't believe my luck. No, wait, yes I could. This was so like me and my luck. If I had half a nerve, I would've just gotten up and walked out, but I wanted to hear what Janice dear had to say.

"Mark and I are getting married," she blurted.

I thought I saw him flinch.

"Well, congratulations, you guys." Town idiot winked at Mark. "You sure have got yourself a real winner."

They now all looked at me, except Mark, of course.

"Well, what do you think?" Janice asked, showing me her ring.

Nice ring; it must've been at least two carats.

I thought for a moment. This really was a blessing. There was no getting out of this one now. He could profess his love to me all he wanted to, but the proof was in the pudding, and I was looking at the two-carat pudding being shoved in my face at that very moment.

I raised my glass of beer.

"This is absolutely wonderful. I congratulate you both," I said as we all raised our glasses to toast.

"So tell me how you met," I said to Janice while taking a sip of my beer. I was going to enjoy this to the fullest.

She told me they had met a couple of months ago at the brunch where she ran into me. Now wasn't that funny? We had just gone out the night before. Boy, he worked fast. So she just met him a couple of months ago, and they were now engaged? She was in for a rude awakening. I then thought about what Char had told me about her being pregnant. She didn't say anything about that, so I hoped that part wasn't true. I still couldn't believe it as she was explaining that they met that day and went out that night. If my memory served me correctly, he asked me out for that same night, too. I guess it was first-come, first-serve. Not to mention he was at Quimby's with Tanya, and while she was busy watching my ass all afternoon, he was hitting on Janice. Stupid bitch. This really was hilarious.

She went on to explain that he had moved in with her recently. Gee, and he told me he moved back into his apartment. Now it all made sense. Ten to one he didn't even have an apartment with his name on the lease. I wondered if Tanya even knew about Janice. Every time she came over to harass me about his whereabouts, he was probably with Janice. Now that pissed me off because while I was getting harassed, like yesterday, he was living it up over Janice's.

She continued to gush over her man who now had a name and face, and I continued to enjoy it. She had no idea what she was getting into, and I wasn't sure I was the one to tell her. I knew one thing for sure; I couldn't wait to tell Char. I knew she would have a howl over this like everything else in this whole fiasco I call my life.

Chapter22

Sunday morning I was going to call Char, but she beat me to it. She wanted to know everything. So I told her all about Mark.

"Is that motherfucker doing this on purpose? Does he follow you around or something?"

"Trust me when I say he had no idea it was me. Then I thought I was going to lose it when she showed me her ring as he turned white."

"Men are so dirty. I don't know how they do it," she said.

"And don't get me started about *my* date," I said. "He was looking all that when he showed up, in the face that is, but I failed to notice that he had on...you ready for this?"

"What?"

"*The red suit,*" I said, and we started cracking up.

"Wait, that's not the funny part; he had on the black muscle shirt under it." We both roared with laughter again.

"And don't forget the matching black shoes to match the shirt," she said. That was it; we were done.

"I can't believe he really tried to get away with that crap," Char said when we finished laughing.

"Are you referring to my date's outfit or Mark?" And the laughter started all over again.

"Then, he got drunk as hell. He kept drinking shots all night and was supposed to take me home," I said.

"Did he take you home?"

"No way. I called a cab for me *and* him. For all I know, his car is still there."

When I got off the phone with Char, I went to the gym. I felt like it was time to trim the fat—in more ways than one. The entire time in aerobics class I just kept thinking about the previous night's events. I spent the whole forty-five minutes thinking about how everything now added up. Mark needed to tell Tanya the deal because if she was going to continue to call and harass me as she had been, I was going to tell her my damn self. I had four hang-up "ANONYMOUS" calls on my caller ID when I got in that night, and I refused to have some psycho bitch stalking me for somebody else's doings. I had no time for that.

Char told me I should say something to Janice, but what good would that do? I did confirm with Char that Janice told her she was definitely pregnant. I had no idea why Janice didn't say anything about that the previous night. I didn't even know if I was going to say anything to Janice; I'd have to think on that one just a bit longer.

When I finished my aerobics class, I decided to lift weights. I started out going hard until some dude came up and decided I was the one he was going to hit on this week. That pretty much ended my weight session, so I showered and went home. When I got home it looked like it was going to rain, so I decided to stay in for the remainder of the day. I had no problem with that. I headed for the TV and for the rest of the afternoon I watched movies starting with the remaining *Romeo and Juliet* that I had started on Friday—this time with no interruptions.

I fell asleep on the couch and woke up when I heard someone knocking on my door. I immediately ran down a mental list of people it could've been while getting up to check the peephole. It couldn't have been Char because I had just talked to her, and she wouldn't have come over without calling first. It could've been a crazy bitch, but she never paid afternoon visits; she was a night stalker—it's sad when you know a psycho's stalking routine—so it had to be none other than...

"What do you want, Mark?" I said through the door. I was really getting tired of this crap now.

"I want to talk to you."

"What? What could you *possibly* have to say now?"

"I just want to talk. Let me in, please."

Dammit!

I opened the door and he stood there waiting for me to invite him in. He could wait all he wanted to.

"Look, I want to apologize for last night. I didn't know it was you that was coming," he said.

Obviously.

"So that makes it better? Who cares, okay? Just let it go. I don't want anything else from you. No, wait, I do want something else from you. Tell your stalking bitch ex-girlfriend, girlfriend, soon-to-be mother of your child, fiancée, whatever, to stop stalking me, or *I* will tell her the real deal, so someone else can be the recipient of her psychosis."

"What? She's still been harassing you? Why didn't you tell me?" he asked.

"I'm telling you now, and if you don't tell her, I will."

He shook his head. "Anyway, that's not why I'm here. I came to tell you that I can't see you anymore."

Someone please tell me that this jackass doesn't have a straight face while saying this. "What the fuck are you talking about?" I asked incredulously.

"I'm in love with Janice and it's going to have to be over between *us*," he said with his straight face still intact.

Was he delivering this speech for *my* benefit, or was this just something to say to me in case I told Janice about him? He'd tell her the same thing he told me about Tanya, that he broke up with *me* and that *I* didn't want it to end.

"Get the fuck gutta my doorway," I said and slammed the door, barely missing his face. This nigra must be crazy. They all were. Well, there you have it folks; Mark finally broke it off with me after I had been pining for him for so long. I know it must've been hard for him and I have no idea how I was going to accept this, but I couldn't do anything but try. The love of my life was finally gone. What was I to do now? *Dumb ass motherfucka!*

Chapter 23

Monday morning rolled around quick. The whole weekend had been a blur that I would've liked to have forgotten. I still hadn't told Janice and I still hadn't decided if I were going to do so. I had more important things to think about.

We finally had our sales team fully together, and it was working out for the better. I'd been spending most of the days in the new Virginia office helping to set it up, so I was rarely at my desk in case Mark, Tanya or anyone else decided to call me. That was a good thing because I didn't need the aggravation.

Neal and I stuck to our deal of calling each other on Mondays, Wednesdays and Fridays. I really looked forward to hearing from him. My feelings for him didn't go away, but they were somehow changing. I couldn't explain it, but it was like we had such an amazing time even though I didn't even see him.

For the next few weeks I didn't go out at all. I probably went out to happy hour once with Char but ended up leaving early because I just wasn't in the mood. Besides, it was on a Wednesday night, and I had to get home for Neal's call. I didn't want to miss that.

My business life had been picking up while my social life was at a standstill. I really didn't mind it. My weekends consisted of ordering a pizza, grabbing a beer and watching movies I had rented from Blockbuster. I think my hanging-out days were finally over.

It was now mid October. The leaves were a beautiful shade of brown and orange and were falling from the trees. Last month, I had turned the big three-oh but felt no different. I wasn't sure if that was a good thing or a bad thing. Char had wanted to take me out, and I felt obligated to go. Yet, I couldn't muster up the energy to go to yet another club and meet the same guys with the same tired lines. So I ended up going to my sister's house "by accident" where she had a surprise party for me. My whole family was there. It was wonderful. Char had this planned the whole time. She knew I wasn't going to any dead ass club. That was the best birthday I could've had, except for one thing, of course. Neal wasn't there. I still missed him so much. He did have flowers delivered to my office, which was nice. They were a beautiful arrangement of red and white roses. I thought that was really sweet. In the few weeks that had passed, I had not heard from Mark, crazy bitch *or* Janice. Fancy Red Suit tried calling me once, but I didn't pick up. He left his number, but when I didn't call back I think he got the message because I hadn't heard from him since.

Aw, too bad, so sad.

When Thanksgiving rolled around, I ended up going back to Philly and staying with my parents. Besides, I hadn't seen my little brat nephews in a while. Neal and I continued to call each other, but as I predicted, the calls were now pretty much limited to twice a week and on no set day; it was now back to when we caught each other. (See, I knew this was gonna happen.) I had been out on a total of three dates within the past couple of months.

There was Rich, who wasn't. I ended up going Dutch that night. Then there was Alex, this white guy I met at the gym. I wouldn't classify that as a date because we just went for coffee after a workout. He was nice, but so not my type, and then there was Michael who was a closet freak. On our first date, he told me that he liked handcuffs and whips and chains. Whatever, but don't tell someone on the first date. Then as he had a few more drinks, he told me that he loved golden showers. I didn't even know what that was until Char told me the next day, and I wish she hadn't.

That was it; I was done with dating.

Neal and I had talked about my going to the Bahamas for Christmas a couple of months ago, but neither of us had mentioned it anymore, so I just assumed it was off. I guessed I would see him when I saw him.

"You need to stop thinking about that little boy and move on," Char had told me one night. "I just don't get it."

I didn't either.

Chapter**24**

The first week in December was always the craziest. It was right after Thanksgiving and everyone was doing their Christmas shopping. Char and I decided to be part of that everybody by going shopping at the overpriced, over-materialized mall.

"Have you heard from your man yet this week?" Char asked while we were walking through the mall, dodging baby strollers and hordes of people.

"He isn't my man and no, I haven't." I was irritated. Not by the fact that she called him "my man" for the umpteenth time, but by the fact that I hadn't heard from him in a while.

"Oh, well, you knew it was bound to happen some time. You even said so yourself."

"So what's up with you and James?" she asked.

James Whitmore was a guy I had been sort of seeing for the past two weeks. He was okay, but as usual I wasn't really interested in him like that and assumed he knew because he didn't push it.

"Things are cool. We're supposed to be going out sometime next week. You should come with us and bring your new guy, what's-his-name."

"His name's Eric and maybe I will. I think it's about time I met James. You've been with him a whole two weeks and haven't complained once about his nose being too big or his hands being too small. This must be love," she said, laughing.

"Not hardly."

"Oh, I forgot to tell you; I spoke to Janice earlier this week," she said.

"Yeah, and what did she have to tell you?"

We only spoke once since that horrific double date a couple of months back. I never did tell her about Mark, but I think he said something to her in fear of me beating him to the punch and ruining his current sucker. He told her exactly what I knew he would—that I had been out with him once or twice, but that was it and that nothing had ever progressed from there. I knew this because she called me a week or so after the date that I now refer to as Pearl Harbor, and I told her the truth. I did my part; now it was up to her to decide what she wanted to do with it. She chose to stay with him, and I haven't really talked to her since. He even had the nerve to call me a couple of times and leave messages on my machine "just to say hi" and see what I was up to. I didn't appreciate him lying on me and then calling as if nothing happened, but the ballsy thing was that he usually made these calls late at night, indicating that he was trying to get some. This asshole never gave up. Maybe he had it like that with his other women, but not here.

"I heard they got married last month, but she didn't confirm or deny," Char said.

"Oh, really?"

"They supposedly went to the justice of the peace on the sneak tip. No one knew about it."

"Well, if that's true, that's too bad for her," I said.

"Is he still calling you?" she asked.

"Still. It's really pathetic. She'll find out one day; unfortunately, it may be too late."

"Mmmm-mmmm-mmmm," Char said while stuffing her face with the cinnamon soft pretzel she had just bought.

We continued walking to the end of the mall until we reached Nordstrom.

"I also heard that Tanya is now seeing someone else, and I'll give you one guess who it is," Char said with a sly grin.

Oh, Lawd, did I even want to know?

"Who?"

"Red Suit," she said. She burst out laughing, spitting out pieces of her pretzel.

I started cracking up with her.

"No surprise there."

"She had been seeing him for a while, at least three months or so. When Mark found out, he was pissed off. He was telling people she only did it to get back at him."

I thought about what Red Suit told me before, about trying to get with Janice. I'm sure they did that sort of thing back and forth all the time. That was probably why he didn't want me; he didn't know I had been involved with his buddy Mark. If he had known, he probably would've been all up on me, too. The thought of that made me shudder.

"I can't be shocked; it seems like whoever I meet has run up all in that girl," I said.

"Yeah and you've already been behind her once with Mark; you don't want to take that chance again," Char said, laughing.

Yuck! Thanks for the visual.

~❤~

We finished our Christmas shopping and met Stacey and Jaleesa for lunch at Friday's. I was the one who suggested it because I was feenin' for chicken fingers and fries, and they made the best. Even their honey mustard was better than all the rest.

When we got there, they were already at a table waiting for us.

"What's up, girl?" Jaleesa said, looking at me. "I haven't seen you in a while."

"Ain't nothin' goin' on but the rent," I said.

"That's not what we heard," Stacey commented.

I knew she couldn't wait to find out my business, so I chose to ignore that comment and sat down. I wasn't in the mood to have her get on my nerves. I saw her but once a month or so, and each time she managed to irk me.

"So give us the 411; I heard you and Mark are no more," Jaleesa said.

I turned to Char.

"Why don't you do the honors since you obviously already started the story without me," I said, giving her the floor.

Char began to tell the whole story.

Okay, I was kidding. Evidently she wasn't.

"That's exactly what happens when you date dogs," Stacey said on her high and mighty horse. "That's precisely why I stay away from them all."

"You stay away from *them* or they stay away from *you?*" Jaleesa said, and we all laughed.

That had to be the truth. No man in his right mind would stay with her for too long. She would nag the poor fool to death.

After lunch we all said our goodbyes, separated and promised to do it again. Since Char and I came together, we walked in one direction, and they walked in another.

"I wasn't going to tell you, but I'm not seeing Eric anymore," she said out of the blue.

Why was that such a big secret?

"Why not? What happened?" I asked.

"I've started seeing someone else, and it's pretty serious. I'm talking this is it, serious."

"Who?" I asked, now *really* interested.

I had no idea whom it could be since she had only been seeing Eric for a few weeks. Who did she find in this short time?

"I'm seeing Christopher again," she said with a guilty grin.

"You mean dude that we caught cheating on you? That same Christopher?"

"That's the same one," she said, still grinning at me.

This is the guy we caught cheating on her with some girl, and she was all broken up about it. She wouldn't go out for months. Ever since then she had been dating several guys, one after the other, and now she has chosen to settle down with the worst one.

"That was a long time ago; he has since grown up and is ready for a commitment."

Somebody zap me away from this girl.

"When did you meet up with him again? How long has this been going on?"

"For weeks now. When I told you that I was going out with Eric, I was really going out with Christopher. The truth was I didn't feel like hearing your mouth," she said.

Oh, she wasn't going to hear my mouth. I was done with that one. I had no more strength in me to argue with anyone about some damn man. The same way she wasn't going to hear my mouth was the same way I didn't want to hear hers when he started acting up, which he would. I knew this. That wasn't all I knew; I also knew that he had slept with Stacey one time when Char was still seeing him. Back in the day when Stacey and I were closer friends, she confided in me in tears one night. She told me that it just happened. Exactly why she was telling me I wasn't sure, but it was now too late. I already knew. He and Char ended up breaking up a week later, so I didn't have to say anything. Now this was back up in my face again. I just didn't have the strength anymore.

When we got to my car, I drove like a mad woman to get home and to get under the covers, leaving all the bullshit behind me. I didn't want to deal with these women and their men problems any longer.

I had my own issues.

Chapter**25**

C hristmas came and went. Neal and I had only spoken to each other maybe ten times that month. He seemed like he was really distant, which in turn caused me to be distant. I think I could safely say that it was pretty much over. It really hurt, too. I still thought about him *all the time*.

James and I were still seeing each other, but I was ready to call that quits, too. For Christmas, I got him a pair of socks. He got me a beautiful diamond bracelet. That right there allowed me to believe that we were definitely not on the same page. Too bad. He was a nice guy. But there was no interest, on my part anyway. Of course I kept the bracelet.

Char was still seeing Christopher, and she had already started calling me on the little things he did that irritated her. When she called to complain about him not returning her pages, I told her I didn't want to hear it. When she informed me about him not inviting her over to his house for Christmas, I told her I didn't want to hear it. Of course, I listened to it all anyway because she was my friend, but I let her know I wasn't far from the I-told-you-sos so she'd better get prepared.

It was Sunday afternoon and I was so prepared to spend the rest of the day inside because it was cold as ice outside. That weekend I had gone out with James, which was a total bore. I had to let him go, so I did Friday. I'd rehearsed what I was going to say, but of course it came out all wrong and ended up like the it's-not-you-it's-me and the I'm-just-not-ready-for-a-relationship-yet, but the best line was the we-can-still-hang-out-and-be-friends. I didn't know it then, but I was never to see or hear from him again.

Saturday night consisted of hanging out with the girls. We went to some new club Jaleesa had heard about. I ended up seeing Mark there with some girl who was not Janice *or* Tanya. He and Janice had gotten married in September as rumor had it, so I had no idea who this new girl was.

Damn, it was only December and he was already steppin' out. Whatever, that wasn't my problem. He had come over to our table and tried to act like he was talking to Char. I just excused myself to go to the bathroom, and when I got back he was gone. Just the way it needed to be.

Char asked me what I was doing for New Year's Eve. I didn't have anything specific that I wanted to do, but I sure didn't want to hang out at some party with more triflin' people. I decided I was just going to stay home and watch some Dick Clark. I said that every year, and every year I felt that pressure on the thirty-first and ended up going to some last-minute party with Char, but I wasn't doing that this time. I wasn't in the festive mood. I didn't want to ring in the New Year doing the same thing as last year—getting drunk and meeting some lame dude, who at the time would give my number, but then I'd spend the rest of January avoiding his call until he got the message. For some of those guys it took only a week to get the hint, but one year this one dude called straight through Valentine's Day.

When will this madness end? I was thirty years old and had no real relationship prospects. I'd end up dying an old spinster with ten bitch cats who'd eat my face for food when I collapsed and died, and no one would know until some neighbor smelled the rotting corpse from my apartment and called the police.

"Are you sure you don't want to go out?" Char asked.

I was sitting on her couch watching her put on her usual hoochie dress for some big New Year's party she was going to.

"Are you sure you want to wear that dress?" I asked.

"Girl, this is gonna drive the men wild. Watch," she said while admiring herself in a full-length mirror. "You should come; you may meet someone."

"I know. That's precisely why I'm *not* going."

"You need to stop thinking about that boy is what you need to do," she said, still admiring herself in the mirror.

I looked up in surprise at her last statement. I thought I was hiding it pretty well. I guess she could read me after all. Either that or I had just been that painfully obvious in my withdrawal from her. She'd been asking me to clubs and happy hours for the past few weeks, but each time I declined.

"I can't help it. I just had such a good time with him here, and now it's as if he never existed," I whined.

"You still talk to him over the phone, don't you?" She looked through her closet for something else to wear.

I guess it wasn't revealing enough for her.

"Yeah, but it's not like it used to be. Now it's just a quick call here and there. I just want more."

"How can you have more with a guy who lives in another country? What did you expect?"

What did I expect?

"I know," I said again. "I just don't know what to do."

"I'll tell you what you should do. You should get off your lazy butt and come with me to the party," she said.

"I'm not going so stop asking," I said as I stood up. "You go ahead and have fun though. I gotta go."

The last thing I heard when I shut the door behind me was her yelling that I was pathetic.

I had no sarcastic comeback for that. The truth was the truth.

When I got home it was seven o'clock. I checked to see if I had messages and I had none. It had been three months since I'd gotten a call from crazy Tanya. She must've been stalking Janice now.

Good.

Mark must've been working on a new conquest because even *he* wasn't calling anymore.

James and I'd just broken up and I'd just left Char's, so I guess I *wouldn't* have any calls. Not even from Neal.

I settled down on the couch with my blanket and turned on the TV. I'd bought a few things at the store. Popcorn, pretzels, potato chips, and later I was going to order pizza. I was set. Diet would start January 2, you know, after the New Year's celebrations.

I even went to Blockbuster and loaded up on movies. I felt like watching some classics, so I got *Pillow Talk* with Rock Hudson and Doris Day; and *Imitation of Life* with Juanita Moore and Lana Turner.

I looked outside. It had started snowing. It was beautiful with the snow highlighting the earth. I fixed myself a drink and thought about how perfect this would be if Neal could've been there, but he wasn't, so get over it.

Before I knew it, I fell asleep and woke up at eleven-thirty to Brandy on *Dick Clark's New Year's Rockin' Eve.*

Riiiiiiing.

Probably drunk Char calling me to tell me Happy New Year. I picked up and heard a faint male voice through static.

"Hello?" I said loudly into the phone.

It was Neal.

"Happy New Year," he said.

He sounded strange.

"Happy New Year yourself."

There was silence except for the static.

"Where are you?" I asked.

"At the hospital."

"Are you okay?" I asked, now worried.

There was only silence. I could tell he was trying to get himself together before replying.

"My mom..."

"Is she okay?" I asked alarmed. "What's up, Neal?"

"She just passed," he said.

Tears immediately streamed down my face as I thought about how much he must've been hurting right then. We talked for another thirty minutes, and I found out that over the past few weeks, his mom had been really sick. That's why he hadn't called. He was trying to take care of her because he knew that these were going to be her last days. He wanted to tell me but didn't want to ruin my Christmas or New Year's. She had just passed a few minutes earlier and he called me first. Since the death was expected, his whole family was there to be with her. She didn't die alone, but I could still hear the pain in his voice.

"I can come down to be with you if you want," I said.

The words even surprised me.

"I'd like that, but I don't want you to go out of your way," he said.

That wasn't even an issue. If he wanted me there, I was going. When I looked up at the clock, it was 12:01. It wasn't under the best of circumstances, but I had ended up spending New Year's with Neal, *the man I loved.*

Chapter 26

"That's a shame," Char said to me over the phone the next day. I'd just told her about Cornelius. She was shocked.

"I didn't even know his mom was sick," she said.

"That's why they left early the last time they were here. Don't you ever talk to Broadus?" I asked.

"Man, I haven't talked to him since the last time he was here. You probably know more about what he's doing than I do," she said.

The sad part was that I did and the even sadder part was that she probably didn't care that I did.

"The party I went to last night was whack," she said.

"I could've told you that," I said. "Oh, wait, I did."

"Oh, shut up. I couldn't believe the tired ass men that had the nerve to walk up in there last night."

"So you didn't get any numbers?" I asked.

"Of course I did," she said proudly.

"Then shut up! Obviously all the men in there weren't all *that* tired. Who's the flavor of the month now?" I asked.

Thankfully she had decided to put Christopher on the back burner.

"His name's Teddy," she said.

"Jaaaaaam, oh Jaaaaaaam, Teddy, jam for me now," I sang jokingly. "Whatever happened to his group Blackstreet anyway?" I said, laughing.

"Shuddddup. Anyway, he seems cool—only he said he's a mechanical engineer and you know what that means."

"*Janitor,*" we said in unison.

"So what are you going to do about Neal's mom's funeral?"

"I told him I'd go," I said.

"You're going to go all the way to the Bahamas for a funeral? People go to the Bahamas for vacation, not to a funeral."

"I told him that I'd come. He just sounded so upset, and it hurt to hear him sound like that."

"You must really like him. Wow, I had no idea," she said.

"I know; I had no idea either," I admitted. "It just sort of crept up on me."

"What about Mark?"

"What about him?" I said.

I couldn't believe she actually brought his name into it.

"It's definitely over between you two?" she said.

"Over? It never began. I can't believe you asked me that stupid ass question. I should hang up on you for that," I said.

I was about to remind her that he was now a married man, but that would mean nothing to her. She sure knew how to ruin a good mood.

"My, my, my, you seem to be quite upset by the mere mention of his name," she said smugly.

"I'm not upset, I just don't appreciate him being mentioned in the same sentence with Neal."

"Well, then you probably don't care to hear about the latest," she said.

This girl always had "the latest."

"Nope."

"Then you probably don't want to know that I heard he's still sleeping with Tanya," she said.

"Nope." "He had the nerve to call me the other day," she said, pausing. Silence.

"I don't know why though. He said he just wanted to catch up, but we both know the truth," she said.

"No, I don't know the truth, but I'm sure you're gonna tell me anyway," I said.

"He asked about you and if you were seeing anyone," she said.

"And what did you tell him?"

"I told him you were fine."

"And?"

"And that you weren't seeing anyone."

Although I did have strong feelings for Neal, you could hardly classify us as seeing each other.

"So when are you going to the Bahamas?"

She changed the subject. *Good.*

"The funeral isn't until Friday, so I'm gonna tell Sam at work tomorrow and fly down there Thursday night. I'll just stay for the weekend."

"I wonder what the weather is like there in January? It's probably still like ninety degrees. It's probably like that all year-round," she said. "Well, have fun."

Chapter 27

I went to work Monday and told Sam about the coming weekend. He said it would be fine. Sam was a cool manager to work for.

I kept busy all week training in the Virginia office, so by the time Thursday came I was "ret ta ta go." I was really looking forward to seeing him but not under the circumstances. As I started packing on Thursday after work, I realized that I had never even gone to a funeral with *any* of my boyfriends. I'd gone to weddings and Christmas parties, but I'd never gone to one funeral. This would be my first.

My flight was leaving at ten o'clock, and it was a direct flight, so I'd arrive in the Bahamas at approximately midnight. Not bad. Neal was going to pick me up at the airport and then take me to the hotel where we were staying. He booked me a hotel room because there really wasn't enough room at his house. His older brother has a house that Neal temporarily moved into until he found his own place. This was something that they had agreed upon. Come to think of it, I'd just assumed he'd be staying with me at the hotel, but if he didn't, I understood. He might've wanted to stay with his family. Either way, I was okay with it.

I got to the airport in plenty of time and my flight left as scheduled. I couldn't wait to get there. I'd talked to Neal throughout the week, so he knew exactly when I was coming. I had no idea when this had happened, but I guess we had become more than just friends. I didn't want to put too much thought into it, but just think about it: I was flying to another country to be with him during his time of need. I'd do that for anyone in a time of need, but this relationship by far wasn't like any other relationship. Could I even say relationship? What exactly was this? I had no idea and quite frankly, I was too tired to dwell on it, so I fell asleep. When I awoke, I would be in the Bahamas looking at Neal's face. I couldn't wait.

We got there on time and Neal waiting for me at the airport. It wasn't hard to spot him because the airport there was much smaller, plus it was a late-night flight, which meant fewer people. When I saw him, I immediately ran to him and gave him a big hug.

"How are you doing?" I asked.

He looked tired.

"I'm okay. How was your flight?" he said warmly.

"Fine, but I'm a little tired."

"Do you mind if we go to the church for a little while tonight? The night before the funeral we have an all-night celebration with singing and food to celebrate the passing of a loved one."

Although I was really tired, it was okay. If it was their tradition, I wanted to go.

"We don't have to stay all night. I just want to go for a little while," he said.

"That's cool. Can we go back to the hotel, so I can freshen up a bit first?" I asked.

"Let's go."

When we got to the hotel, it was beautiful. The hotel was right on the beach, and our room was a suite. It had two bedrooms, a kitchen and an upstairs and a downstairs.

"This place must be expensive," I said.

"No, not really. My cousin owns it, and I got it for a discount," he said with a wink.

"Must be nice to have friends in high places," I said, laughing.

I showered and did my hair in record time. When we walked out of the door to go to the church, it was one o'clock in the morning. As we drove, I just remembered that I'd be meeting his brothers and sisters for the first time. Talk about pressure.

"We don't have to stay long," he said again. "I know you had a rough flight."

Just like him to think about me.

"I'm fine. Don't worry about me. I'm just a little nervous about meeting your family for the first time tonight," I said.

He started laughing.

"You'll love them. They're really cool."

That did little to relax me, but I would try. I felt like I was sixteen and meeting my boyfriend's family for the first time. It wasn't a big deal; I was thirty, for God's sake. Why was I so nervous? They would probably look at me like, who does this American girl think she is dating our younger brother?

"What are you thinking about?" he asked.

"Nothing, why do you ask?"

"You just look like you're deep in thought someplace else."

"I'm just enjoying the ride," I lied.

He grabbed my hand and squeezed it softly.

"You don't have to be nervous. I told my family all about you, and they can't wait to meet you."

"I'm okay, but I'll admit I'm a little nervous. This all just happened so quickly."

"We don't have to go if you don't want to," he said.

"No, I want to go," I said, looking into his eyes.

For the rest of the ride, he held on to my hand and that reassured me that it was going to be okay. I felt bad for him having to baby-sit a grown woman when I should've been the one reassuring him that everything would be okay.

When we got to the church there were cars everywhere. I could hear music in the background, and there were people both inside and outside the church. The place was packed. The night air felt good. It wasn't like the winter wind I left back in Maryland; it caressed me softly and felt refreshing. I thought it would've been much colder than this, but I felt comfortable though all I had on was a light jacket.

When we walked into the church I smelled something delicious. The scent was like some type of seasoned chicken. He must've seen my expression because he told me it was chicken, peas and rice. We walked further into the church and saw everyone celebrating with song and dance.

He grabbed my hand and we immediately walked to the back. There were some women sitting in the back of the church playing the tambourine and other various percussion instruments. We walked up to them and he introduced me.

"Sophie and Yvette, this is Monica," he said.

They immediately stood up and gave me a big hug.

"Nice to finally meet you," Yvette said, showing beautiful pearly-white teeth.

"Make yourself comfortable and get something to eat," Sophie said.

I did just that. The peas and rice were delicious and the chicken just fell off the bone. I looked around and everyone was having a great time celebrating the death of his mother. At first I thought it was kind of odd, but when I thought about it, this was how death should be. You celebrate someone crossing over and going into Heaven.

We spent about three hours there, and I didn't even look at my watch once until four in the morning. Even then there were still plenty of people there singing gospel songs and celebrating.

"Are you ready to go?" he asked, yawning.

"I'm okay. If you want to stay, we can," I said.

The truth was that I was beat-down, but I didn't mind staying if he wanted to.

"No, I'm tired, and we need to get some rest for the funeral tomorrow."

"What about your sisters?" I asked, noticing them still serving food and singing and dancing. "They've got to be tired by now."

"Yeah, and they've been here since seven this morning and more than likely wouldn't leave until the break of dawn," he said.

We said our goodbyes to everyone and left. As we walked out of the church, I looked back at all the celebrating that was going on. Never in my life had I seen anything like it. This would definitely be something that I'd remember.

~❤~

The next morning we got up at eight o'clock. The funeral was at ten, but since he was part of the immediate family, he had things he had to do in preparation. I noticed him getting dressed. He just kind of walked around blindly without saying too much.

I knew this was extremely hard on him, but I lacked experience, so I wasn't sure of what to say or do.

"Are you hungry?" he asked. "If you are, we can stop and pick up some breakfast."

I told him that I wasn't hungry, so we just proceeded to get dressed. I'd brought a black suit because I wasn't sure what to wear. He dressed in all black himself. I guess, in that respect, all mourning people, regardless of culture, wore black, but when he saw my suit he told me that in the Bahamas, the women in mourning usually wore all white.

Oh, jeez. I had no idea.

"I'm sorry, I forgot to tell you. I wasn't thinking," he said.

"That's okay, but am I still okay to go to the funeral? I didn't bring anything white."

I certainly didn't want to offend anyone.

"Oh, yeah, that's fine. That's how it is usually, but there are some women that still wear black."

When he saw the disappointment in my face, he pulled me toward him and hugged me.

"Thank you so much for coming," he said and kissed my cheek.

I could tell that he really meant it, too. I didn't mind at all. It was the least I could do for him. I should've been thanking him for restoring my faith in men when I thought all was lost. That was where the real thanks came in.

"You ready?" he asked when we were all dressed.

"I'm ready," I said, hoping that I was truly ready to experience this type of situation with him. We'd see.

The funeral was beautiful. The whole town must have come. As usual, most people gave their condolences to the immediate family members. I didn't know if I were going to be sitting upfront, which was reserved for family members, or if I was going to join the rest of the attendees in the pews in the back. When we got there, his sisters immediately directed me to the front of the church to sit next to Neal. The church was delightfully decorated with an assortment of flowers and a poster-size picture of his mother. I'd never seen her before. He looked exactly like the male version of her. He had her strong features and high cheekbones.

When the service ended, we all had to go to the cemetery for the burial. Neal had held it together pretty well. He did break down and cry a couple of times, and when he did, I would reach over and put my arm around him. I knew he was truly going to miss her.

At the cemetery they laid her to rest and said a prayer over the grave. By the time everything was over it was well past eight o'clock. I didn't realize it had taken that long.

"My sister is having a small dinner tonight, and you can meet my brothers," he said.

I didn't really meet them the previous night because most of them were living in Florida and didn't come in until the next morning. He did introduce me briefly at the funeral to some of them.

I thought all of this was really nice. His family was really close, and I wasn't used to that. My family lived in different states, so it was rare that we all got together and had family dinners, even in this type of situation.

We quickly showered and changed and headed over to his sister's house.

When we got there he introduced me to his sisters' kids, his brothers, his brothers' wives, their kids, everyone. He also introduced me to his niece who was fourteen and was described by him as "sassy." I could see why. She had a huge load of makeup on her face, and when he introduced me, she just gave me the up and down.

His sisters sure knew how to cook some food. We had peas and rice, which was a Bahamian specialty, and fried fish and ribs all cooked on the barbecue outside. It was delicious. We spent the next few hours talking and playing dominoes. It was kind of hard for me to understand some of the things they were saying because they were talking so fast and with the accents. Neal must've given me the watered-down version of his accent because I understood him perfectly when we were alone. But I noticed when he was with family and friends, his accent went into full gear, and I could barely understand him either.

"Are you ready to go?" he had asked somewhere around eleven-thirty.

I was having a good time, but I really was tired from the day. I just wanted to go back to our room and get some rest.

When we returned, we showered and jumped into the bed that now had fresh, clean sheets. We ended up falling asleep almost immediately in each other's arms. I was really glad that I had gone down there to be with him. From the looks of it, he was glad, too. There really wasn't anything I wouldn't do for him. I was pretty sure the feeling was mutual.

Since I was only going to be in the Bahamas for another day, his whole family wanted to take me out to dinner at the restaurant where he and his sister worked. So there, I met with all of his co-workers and his managers. He pointed out one of the waitresses he used to date in high school. She was *ai-ight* looking, but I beat her out.

"You see her?" He pointed to a thick, pretty girl. "She's doing the owner of the restaurant."

"Yeah, right, and how do you know that?" I asked.

"It's a known fact. Everyone knows it," he said.

I started laughing. Good to see that the Bahamian work ethic was pretty much the same as the American work ethic.

"After dinner tonight, I want to take you to the beach I used to go to when I was a kid," he said. "You have got to see it. When the sun sets, it turns the water this pretty pale shade of blue, and then it gets darker and darker as the sun goes down until it eventually turns the water to a deep, dark green."

I looked at him and saw that he was in another world as he reminisced.

"My mom told me that my dad used to take us there as kids," he said, still looking off into the sky.

"What else do you remember about your dad?" I asked.

"I don't even really remember that. I just know this because my mom told me. I was too young to really remember anything. It just makes me feel..." He looked up toward the clouds and searched for the right words. "It just makes me feel...comfortable every time I go there."

I felt kind of sorry for him at that moment. I could see that he had some regrets about not having a father figure throughout his life. Maybe that was why his family was so close. Now that his mom was gone, they would probably become even closer.

I saw as he hugged his sisters constantly and how he lovingly interacted with his brothers. He claimed he hadn't seen his brothers in years, but you couldn't tell. They joked and laughed like this was an everyday occurrence.

When the sun started to set, he scooped me out of the chair and brought me around to everyone to say goodbye. He was taking me to the beach as promised.

When we got to the car, he swung me around and put his arms around me and kissed me.

"Did I thank you for coming?" he asked, smiling.

"Yes, you did, but you can thank me again if you want to."

He leaned into me and kissed me again, only softer.

"Thank you for coming...again."

"You're welcome...again," I said, smiling.

He gave me another kiss and then opened my door. I hopped in and off we went.

It was a beautiful evening. The sun was just starting to set and the sky was a spectacular shade of orange and yellow. Wintertime in the Bahamas was incredible. Although I had to wear a light jacket, the breeze was extraordinary. It wasn't cold and windy; it was more like a summer cool, whispering one.

As we drove he held my hand. I was certainly having a good time and didn't want it to end. I tried not to think about the next day and getting on that plane to go back to the States, but it was inevitable. Every time I thought about how much fun I was having, I had to think about that fun ending and very soon.

When we reached the beach, it was as beautiful as he had promised. It was a private beach, so it was completely empty. We had to drive through a pathway of trees and bushes to get there, but that just made it even more stunning. We were able to pull right up onto the beach and could have driven in the water if we had wanted to. I couldn't believe it. It really was exactly as he had described it. The sun shone on the water and it did make it this brilliant bluish color. When I turned to look at him, I saw that he was looking at me with an expression of anticipation.

"See, isn't it as I told you?"

"Magnificent," was all I could say as I stared out at the ocean.

I looked out over the horizon and could've gotten lost for days out there. It was so peaceful. I couldn't believe I complained as much as I did back in Maryland. Nothing seemed to be able to bother me now.

After a few minutes of silence, he spoke again.

"I don't want you to leave," he said.

"I don't want me to leave either," I said, laughing.

"I'm serious," he said. "I wish you could stay longer."

"I know," I said, getting serious. "But I can't. It wouldn't be feasible for me to stay."

"I know, but it would've been nice, wouldn't it?"

It sure would have.

~❤~

When we got back to the room, it was completely dark. His cousin, who also worked at the front desk, told us that we had a message on our door. It was his sister wanting to hang out.

"What do you think?" I asked.

"Hell, no," he said. "Tonight I want you all to myself."

He opened the door and went in. He immediately pulled me to him and started kissing my neck, my face, breast, anywhere his lips could find. He then hurriedly pulled my shirt over my head, then took off his shirt. He must've had the same thing on his mind that I had on mine all day. We fell to the couch but missed it and ended up on the floor. We started laughing as we plopped our bodies back on to the couch.

"Why are we on the couch?" I said, laughing. "There are two perfectly good bedrooms upstairs."

"I can't wait that long." He was almost out of breath in between kisses.

It was like we were two dogs in heat. We tripped all the way up the steps until we steered our mashed bodies to one of the bedrooms. We immediately started making ferocious love like this were to be our last night together, and who knows, with me leaving the next day, it just might've been.

The next morning we made love again and again. We had to. I felt desperate, seeing as I was leaving in a few hours and didn't know when I would be able to see him again. I had the same aching feeling in my stomach as before when we were about to part. He didn't want me to leave, and I didn't want to, but we had no choice.

We took our showers and got dressed. Since I didn't even bother to take my clothes out of the suitcase, I didn't need to pack, so we had some extra time. We decided to go to breakfast and then straight to the airport where my plane would be leaving in another two hours.

"So are you all set?"

"All set for what?" I asked.

"All set for going back to the ice and the snow?" he said.

"I'm never set for that."

Silence.

"Maybe I could come visit you in a couple of months," he said.

"Yeah, maybe," I said, not wanting to hold him to that.

"I'll write you a letter tonight," he said.

"Yeah, and it'll only take six months to get to me," I said jokingly.

He must've sensed that I wasn't really in the mood to talk anymore, so we just shut up and ate the rest of our breakfast. When he took me to the airport he could only drop me off because he had to go back and get ready for work. The goodbye was really short and sweet. I didn't want to dwell on anything. It was just the call-me-when-you-get-home-so-I-know-you-got-home-okay thing. I told him to tell his family goodbye for me, and we gave each other a hug and a kiss, and that was it. I could sit here and tell you that that's the way I liked it, but I'd be lying if I did. The truth of the matter was that I didn't want to say goodbye at all, but if I had to, make it as short and sweet as possible. That's precisely what we did.

Chapter 28

When I finally got home I gave Kitty a big fat kiss. She's what I missed the most about going away. She just hissed at me (she hates kisses, which is why I do it all the time) and jumped from my arms. See, I told you she was a bitch.

It had been raining all day and evidently it snowed too because there was still remains of the snow on the ground being washed away by the rain. It sucked. I put my suitcase down and took another shower. Traveling always made me feel dirty. I put on my Bjork CD and sat down to just reflect on my wonderful trip under not-so-wonderful circumstances. I then called Neal at work to tell him I made it home okay. They couldn't find him on the floor, so I just left a message. As soon as I hung up, my phone rang.

I looked at the caller ID.

"Hey, Char," I said as I picked up.

"Well?" she said.

"Well ,what?"

"Don't play with me, girl. How was your trip?"

I started smiling. I couldn't help myself.

"I had a good time," I said, downplaying it.

"Just good?"

I couldn't hold it in any longer.

"Okay, I had a great time," I blurted out. "I met all of his family, and we had a wonderful time."

"Did his sisters act all ignorant toward you and not speak to you?" she asked.

"Just the opposite. They were real nice. As a matter of fact, we spent so much time with his family that we had to find time to ourselves."

"How about the brothers?" she asked.

"What about his brothers?"

"Are there any for me?"

"Please. They're all married and have kids. Besides, most of them are older."

"I like older," she said.

"I also said married."

"I like married, too."

"So anyway," I said ignoring her, "I just got home and I already miss him."

"You really sound pitiful. You must really like him because I haven't heard you sound like this since Kenny."

"I don't think so. Kenny was nothing like this. I mean seriously, Neal is the nicest guy I've met in a long time, and it really feels like we have known each other for longer than we actually have," I said.

"Is that good?"

"In this case, yes, it is."

I sat down on the couch in defeat.

"I don't know what to do," I said, whining.

"When are you two going to see each other again?" she asked.

"I don't know," I admitted.

I had no idea when and even *if* we were going to see each other again.

"Well, on that serious note, I'll bring you back to the real world," she said.

"Uh-oh, I was only gone for a weekend. What could've happened in that little time?"

"I'll tell you. Your boy Mark was caught in bed with Tanya by his new bride." She waited for my reaction, but all I could do was shake my head.

"She threw a fit and threatened to annul the marriage. Oh, yeah, and Janice is pregnant, too. They are both about five months into their pregnancy, so you know what that means," she said.

"They just got married a couple of months ago and he's already cheating?"

"Just think, that could've been *your* husband," she said, laughing.

"Oh, no, it couldn't; I barely dated the idiot."

"Then you could've been the baby's momma," she said still laughing.

No more Jerry Springer for her.

"They're called condoms, sweetie," I said. "You should try 'em."

"Speaking of condoms," she started, "I forgot to tell you that Stacey is pregnant."

"She is?" I said in disbelief. "By who?"

I really wanted to ask who was the poor schmuck that just signed his own death sentence but decided against it. Too ignorant.

"I don't know. She's not telling anyone for some reason. It's probably Mark," she said, laughing.

I wouldn't have been surprised. He'd had everyone else in town, unfortunately including me. I couldn't believe that I actually had such bad judgment. This was one of those life experiences that you have and learn from but shall never ever mention again.

How did I go from looking at a beautiful sunset in the dream world to infidelity and ignorance in the real world?

Mark and Neal were complete opposites, and I wondered how I could've been attracted to both at the same time. That's a mistake that won't happen again. You can bet on that.

I went to the kitchen and pulled out some bread for a sandwich. I was also in the mood for chips, so I pulled those out, too. I was supposed to be cutting out all white bread on my newfound diet but I figured I'd start the diet tomorrow. I grubbed all weekend, so I might as well have finished the weekend off. I decided to put the white bread back and pulled out a hoagie roll. If I was gonna do this, it was gonna be done right. I pulled out ham, turkey, lettuce, tomatoes, onions, cheese, pickles and real mayo. I do have to say that this was going to be the best sandwich yet. I might as well have enjoyed this one last sandwich. When I finished making the colossal sandwich, I went out to the family room to enjoy it in front of the TV. Just as I was about to take a bite, my doorbell rang. I should've just ignored it. Every time you are ready to throw down, someone is either knocking on your door or ringing your phone trying to sell you something you don't want or need.

I opened the front door and saw Neal standing there. Ohmigod!!!!!! What was he doing here? I couldn't say anything. I was totally speechless.

"You said it wouldn't be feasible for you to stay in the Bahamas," he said, "but it is feasible for me to come here."

Was he serious? He had to be serious; he was standing on my doorstep right there, right then. I hugged him so hard it hurt. I was going to do this. *We* were going to do this and I was ready. We kissed and hugged and tears streamed down my face. I couldn't have been happier. We had things to work out with him coming to the States and all, but it sure enough was do-able. It was *feasible*. We could do this and we were *going* to do this.

He looked at the sandwich and chips on the table.

"I'm sorry. Were you eating?" he asked.

I started laughing. That was the last thing on my mind.

"I don't need that anyway," I said to him, still laughing. "Besides, it's official; I'm on a diet to trim the fat." Now I was ready to eat healthy. No more empty calories consisting of chicken fingers and fries, and the Marks of the world. It was now nothing but healthiness for me. My diet finally began.

ABOUT THE AUTHOR

Laurel began her first novel in 1998 with no real intentions of getting it published. Upon moving to Freeport Bahamas, a decision was made to finish the book and get it published on the insistence of her family and friends who had read the first few completed chapters.

Now living in the sunny and beautiful Bahamas with her husband and daughter, she has completed her first novel, *My Diet Starts Tomorrow*. Her second novel, *Mirror, Mirror*, will be released Spring 2004.

You can visit the author at http://www.laurelhandfieldbooks.com or email her at author"laurelhandfieldbooks.com.

Excerpt from

Mirror, Mirror

Coming Spring 2004

Chapter 1

"JORDAN!!!! Coffee for Trent NOW!" Mr. Hines, her boss, yelled from the intercom he rarely used sitting on her desk.

Jordan jerked up from her desk and immediately ran to the coffee room. She would do anything for Mr. Prescott, even if it was at the request of that ass Hines. Anything he wanted was anything he got. Especially if he wanted her in a long sleek, flowing see-through teddy just like last night.

Ahhhhh. Last night. It had been so special, so ideal. They had concluded the perfect evening at Trent's penthouse apartment where he made feral, passionate love to her all night long.

She opened the top counter and reached for a coffee mug.

She remembered each detail vividly. When she peered into the apartment, she saw a wildly gigantic open space mutedly lit with scented candles scattered throughout the immaculate room.

Earlier that evening they had shared a candlelit dinner at a cozy little restaurant aptly named L'Amour. It was there he donned her with a sparkling diamond bracelet from Tiffanys. The dinner of lamb, new potatoes and a vegetable medley had been delicious. When he brought her back to his place for the "dessert," she'd been more than willing to accept his love. He had opened the door and scooped her up in his arms to take her through the front gates of his kingdom as if they had just been united in holy matrimony. He delicately placed her on top of the bearskin rug in front of the blazing fireplace and kissed her softly.

Ah yes, the memory was so clear now.

Wait, no; she took the fireplace out of her gilded reverie because there was no need for one in the middle of July.

Start over.

Before she could mentally redesign her vision, she heard her name being called from down the hall.

"JORDAN!"

She reached into the drawer, pulled out a spoon and quickly mixed the steaming liquid in the cup. She would have to finish her fantasy when she retired for the night. Hopefully it would replace the nightmares she was having for the past few evenings. As for right now, she had to get his coffee to him pronto.

When she reached Hines' door, she tapped quietly and waited for a response. There was none so she knocked a little louder.

"Come in!" the voice boomed from behind the large oak door.

She carefully placed her free hand on the doorknob and balanced the coffee in the other hand while slowly turning the brass knob. Before she knew it, impatient, Hines thrust open the door from the other side and immediately sent her plummeting into the office spilling the extremely hot liquid down the front of her new white J.C. Penney blouse.

Jordan winced in pain as the coffee seethed its way through the blouse and onto her skin. Hines, who was on his headset phone system, cut his eyes in disgust and said nothing to her and continued with his phone call. On the floor, Jordan looked up for Mr. Prescott. Thank goodness he was no longer in the room to witness this humiliation.

Hines walked toward his desk and grabbed some tissues. He walked back over to her practically shoving them in her face, all of this while still talking on the phone. She reached out for the tissues with some slowly flailing to the floor. As she bent down to pick up them up, her glasses fell from her face and landed lens down in the moist section of the floor where the coffee stained the gray carpet.

"I'm sorry. I'll get this cleaned up right away." She was on her hands and knees dabbing the wet spot with the dilapidated tissues.

"Just leave it and get me another cup," Hines said, shooing her off. His face was now a deep shade of red. This was a tremendous feat considering his dark, rich complexion.

Mr. Hines was a true jackass. Everyone in the small office thought so. That could be why he wasn't married, although he kept a picture of some butt ugly woman on his desk which they all knew wasn't his wife. According to rumor, he never got married. He did keep a bevy of women on the side. For whatever purpose she didn't know and didn't want to know. The thought sickened her to her stomach.

Hines was neither handsome nor repulsive. He was just there. She guessed him to be in his mid forties but he had a perpetual crinkle right between his eyes that made him appear much older. He was extremely tall and his stature made him even more Goliath-like. He could be considered attractive if you didn't know him, but to Jordan there just wasn't anything physically eye-catching about him at all. After all, she knew him and knew him well. He was one of those men that was always right and never thought twice about telling everybody so. He was also a callus man who had no people skills whatsoever and didn't give two hoots about anyone or anything but his checkbook. That was probably another reason why he wasn't married, the whole alimony factor after the inevitable divorce. To her, it was like he was the devil incarnate.

As she got up and headed toward the door to retrieve him another cup, she heard him say something behind her.

"And this time, be more careful! The cleaning of my carpet will definitely be coming out of your pay."

Jerk! she thought as she closed the door behind her.

This seemed to be the direction Jordan's life was headed in. That is, until the murders took place and that changed everything.